Souls of the Soil

This book was
adopted by
Joan Q. Horgan

· A NOVEL BY ·

Gloria Waldron Hukle

Book design by The Troy Book Makers
Cover design by Donna Lama

Printed in the United States of America

The Troy Book Makers • Troy, New York • thetroybookmakers.com

To order additional copies of this title, contact your favorite local bookstore or visit www.tbmbooks.com

ISBN: 978-1-61468-354-4

Also by Gloria Waldron Hukle

Manhattan: Seeds of the Big Apple

The Diary of a Northern Moon

Threads—An American Tapestry

For My Father

William Waldron
(1917 – 1958)

From the earth's loosened mould
The sapling draws its sustenance and thrives
Though stricken to the heart with winter's cold

From "An April Day"
By Henry Wadsworth Longfellow

Waldron Coat of Arms

PREFACE

Biblically speaking, the *Book of Genesis* opens with God creating both heaven and earth at the exact same moment. For believers, the written word could imply that our planet—every grain of sand and drop of water—is composed of the same constructive material as is heaven. If we accept this possibility as a truth, all life—past, present, and future—was meant to dwell harmoniously within a universal, never ending, *Garden of Eden*. History tells a different story.

Scientifically we acknowledge that every atom from the beginning of time to the current moment still exists today. Therefore, one might easily theorize that Mother Earth holds within herself something spiritual or heavenly, which is, of course, the concept that many primitive cultures embraced. It should then follow that God's most complex mix of atoms and molecules—called man—would be happy to dwell within this perfectly arranged, wondrous design, yet rare is the contented mortal. Contentment doesn't seem to be mankind's strong suit.

The 21st century seeker reaches out across our planet in the same way as did his ancestral grandfathers, although using modern technology rather than just following the stars. The fact is that emigration is a never ending expedition. Discontent, whether forced by exile or simply by a desire for a better life, is the catalyst for global movement that continues to make history. In a very real way dissatisfaction is my foundation for writing this New York narrative where a struggling 18th century past overlaps a confusing present.

INTRODUCTION

On October 3, 2012, the Albany, New York *Times Union* newspaper published an article by Kenneth C. Crowe II titled "Sacred Site will have Iroquois Homecoming" in which readers were mini-educated about the Native American spiritual significance of the Cohoes Falls (Cohoes, New York) and plans for a Native American permanent educational facility there. As it happened, I was in the midst of researching my fourth historical novel with a focus on past peoples of Upstate New York and how their migration story might impact a modern-day family. Mr. Crowe's passion for a future site dedicated to cultural remembrance rekindled what I have long believed: the lands in the vicinity of the Cohoes Falls, those nearby in the general area where the Mohawk and Hudson Rivers come together, and complementary areas of the Rensselaer Plateau on the east side of the Hudson River, possess a mystical presence.

The powerful waterfall called by early Native Americans "Coho" or "Cohoos" or sometimes "Oa-ha-oose", which meant 'shipwrecked canoe', was soon the visual awe of 17th century Dutch New Netherland explorers. Holland-born Reverend Johannes Megapolensis, a mid-1600s Mohawk-speaking resident of both Dutch New Amsterdam (later New York City) and the small settlement 150 miles to the north that would later become Albany, wrote of the falls with adulation, obviously mesmerized by surrounding rainbows and Indian lore.

Jasper Dankers and Peter Slyter, members of a religious sect called the Labadists, were travelers from Holland scouting out new lands for a community and while doing so visited the falls, describing it as perhaps the greatest in all the world. (Niagara Falls was until that point undiscovered by Europeans.) Later, Dankers would spend a night in the village of New Harlem (on Manhattan Island) at the home of Constable Resolved Waldron, and Dankers would write an account of that visit as well.[1] In March of 1637, decades prior to the coming of Dankers, Slyter or Waldron, the ship *Rensselaerswyck* arrived at New Amsterdam's wharf. Aboard the cramped vessel were several craftsmen, bakers, brewers, and mid-wives, men and women who would in time significantly change the look and feel of provincial New York. These new Americans and their descendants are the people who populate my novels.

In following the steps of these early European immigrants, who would not be impressed by the magnitude of their accomplishments? The exhausted immigrant arriving at New Amsterdam was often transformed from a common worker to a prominent member of the growing community. History detectives are often fascinated by the discovery of how many early settlers eventually turned away from their learned-trade and jumped into the then lucrative fur trading business. Despite their inexperience with the linguistics or the customs of local tribal peoples, the newcomers were anxious to engage in this New World endeavor, convinced they had landed on heaven's doorstep.

One colonizer arriving on the *Rensselaerswyck* was Goosen Gerritse Van Schaick, a Dutch brewer under contract with the Van Rensselaers. Van Schaick, who fathered ten children and ultimately served as a magistrate, did make beer in New Netherland.

However, while utilizing his rudimentary carpenter skills Van Schaick also developed a healthy knack for real estate around Albany and the hinterlands. Soon this newcomer was also making

---

1. The lives of Resolved Waldron, his family and neighbors are explored in my novel *Manhattan - Seeds of the Big Apple.*

money trading for furs and working in the complimentary tanning trade. A courageous visionary, Goosen Van Schaick's interest in land acquisition was broadened when he met another carpenter, Holland immigrant Philip Pieterse Schuyler. The son of a baker in Amsterdam, Schuyler, also a fur trader, would eventually be one of the most important men of his time in New York. Schuyler's rise to power was enhanced no doubt by his marriage in 1650 to Margarita Van Slichtenhorst, daughter of the Director of the Colony of Rensselaerswyck. However, he, like his friend Van Schaick, was also a shrewd businessman, parlaying his profits into lots, homes, and the rich wilderness land far beyond Albany. Surely, neither of these men thought of themselves as "prophets", but their relentless ambitions fueled by old world discontent would make an impact on thousands of future Americans.

In 1665, only fifteen years after Schuyler's arrival, the two partners took a giant leap of faith when, with the blessing of the new English Governor, Richard Nicolls, they purchased from three Native American chiefs a large track of land about 170 miles north of Manhattan. The area became known as the Halve Maan (Half Moon) Patent. Phillip Schuyler later transferred his interest in the waterfalls and rich delta wilderness lands of the Halve Maan Patent to his partner, Van Schaick. Their professional liaison eventually altered somewhat, yet well after the death of both men, personal relationships flourished between the families through their children. In 1681 the Van Schaick and Schuyler families would unite with the marriage of Van Schaick's daughter Engeltie (Angelica) to Pieter Schuyler. The marriage produced four children before Engeltie's early death during childbirth at age thirty.

Goosen Van Schaick's lands embraced a bevy of various river islands known in his and Schuyler's time as Long Island (not to be confused with the Manhattan area Long Island). After Van Schaick's death the island of the Cohoes Falls became Anthony's Island, named for Goosen's son. Anthony built a formidable mansion (circa 1735) that stands to this day. Eventually Van Schaick's

Half Moon lands including today's Cohoes, Peebles Island, Waterford, Half Moon, and Stillwater became part of Albany and Saratoga Counties in Upstate New York.

The area where the Macques Kill (Mohawk River) and the North River (Hudson) join, presently the village of Waterford, New York, is significant to the setting of this novel as is the village of Schaghticoke sitting to the north across the Hudson in Rensselaer County. In earlier times, Waterford, an hour walk from the city of Cohoes, was known as Half Moon Point. Were archeologists to scrape away the layers of time beneath Waterford, they would find remnants of an ancient Native American village once called Nachtenack. Because of its excellent location, Nachtenack was an acceptable place for active fur trade between the Dutch and the Mohawk Nation during the early 1600s.[2]

Seeing opportunity, by the dawn of the 18th century several Albany residents had either moved to or purchased Half Moon Patent lands. From early documents we learn that one hundred persons made their homes in that vast area. These early settlers included farmers and tradesmen such as Evert Van Nes, Pieter Waldron (grandson of afore mentioned Resolved Waldron), Daniel Fort, Cornelius Vandenbergh and Wouter (Walter) Quackenbush. Many of these were early settlers at Schaghticoke.

The formidable stone home of Killian Van Den Burg, bearing his initials and dated 1718, once stood on the bank of the Mohawk River near the present day hamlet of Crescent. In 1721 Cornelius Van Buren worked his sawmill near present day Mechanicville, New York. This area would see turmoil throughout the 1740s as Abenaki Indians banded with the French, burning farms and scalping settlers. The original Van Schaick lands became ground zero for the French and Indian War. Revolutionary War troops would be encamped behind Anthony's mansion in present day Cohoes not far from the site where, years later, a prehistoric mastodon would be unearthed.

---

2. The village of Waterford was laid out in 1794 and was incorporated March 25th of that same year. Waterford holds the distinction of being the oldest continuously-incorporated village in the United States.

Both the English and the French continued to push west into the rich wilderness areas of what would ultimately become Ohio. This continuous lust for land was the underlying catalyst for the French and Indian War which eventually seeded the American Revolution.

Albany, New York and its surroundings retained its Dutch character well into the early 19th century, yet early on, Irish and Scottish immigrants would intermingle with the American descendants of the original Dutch settlers. Patrick Clark, a member of St. Peter's Anglican Church in Albany, would marry Cornelia Waldron (a great-granddaughter to Resolved Waldron) who was a member of the Albany Dutch Church where all their children would be baptized.

John Clark, believed to be a descendant, was an early resident of Waterford, sometime before 1790. He had two sons, Stephen and Daniel. Stephen owned a factory and furnished shoes for the army during the war of 1812.

Another notable son of Ireland, William Johnson, immigrated in 1737 with the intent of running his uncle's northern plantation on the banks of the Mohawk River northwest of Albany. His life in America would be a collage of intricacies that formed a remarkable legacy. Sir William Johnson became a renowned Indian Superintendent and was the hero of the Battle of Lake George during the French and Indian War. Upon his death in 1774, Johnson would leave to his children, born of relationships with both white and Native American women, over seven hundred thousand acres, two mansions, and many slaves.

Toward the end of the 18th century, the Irish found work based on an idea that had for generations braised the lips of forward thinking Albany Dutch settlers. As the acquisition of local pelts became less possible and profitable, the Seneca lands to the west became more alluring. Many Dutch entrepreneurs had dreamed of building an inland navigational system similar to that of their Fatherland. It would take the minds and hearts of a few sons of Ireland to turn the ancient Dutch dream of binding east and west into reality. One such man, New York City merchant

Thomas Eddy, who during hard times had gone bankrupt, would later be appointed treasurer of the Western Inland Lock Navigation Company, twenty- eight years before the Erie Canal would be completed.

Of course, the man credited with the successful construction of the Erie Canal, DeWitt Clinton, was put to the task years before he would be elected Governor of New York. For the most part it would be the brawn of the Irish who would build the marvel that was referred to as "Clinton's Ditch". The canal was completed in 1825. Thus another layer was added to the European emigrational impact on America.

In 1836 Peter Harmony founded a textile factory by applying the power of the Cohoes Falls. Harmony's venture went bust, but was picked up in 1850 by two others, Thomas Garner, a merchant from Manhattan, and Nathan Wild, who owned a mill at Valatie, New York. By 1872 the "Harmony Mills of Cohoes" was acknowledged as the world's largest cotton-mill complex, and Canadians by the hundreds immigrated, joining forces with the Irish and other newcomers, to work in the mills and local shops at what became known as "Spindle City".

Men such as former Chambly, Quebec innkeeper Moses St. Alban Benjamin were among the ranks of 19th century Canadian entrepreneurial immigrants. Arriving in New York in 1871 at age thirty-one, Moses and his wife Celina would raise a large family while owning and operating a haberdashery on Main Street in Cohoes. However, Moses was determined to expand his clientele beyond gentlemen's hats. From family lore we learn that Celina Benjamin's hats were sold as far away as Manhattan. In the 20th century St. Alban's great-great grandson would become Mayor Mahoney of the Village of Waterford, New York, and the Canadian immigrant's great granddaughter is the author of this book, the fourth of the "American Waldron Series" historical novels.

The 21st century continues to bring prosperity to Schuyler and Van Schaick's original land holdings. New York stays true to a "Dutch West India Company" frame of mind, attracting promising new business. Global Technologies, involved in the manufacture of the latest technology—computer chips—is a multibillion dollar complex and would surely boggle the minds of the original Dutch partners and their descendants.

In 1709 Col. Peter Phillip Schuyler ordered a blockhouse and stockade built along the Hudson, calling the site Fort Ingoldsby. The fort would later become Stillwater, New York, and from Stillwater would come a forested, sleepy little village near Round Lake called Malta, today the site of one of the largest technology parks in the world, computer chip boards replacing animal pelts.

* * *

As America and countries around the world struggle to resolve difficult issues of immigration, the vision seen by this storyteller is layer upon layer of dreamers born afar who made what became the United States of America their forever home.

Standing before New York's Cohoes Falls, everything fades as Wolf people or Mohican, the descendants of the Delaware or Lenni Lenape Native Americans, forgive and stand shoulder to shoulder with immigrant voyagers of every color and creed.

We listen to the voice of the ancients; the *Souls of the Soil*. They whisper of a new time soon to be born. Perhaps this catalyst for change that we continue to seek sleeps within a newcomer—upon sacred ground beloved by the indigenous people—the place that captivated the European visionaries.

CHAPTER 1

Provincial New York, 1679

Two miles from the northern frontier city of Albany, a snowy mist has begun to fall this still, grey November morning at Papscanee Island. Except for the repetitive *rat-ta-tat-tat* of a North American woodpecker methodically jabbing at a dead tree limb somewhere deep within the thick of the forest, silence prevails. The bird's perseverance signals the birth of a new day on the land that Cornelius Vandenbergh and a few others like him believe to be another "Garden of Eden." Here, far beyond the intrusive populous sounds and smells of Manhattan, this tenant farmer, along with a hardy patch of old world immigrants, has for decades toiled the rich soil belonging to the powerful Van Rensselaer family. Here, situated along the east side of the great North River, Vandenbergh had loved, married and fathered three children.

But his happiness had been severed when six years ago his young wife traded her life for that of their newborn child. With two small, baffled boys standing by his side, he'd stood beside her still body and cradled his sleeping infant son. For his children he knew he must live, yet there would be no true living without their mother. The midwife left, and he wept until nothing more would come from him.

Late that same afternoon, the attending mid-wife had returned bringing back a neighbor woman who had recently given birth to a daughter. The young mother, who had been like a sister to his wife, approached him with a generous proposition. She would be blessed to nurse his baby with her own, and she and her husband would care for his little ones until such time that Cornelius would remarry. From the front door of his house Cornelius fought renewed tears as he'd watched her guide his children away, knowing that it was the best he could do, as it would be impossible for him to work his farm and care for his children at the same time.

With the help of neighbors and shrouded in sadness, the following day he'd buried his precious love, the only one whose sweet lips he had ever kissed. Almighty God had cursed him with irrevocable sorrow. Those had been Cornelius's thoughts when they had lowered his beloved into the ground at Papscanee. With every shovel of dirt thrown into her grave, he felt the meaning of the words "sick with grief". One day had passed into another. *Rat-ta-tat-tat.*

But The Almighty had not forsaken Cornelius Vandenbergh, for while still in the midst of a lonely widower's misery, and by way of Albany's kind Dutch Dominie, he'd found a second good woman. From the beginning when she'd first accepted him he was grateful for the consistent Cornelia, a childless widow. Because of her he'd been able to retrieve his children and to keep his family together. For her part, Cornelia had always endeavored to be a tender loving mother to his orphaned children.

Early in the mornings she instructed his boys in prayer. She taught the children how to pluck a fat hen. A hard day of working in the fields was always followed by warm bread and beer on his table. On occasion he'd watched her as she efficiently cleaned the hefty sturgeon he'd caught in the river. Rarely ever silent, Cornelia would sing her chanty—a familiar sailor's ballad—in a strong alto voice which he found to be a fond reminder of "Fatherland".

Later in their bed, he was comforted whenever he wished. His wife made no complaints or excuses as he'd heard some wives did. After a year's time, his gratitude had lapsed into a quiet, unbending love, and so when his wife's elderly blind mother needed the care of her daughter, he had welcomed his mother-in-law into his house.

His young daughter, Catherine, born of this second union, has been the sweet joy of his elder years. A Dutch immigrant who had come to this wilderness land with nothing, the once fraught widower had prospered as he heartily embraced his second chance, and, until yesterday, he had thought himself the most fortunate of men.

Now exhausted, Cornelius sat beneath the sturdy singed trunk of a tall elm, a safe distance from the smoldering heaps of ash, the remains of his house. Yesterday's wind-driven, smoke-filled afternoon, punctuated by the pitiful sound of choked voices, had passed into a frenzied night. Scores of neighbors from surrounding farms had fought to corral irrepressible flames. Despite the brave comradery of many, Vandenbergh's house, barn and outbuildings were gone. His precious wheat and corn crops had also perished. Most of his animals were either burnt or dead. Even so he praised God that at least all of his family lived.

Dawn worked hard that morning to push away the darkness. Now, as raining snowflakes melted into the scorched earth, a bewildered Cornelius heard the prayerful who had stayed behind to help through the night. As those assembled chanted reverently, their voices meekly rising above the call of the woodlands, Cornelius grew irritated. Although he was relieved that his family survived and the wind has been replaced by a gentle snow, the soulful supplications seemed senseless. His swollen head erupted with every crescendo, and he wished to God that the prayerful be silent.

Looking over his burnt fingers he saw that little flesh was left on some, and a true anger rose within his heart. *What sin have I committed this time that I should deserve this? Have I not been a just man and done all that I should do? How will I be able to work with hands like these?*

While struggling to remember what had happened during the past crazed hours, Cornelius was hardly cognizant of the approach of a Mohican, the River Indian whom colonists hereabouts had long called Abram. Cornelius knew him to be a medicine man and friend, one who had lodged with him and his family on many occasions.

Now, eager for relief of his searing pain, Cornelius extended what was left of his hands.

Acknowledging the white man's invitation, Abram, barely touched him with a poultice—a handful of river soaked, muddied herbs. Another Mohican tried to cover Cornelius with a blanket while a squaw came forward offering a hallowed gourd filled with sweet hickory nut milk, but Cornelius wrenched away from his Samaritans. He could not endure the poultice, nor the slightest weight of the cloth the elder of the men wrapped around his shoulders. Although he thirsted and though he tried, he could not drink the milk.

Abram pointed to a festering blister on Cornelius's forearm and offered the prepared salve, persisting in broken Dutch, "It is good... will help heal."

Stubbornly, Cornelius shook his head and waved him away, but as he did so he suddenly remembered something that made his head ache all the more. During the night it was Abram who had assured him that his children, his wife and her mother, along with their servant girl, had been taken to a neighboring farm. Word had come later that the women there were tending them.

Slowly regaining his presence of mind, Cornelius recalled the name of the man whom Abram said had offered shelter to his family. In absorbing the Indian's words meant to comfort, he was jolted to his core. How could it be that the combatant John Thomas, who had always acted toward him like an enemy, would step forward to do anything for him or his family?

Although he should have been relieved, he was greatly disturbed thinking of his wife and children at the Thomas place. Last spring he had brought this same neighbor to court, the two of them arguing bitterly over the fencing of the pastures between their farms. Several times they had openly cursed one another and had nearly come to blows, and would have, had it not been for the intervention of officials in attendance. Cornelius thought John Thomas an unreasonable, lazy sort, and he couldn't understand how the Van Rensselaers permitted him to stay on their lands. He knew from private conversation with the overseer that he had agreed with him, but of course, it was up to the courts to decide.

Cornelius felt he saw his and Thomas's situation plainly. He had taken care of the fencing in the past with the help of no man, but his bones had grown stiff; he could no longer take on the task without any assistance, and his boys were still too young for a grown man's work. It was only right that each man do what he should do because the fence was a shared boundary.

Thomas's indignant counter complaint was that the previous owner of his farm had never been made to help with the mutual fencing so why should he be ordered to do so?

Cornelius had argued back that the previous owner had offered to help with the fencing, but he did not need his help at that time. He'd also told how the previous owner had been a good master over his own pigs, and they had never plundered through freshly sown fields in springtime, nor rooted through his wife's vegetable garden as Thomas's had done throughout the previous summer.

Cornelius considered himself a patient man, but seeing the mother of his children weeping over her garden losses every other day was more than he could tolerate. No man should allow such an offense. He'd taken his complaints to the land owner, Jeremias Van Rensselaer's widow, and Mistress Maria had agreed that right was only right.

He had won in court, but John Thomas blatantly continued to ignore the court ruling. Since that time no Christian love had remained between them. In truth, Cornelius had long wished that his aggravating neighbor would move far away so that he would never see or hear from him again. But his Cornelia was not happy to be at odds with anyone for any reason, and she had gently urged him to find a way for reconciliation with their neighbor. When they had prepared to joyously celebrate his aged mother-in-law's birthday in conjunction with one of the best harvests that they had ever experienced, his wife had suggested they invite all their neighbors without exception. Ashamed, he remembered how he had been furious and refused her request to try again to talk over their dispute with Thomas and make amends. He'd have none of it, and instead, again he'd angrily cursed him.

Now, as the prayerful chants of his neighbors continued to assault him, he pondered all of what had happened during the past year. It was hard to believe that this same man who had once quarreled with him would take in his desperate, injured family. He wondered why his enemy would show such compassion. Perhaps he had judged him too severely, or perhaps God had sent an angel who had shamed John Thomas into taking action as a way of amends.

Cornelius's hands seared with pain. As if Abram, still kneeling beside him, could see into his tormented soul and understand, his friend lightly touched his shoulder before withdrawing. As Abram disappeared Cornelius attempted to stand, but stumbled backwards, his legs collapsing. The Indian woman returned, this time with a moist cloth, and he allowed her to barely dab his lips. Without speaking, he thanked her with a slight nod of his head and drifted back into thought.

It must have been near three o'clock in the afternoon yesterday when the fire started. The sky had had a strange look to it all morning, especially for early November. As the wind picked up, he and a few of the neighboring men finished splitting logs at the edge of the back woods while his young sons wove in and out of the forest collecting smaller branches.

The cart behind his oxen was nearly full, and as it was nearing mealtime he'd picked up his musket preparing to return to the house. At that moment a series of lightning strikes lit the sky followed by ominous crashing thunder. Van Rensselaer's hired Indian who had been sent along to help him had shuddered fearfully. "The *sky world* is angry," he'd said.

About that same time, one of his neighbor's Negro women came to fetch him. Out of breath, she dropped to her knees before him, frantically announcing that Cornelius's house was on fire and her mistress begged him to come in all haste.

Leaving the full cart and the pair of oxen in place with the distraught messenger, he and the others ran as swiftly as possible, arriving at the plantation no more than ten minutes thereafter. Black smoke billowed high into the sky, and what Cornelius had most feared was soon confirmed as they approached the outlying fields. His family's dwelling was already falling.

Panic struck his heart when he saw his terrified wife frantically beating at flames that had attached to her skirt. He raced toward her, and, ignoring the delirious talk he couldn't understand, brought her hard to the ground, rolling her, smothering the flames with the palms of his hands. The flames out, he looked closer now and his heart sank. Cornelia's face was blistered red, her golden hair partially burned away from her scalp.

Please God, do not take my wife from me.

He remembered now that as he worked to save Cornelia one of the Indian women had rushed toward his boys with his little Cate clasped within her arms. She had fled with them all toward the river though the boys resisted, not wanting to leave their mother. In the confusion of the moment Cornelius recalled holding onto his dear wife, fighting with her to come away, insisting that he would go back into the house for her mother, but she would not hear him, and urged him to go instead to free the animals. She would go through the flames and find her mother. Precious moments ticked by. Finally, taking a bucket of water from one of the Indians running past, Cornelia quickly spilled it over herself. They had no more time to argue. They could not save both unless they split up.

Cornelia had found her mother crouched down behind her bed, and the two miraculously made it out of the house, but her mother was badly burned. Cornelius feared that his mother-in-law might not live to celebrate another birthday. The delay was his fault. He was to blame for the old woman's additional suffering. Each of them had done as they must, and yet, Cornelius did not know if he would be able to live with his guilt.

As the fire raged, he was able to shoo three horses and eleven of his cows out of the barn. Finally out in the open, they most willingly ran from the flames into the woods, but the pig sty along with all his well-fattened hogs near ready for slaughter had burnt.

His neighbor, Henry Van Ness, and Van Ness's friend, Will Waldron, up from Manhattan, had come running down the road to help just after he'd arrived. However, by the time they'd reached the farm the fire was already well along the path of total destruction.

Throughout the afternoon and into the night all anyone could do was form a long human line from the river to the burning structures and pass water-filled or empty leather buckets back and forth.

Vandenbergh was beginning to comprehend the extent of his losses. Besides his field crops, two barracks filled with grain had also burned. His barn was lost, as were the rest of the cows, along with his rope maker and other tools. His home...a complete loss. Some things were not easily replaced—his precious, great leather bound Dutch Bible with its meticulous list of his birth and the births of both his wives, his marriages, his first wife's death, and the listing of the births of each of his children. A replacement list would take time, but God's holy word as well as the significant dates that had marked his life were all clearly etched in his being. The furnishings—beds, his wife's spinning wheel, every cooking pot that had melted in the intensity of the fire, even the expensive hearth tiles he had purchased for Cornelia from Peter Quackenbush's kiln in Albany—would be replaced with time.

But the loss of his ledger book was far more worrisome. How would he make sense of his costs to the Manor's mistress, Maria Van Rensselaer? Cornelius grasped the dire predicament of his circumstances. He had nothing left with which he could pay his annual rent in May. He had nothing to feed his family. He was ruined. Bitterly he recalled his Dutch grandfather's ominous prediction. *In New Netherland, a man would shovel dung against the wind for naught.* And so it seemed that his grandfather's words had come to pass.

Fixing his eyes on twelve-year-old Henry Van Rensselaer, sleeping soundly on the bare ground not far away, Cornelius sighed in utter helplessness. This morning, by way of messengers, the boy's mother, the Mistress of the Manor, had promised her support. At dawn, Henry and two young men had arrived by canoe from the manor. Henry had run to him eagerly, right away conveying his mother's genuine concern for Cornelius and his family.

Vaguely now Cornelius remembered young Henry, second of Maria and Patroon Jeremias offspring, standing over him, weeping. The boy, only a few years older than his own son, had, since the death of his father, often been a visitor to Vandenbergh's humble house. He loved the horses Vandenbergh kept, especially the big white one.

The messengers had conveyed Maria Van Rensselaer's instructions that they make an immediate report to her of the overall circumstances of this terrible fire; she had seen the smoke swelling into the sky high above the North River. Once an inventory of loss was made and in her hands, Henry had blurted out that his mother promised that she would write immediately to his uncle in New York as well as his father's relatives in Holland, but first she would come herself within a week's time to bear personal witness to the disaster. In the meanwhile, Henry was determined to remain close by with one of the neighbors.

Mistress Van Rensselaer's gesture meant much to Cornelius. The mother of six understood hardship. She had been lame since the birth of her last child and could only walk with the aid of her crutches. Despite her handicap, she was dedicated to the welfare of the people who had agreed to settle on her lands. Though she was privileged in many ways, who among them did not look at Widow Van Rensselaer without both pity and respect? Cornelius didn't know how he would be able to go on. He could barely move, and yet he looked forward to seeing her.

Abram distracted him, excitedly pointing to a place in the distance far past the rubble of the barn. Cornelius followed his direction and watched as human figures led two of what he assumed were his runaway horses out of the woods into a fenced corral that remarkably still stood. As they came closer, he saw that the rescuers were none other than Will Waldron and Abram's brother. Desperate tears filled Vandenbergh's eyes. He was thankful to see his horses, but again worried how he would be able to pay his rent on the land and the animals.

Although his neighbor, Van Ness, had urged him to go to Thomas's and join his wife and mother-in-law, Cornelius balked. He could not leave this place until every one of his animals was accounted for so that a responsible report could be made to Mistress Van Rensselaer. Then, and only then, would he go to be by his wife's side. He begged Van Ness to get word to her that he was well but not to tell of the seriousness of his injuries. And when Maria Van Rensselaer did come to see the ruins, he would talk with her himself so that she would be able to give a firsthand, honest accounting to her brother-in-law.

Looking around at the devastation, Cornelius now wondered if he should have taken the widow up upon her recent offer for him to settle with his family farther north upon her lands near to friendly Indians. He had talked with Cornelia about moving. The farmers there were protected from the Canada French and their Indian allies by good Mohican friends, some of whom were cousins to those on Papscanee.

He had given the widow's proposition serious consideration. He knew some of the farmers who had gone northward to these lands and were now prospering there. It was his understanding that this was why Will Waldron was staying with Van Ness. The two of them had just come back from the North Country, and Cornelius had listened when they shared that this prosperity came not only by way of tilling the soil, but also from the proceeds made from high quality furs. They sold the furs to traders from Albany and bartered with northern Indians who stopped there to trade. Some settlers would even prefer trading to farming if they could. But Cornelius had said no to the good widow's offer and even now meant to keep to his decision to remain as a farmer at Papscanee Island.

Cornelius looked up the hill behind his farm and saw that his beloved apple orchard survived unscathed. Although this year's fruited preserves stored within his wife's cupboard had perished, he would hold onto the hope that the apple trees would blossom again in spring. Next year during September his children would climb the branches and pick enough apples to fill a hundred baskets.

Cornelius met Abram's concerned gaze and reluctantly motioned to the Indian to approach, indicating that he was willing to allow him to try again with a poultice. Abram understood and tended to him. As he did so, Cornelius focused upon a Native woman who had stooped to pick up a large shimmering crystal of the kind that were scattered all over the island. Long ago he had been captivated by the story of the stones that glittered—a tale passed down by Abram's ancestors. According to legend, before recorded time crystals more numerous than the stars had rained down from the sky, blessing the fertility of the land as each one released sacred powers of the Great Spirit.

Tentatively, Abram again extended his brother's colorful blanket, and this time Cornelius accepted it. From a leather flask hanging around his neck, the Indian trickled water over Cornelius's head. Cornelius immediately understood the significance of the anointing. No doubt this was the holy water drawn from the high-rock spring where many of the Natives worshiped. Several Native women had joined their men gathering together with the white men, and all prayed over Cornelius' pained body, each in his or her own way.

Cornelius fought to hold back tears. When his eyes again fell upon the ruins of his home, he wondered where his God was. Did He see him at all? Cornelius appreciated the compassion of his neighbors, but he did not want their pity or their prayers. If the Almighty had abandoned him, he would stand on his own. He was, to be sure, a Vandenbergh, and a Vandenbergh must persevere whilst he drew breath.

Silently, he vowed that as soon as he regained his strength he would begin again and be a burden to no man. And when his time came to leave this troublesome world he would be buried deep within the soil of his beloved orchard that overlooked the river. This was his wish. This was his country. Forevermore this land would be home to his family.

CHAPTER 2

Upstate New York, 2014

Tom Carey again maneuvered his lanky 6'5" frame through the crowded funeral chapel. After a half dozen tries he finally found a good, inconspicuous spot toward the back. Who'd have thought that he'd be back in New York for something like this? Swallowing a Nexium, he washed the capsule down with the remnants of cold black coffee he'd been nursing in the back room and deliberated when he could try for a polite departure.

Shooting a quick glance in his mother's direction, he crumpled his empty Styrofoam cup. Although they'd been there for over an hour, they couldn't just dart in and out. Helen Carey, Catholic to the core, would want to stick around for the comforting voice of her old friend and confessor Father Patrick, who undoubtedly would say a few words about eternal life and heaven opening up the doors to Mrs. Mann.

Tom had serious doubts about the existence of heaven, but he understood what his mother's faith meant to her. There could be no closure this evening without closing prayers, and the retired priest had yet to show. A few minutes before, he'd overheard someone whisper that Father Patrick was driving in from Syracuse and the weather to the west of Albany along the Thruway was black with thunderstorms. Tom pulled his silenced iPhone from the inside pocket of his suit jacket. 6:43 p.m. He returned the phone to his pocket, and straightened and smoothed his navy blue tie.

Gonna be a long night. What the hell was I thinking?

They'd flown in from Phoenix, and of course, Mom... he ... well, they both wanted to show the family more than a dribble of respect. It wasn't as if they hadn't talked this all over days ago after his mother had received the call. They knew this was going to be a tough trip back east, and neither of them wanted to revisit the past. Yet this was Christine Mann dead...his once-upon-a-time second mother who'd always been willing to make his favorite sandwich: peanut butter, mayo and marshmallow minus the bread crust.

Despite his burning esophagus Tom smiled, thinking about all those absent crusts that he, the Mann girls, and Russ Yates kept from his mom and dad who abhorred any form of waste. No worries in those days. Nothing edible ever went to waste while under the Mann watch because Russ Yates, aka "Crusty Rusty", ate everything and anything offered—including hated lima beans. At twelve their other mom introduced him and Crusty to hitting balls at the Schuyler Golf Range. Little doubt that Christine Mann probably would be credited with his passion for the game.

Good times before life became so complicated.

His mother extended her hand to someone else he didn't recognize.

While in flight to Albany, they'd tried to absorb the shock of an apparently healthy woman's sudden death. The details of her passing were wild. According to her daughters, she had no history of heart trouble yet was gone within a breath of serving up her response to Alex Trebek on "Jeopardy". Helen's only explanation had been what Tom remembered as the part of a quote his mother kept framed on her desk at home—something about yesterday already being a dream, and to shoot for living well in the moment. After what he'd seen in the service, he had little to add.

He'd begun to speculate about the parade that filed past the elaborate mahogany open casket. What was Mrs. Mann's relationship with those who viewed her lifeless body, sharing in the intimacy of her death? Clearly, she'd touched more people than she probably would have thought, but that didn't surprise him. Her daughters, Charlene and Lisa, steadfast sentinels by her side, were obviously sedated. Their devotion was no surprise either. Robotically they offered up the same polite smile to each sympathetic word. Charlene's two boys seated up front fidgeted in their seats.

Tom sighed. *It might have been me standing up there with them and not their uncle. It should have been me.* He turned away. It was harder than he'd expected watching them suffer through their loss, but at least the sisters had stuck together. They had always had one another.

Shortly after arriving he and his mother had knelt beside each other in front of the casket, and he'd managed a silent "Hail Mary". For a lot of reasons he felt like a hypocrite, and he was embarrassed that he could hardly make eye contact with either Charlene or Lisa while he expressed his sympathy. It just wasn't how he'd thought it would be after all these years, but nothing had ever turned out as he had once expected. And another huge surprise…he'd almost hit the floor when he noticed what Charlene was wearing around her neck.

The posture was different with the longstanding patriarch of the family. Michael Van Schaick, brother to the deceased, standing supportively between his two nieces. "Big Mick" hadn't changed much from how Tom remembered him—full head of white hair now, but still the powerful, assured presence of a self-made man, the spawn of an old Upstate New York family with deep roots traversing back to the area's 17th century New Netherland immigrants.

Tom remembered mixed "since the beginning" genealogical verbiage from the billboards Van Schaick had put up all over the Capital District. Watching the man now, Tom also remembered how his grandmother had sputtered "uncouth" upon first seeing Van Schaick's advertising signs. She had complained that "Mr. Van Schaick" had capitalized on her fine Dutch heritage to sell his big, custom-built houses in Clifton Park. Nevertheless, that advertising campaign had been successful. According to his mother, Mick did become one of Upstate New York's premier builders. Tom surmised that Van Schaick's crews most likely did build a damn good house. All the same, Nana had good insight into people.

Tom saw that Charlene had taken a few steps in the direction of the ladies room before being squeezed between two sympathetic grey haired women. His chest heaved. He remembered how the little girl whose face he'd once pushed into the snow had grown into a beauty. He was the one who couldn't stay away from those big brown eyes. He was the one who had broken the understood protective barrier around the Mann girls. He had pushed the envelope. He and Char happened. Tom was sure that her Uncle Mick had been infuriated when he realized that they were together. After all, he was Steve Carey's son.

His first memory of Mick Van Schaick was at his folks' dining room table. He must have been about eight. Tom remembered that day in particular because he'd reached across the table for something, knocking over a full glass of milk on his mother's new white tablecloth in the process. He couldn't recall what he'd reached for, but he could still hear his mother yelling clearly, "Tommy...you come right back here!" as he bolted from the table, blubbering, and ran to his room. Nothing she or his dad had said could coax him back. He'd gone without dinner and happily.

Back then his dad and Mick were partners in a window and door store on Central Avenue in Albany. Once in a while on a Saturday his dad took him down to the shop. Mr.Van Schaick had been nice to him then, but the home improvement venture didn't work out, and their partnership had ended badly by the time he entered junior high school.

The end of the partnership marked the beginning of a lot of changes. Mick stopped coming to the house for Sunday dinners, and the Van Schaick name was rarely, if ever, spoken of again in his parent's house Later, he would sometimes see Mick down at the Schuyler golf course clubhouse where, thanks to Mrs. Mann, Tom had bussed tables during high school. But the "King", as many called the founder of Van Schaick Development, had few good words to throw at the tall, skinny kid cleaning his table. Back in the day, he'd wondered about what had happened, but kids then didn't talk to their folks about those things in the open way he and his boy talked. Now that he thought about it, he and his dad rarely talked about anything much.

As a teenager in the 80s, Tom and all his buddies knew that if any of them dated one of the Mann girls more than twice, and then something went on that had to be confessed to the priest in the 'black box' on Saturday afternoon, somehow, someway, the randy sinner would be found out and shadowed by iron-fisted Mick or one of his cousins. Most of his friends wisely passed on asking out the Mann girls.

But, earlier this evening when he'd first laid eyes on Van Schaick, Tom had noticed that the man who greeted Helen Carey was a different man from the fierce ball-buster he had known as a teenager. Van Schaick had taken his mother's hand into both of his own with a trace of a cordial smile; his "good to see you, Helen" was barely audible, yet filled with a tenderness Tom had never seen. For a brief second, amazingly, he'd even acknowledged her son.

Yet Tom wasn't indifferent to the man's vibes. He was ten years a practicing criminal attorney and knew "false" when he felt it. While his misty-eyed mother hugged each of Chris's daughters, their uncle's sullen gaze had washed over him: a long, searing burn accompanied Mick's hostile stare, too. The man wanted nothing more than Tom, the table wiper he'd remembered, gone. Tom thought that "gone" might be an area where he and Van Schaick were on the same page, but for different reasons. Although he was uncomfortable with all of this, with everything pressing on his own calendar back west, he'd be happy to oblige.

Whether or not Van Schaick was a lying son-of-a-bitch as Tom's father had hissed a few nights before he died really didn't matter anymore. Whether or not the ghosts of their ancestors danced around them pleading for attention as his dad often insisted after a few too many beers, none of it was relevant. Anything that had linked the Careys and the Van Schaicks was broken the night his father had given up his soul.

Long ago Tom had given up trying to find reasons. Only facts tumbled across his table, but he did believe that a higher power set the odds. It didn't matter if you were traveling in a convoy in a war zone or relaxing in your recliner watching a game show. The difference between here and there was razor thin. So, on the plane he'd listened quietly, and after his mother had apparently exhumed all that she could, he'd put his head back against his headrest, closed his eyes, and speculated about what the trusting, brown-eyed girl whom he'd once wrapped his arms around at the top of a Schaghticoke Fair Ferris wheel would be thinking. He'd concluded that the grieving woman he'd meet wouldn't know that a heart-broken teenage boy hadn't had a choice. But, then he'd noticed her necklace.

Seeing Charlene after all these years wasn't the nothing he had assured his wife it would be before he'd left Phoenix. Within minutes of arriving at the funeral chapel, Charlene had recharged emotions that he'd sworn to Alison were long dead. Without a spoken word, his first love had made a point of showing him that in part she was still the trusting young girl he'd left behind. He recognized what she wanted him to know as soon as he saw the pewter pendent hanging around her neck.

The day before he had left town with his mother, he'd mailed the medal—a circle of roses intercepting a cross—in a plain manila envelope without a return address. Back then he couldn't bring himself to write a note. He didn't have the right words and was afraid that her father might intercept his letter. Somehow though he'd thought that if God was really up there He would see to it that the cross would find its way into Char's hands. Tom had hoped that she would understand his unspoken message... that he would love her forever. Until today he'd not known if she had ever received the necklace.

Throughout the years that followed their hasty departure from Milltown, Helen Carey had reconnected with Charlene's mother and with other old friends in New York, but there had been little mention of Charlene except a few lines written within a letter he'd received from his mother while serving in Iraq letting him know that Charlene had married. Tom remembered that in part he was relieved. After all, it had been years and he had chosen to remember their good times. He wanted her to have a life...a happy life. They just weren't meant to be. He'd accepted that.

He'd not heard much throughout the years about his old friends in New York which was probably best. A hard journey past several rough milestones had eventually allowed him to put aside his pain and his guilt over leaving his childhood sweetheart. Part of what he'd endured consisted of time in the Corps, resulting in a prosthetic replacing his right foot. It had taken months at the VA hospital and Alison's fantastic smile and then returning to law school before he'd given himself permission to make a life of his own. He'd married his 'best nurse'. Then came the miracle of the birth of their son, Kyle.

On their way to Albany his mother felt she should fill him in about things so that he would be prepared for certain changes he'd be encountering, such as Charlene recently losing her husband to lung cancer, leaving her with two teenage boys. About Char's mother, Tom also learned a few other things. Chris had taken the grandkids on a cruise. Chris still was a golfer who played eighteen holes a week April through October. She line danced and gardened with a passion. It seemed odd to hear a fast summary of so many details about the Mann family, and strange that his mom had kept it all from him.

Charlene's phone call had been a terrible shock to his mother. Apparently she had found his mother's number in her mother's address book. She had called and said that she had dropped by her mom's to pick up a cake her mother had made for the following day when they planned to celebrate Char's younger boy's thirteenth birthday. Pulling the cake from the refrigerator, Char had heard her mother's last words float in from the living room—"I know that one." Then nothing. The ambulance had arrived within minutes. Later at the hospital Mrs. Mann was pronounced dead. *Nobody saw it coming. Nobody was ready for this.*

Tom walked to the lounge and tossed the crushed cup he'd been holding into the trash basket. *Who is ready for anything?* When he'd noticed that necklace on Char something inside of him moved, and it came to him that the final curtain had only just fallen. She didn't hate him. Char's merciful heart had given him absolution. He sure wasn't ready for that.

Returning to the chapel, he found his mother up front still holding Charlene's hand, but staring across the room at a stunningly attractive, dark-skinned older woman. He'd noticed her a few minutes earlier when she'd come in and stopped to scan the room, and for a second they'd made eye contact. Except for a large gold belt buckle with some sort of insignia on it, she was sleekly dressed in black.

Mick, Tom noticed, stood erect, suddenly uncharacteristically dumbfounded, surveying the stranger as she approached the coffin. At the same time his mother leaned toward Charlene, whispering a few words of what must have been an introduction. Tom assumed the woman must be someone his mother had known a long time ago.

"Tom ... hey Tom."

Tom swung around to see Jimmy Goewey, a Van Schaick cousin, heading toward him after signing the guest book a few feet away. He came straight to him, hand outstretched.

"Man oh man," Jimmy exploded. "I haven't seen you for God knows how long. Damn, you sure look fit. Once a Marine always a Marine. Everybody knows that. You're still out west, right? Hey, I heard you finally got married and you're a lawyer?"

Tom smiled. "Yes. Way west ... Phoenix. Married a long time now, Jimmy. My wife and I have a boy, ten—Kyle. And it took me awhile, but, correct, I'm a lawyer. So how about you?"

Jimmy grimaced, then answered while perusing the room. "Well, I'm on my own these days ... divorced since 2004."

"Sorry to hear".

"Well, she got remarried a couple years back, but I still sail single. Just one of those things. All's good though now. We buried the hatchet."

"Glad to hear. Any kids?"

"No kids. I'm still selling cars, but now I'm in Rensselaer." Shuffling through his inside suit pocket he pulled out his business card. "Here. Let's keep in contact. Shoot … I think I'd better get on over there and say hi to Charlene. Sad about her losing her husband so early on top of her dad and now her mom."

"Yes, her mom was a nice lady," Tom squeezed in.

"Terrible, just terrible. Two young kids to raise now, but damn she looks good, don't you think?"

"She always looked good," Tom answered, easing the business card into his pocket.

"Oh, right. Sorry man. I forgot about you two being an item back in the day."

Tom smiled. "Old business. Nothing at all to be sorry about on my score, and I'm sure Charlene would say the same. She'll do fine. She's a strong girl. Hey, do you ever hear from Buddy Vandenberg or Crusty?"

"No, man. I don't know what happened to either one of them. I think Yates went into the Air Force. Oh, and Buddy married one of the Romano girls. They ran a great little Italian restaurant with her father for a while, but that was ages ago." After an awkward pause, "Well, super seeing you, Tommy. Will I see you at the funeral tomorrow if I'm able to make it?"

"I'll be there with my mother," Tom replied, trying to place the Romano girls.

Jimmy nodded back at him while wrangling his way through the crowd. Tom thought of an old expression he'd heard a lot as a kid: *the more things change the more they stay the same.*

As Jimmy faded away the woman in black darted past him and he was able to see the image on her belt buckle…three black bulls. He'd seen that insignia before someplace. Wasn't important, but she was memorable. He'd ask his mother about her later.

Suddenly Tom noticed that Jimmy had stopped to shake hands with someone who seemed familiar. Looking closer he recognized him—Joe Bennett, a guy he'd hoped that he'd never see again. Nothing much surprised him anymore, and stuff sure as hell rarely shook him, but there, just a few feet away, stood the son-of-a-bitch who might just as well have killed his dad. And there he was … Joe Bennett, and wearing the collar of a cleric. *What?*

CHAPTER 3

Helen Carey had come to love the melon fragrance of the white saguaro blossoms of Arizona's cactus, but today, as mourners drifted away from the rural hillside cemetery, all that she inhaled was the sweetness of an Upstate New York spring. She found herself recalling the words of the 19th century author Nathaniel Hawthorne: *Time flies over us, but leaves its shadow behind.* She imagined an arm encircle her shoulder, something Christine Mann had often done when she'd most needed it.

Tom reached out. "You okay, Mom?" His concern was obvious. "You look tired."

"I'm fine."

"Watch these steps going down. They're a bit slippery. Here, take my hand," he urged.

"I'm okay. Really." But she welcomed his firm grip. "You and I both know, son, she's in heaven now." Helen sighed. "If anyone would get in, that would be Chris, of that I have no doubt."

Tom continued his support, only letting go of her after they had descended the last of the crooked slate slabs.

Helen paused. "I'll be along, Tom. I'd just like a few minutes alone. Now go ahead and catch up with Lisa and her husband. They've been trying to get your attention. Over there by the red pickup truck. See them down there?"

"I do." Tom waved back at the couple he barely knew.

"It might be good for you to have a few minutes with them. Lisa seems to have married an awfully nice fella. Any hard feelings she would have had over anything most likely disappeared when she saw you had come for her mother."

Tom responded slowly and thoughtfully. "I sure would hope so. Okay. Then I'll meet you down by the car in, say, fifteen minutes?"

He remembered how Lisa, always her sister's honor guard, had come to their old Milltown house the day before they'd left. His mother had run out to the store for some last minute thing. The doorbell rang, and he'd answered. There stood Lisa with a giant 'Big Joe' soda in her hand. Within two seconds she'd thrown the soda, ice cubes and all, into his face. "Screw you!" were her profound words of departure. He'd never said a word about the incident to anyone.

Tom smiled warily at his mother, and pleased that making peace seemed to be in the air, Helen confirmed, "I don't think I'll be much longer than that. I'm going to take a short detour before I go back to the car. I'd like to drop by your Nana's grave, and then I thought that I'd check my own grandma and grandpa's over in the old section just to see if the stones are still standing."

Tom nodded and headed across the grass while checking his cell texts. One was from Alison. "Plumber fixed the shower. All's good here. Love you."

He responded, "Same."

Helen hesitated, watching her son as he made his way toward the crammed cemetery parking lot, his broad shoulders squared back, and his stride confident. Nobody would guess that he wore a prosthetic. He was, as his wife had once remarked, "a walking miracle".

As Helen deliberated the best way to approach her grandparents' graves she also reflected how super it would be if the kids could make amends. Separating Tommy from all his friends, especially Charlene, had weighed heavy on her heart. She knew how much their move had hurt Chris, too. Turning around for one last glance up the hill where Patrick still lingered with Charlene, she was sure that Chris would have been happy to be the instrument of peace. The feeling of reconciliation was warming.

Above, the priest met her gaze, and Helen knew without any gesture that Patrick would probably call her once she and Tom were back in Phoenix. Last evening he'd found her alone in the coffee room as she made herself a cup of tea, and he'd quietly asked how to get in touch. She'd given him her land-line number at home, but hoped she hadn't sent a wrong message and surely not after all of these years. She didn't want to discuss or confess anything more. Really, what else could be said? But, she couldn't brush him aside. She wouldn't.

This morning had been so stressful for her with her thoughts jumping between past and present. She'd seen Chris Mann only once through the decades when, the year following 9-11, the two of them, along with another high school classmate living in Nebraska, had met in Vegas. It seemed like a perfect neutral place and the right time to reconnect to remind each other that although everyone's life in America was frightfully altered forevermore, living had to, and would continue. She'd calmed her nerves with several fortifying gin and tonics. She'd not been on a plane in decades. Once in Las Vegas, with the mutual promise made not to discuss 9-11 she'd found the renewed support of old friendships.

The three of them had played the slots, caught a couple of good shows, walked the Strip, and laughed as they had as girls. The best part of that vacation, Helen recalled, was that it had felt great to dispel the last images of a tearful Chris helping her pack up the old tan and brown VW Bus, the vehicle that would a few days later transport Tom and her across the country to their new life. Helen suspected that the trip she and Tom had made was much the same emotionally as those made by many of the people buried in the old section of the cemetery she walked through now. None of them knew much of anything about where they were going or how their lives would work out. All they knew was that, for them, like it had been for her, change was the only path to a future.

After the Vegas trip they all had kept in touch, telephoning around the Christmas holidays with follow up emails every so often. However, Helen had gone back to work as an adjunct professor at the community college, and Chris and her husband had begun a second career with a catering business. Later, Chris was busy enjoying babysitting her grandkids. And then her husband died. Helen had regretted that she couldn't get away to attend the funeral. Communication waned though she had reached out to Chris. Recently they had found each other again via Facebook. They had both agreed they should do something together again, but it never came to more than that, and now Chris was gone.

How surreal to think that she would never see or hear from Chris again. How terrible to have to accept that the last time they had shared a thought was on a social network. Her biggest regret was that she hadn't just picked up the phone and called Chris when her inner voice had told her to do so. Long ago she should have told her the whole truth about why she had had to leave New York or at least the truth as she had come to believe it. Now there was no one left to tell. What remained was (as she had once confessed to Patrick) a truth better left unsaid. *Maybe I shouldn't have given my number to Patrick after all.*

Her mother's simple stone was unblemished as were those of her grandma and grandpa. Surprising, because as her mother had once pointed out there was no perpetual care for this cemetery. Many of the stones that covered the town's first settlers had deteriorated. Helen remembered that her mother had felt a sense of responsibility for those graves because she knew that many buried there were her ancestors.

Twenty minutes later, satisfied with her pilgrimage, she found Tom waiting patiently behind the wheel of their rental. Her thoughts had already returned to Steve, the husband who at one time had been both lover and the best of confidants, a soulmate whom she had lost to an unseen world long before she and her eighteen-year-old son were left to bury his physical remains. God knows, Steve had his troubles, but she'd never stopped loving him.

Most likely Tom thought that she would cave from grief over Chris, but it was Steve whom she had been thinking of when they'd boarded the plane at Phoenix, and God forgive her, it was Steve she thought of when she knelt to pray for Chris. She wondered if Chris would meet him in heaven or if he would be someplace on "the other side of the veil" as he described what she thought was Purgatory. What about Heaven? Was Steve right about the afterlife? Does everyone live dead center in the midst of an unseen world that blends the past with the present? For Steve his new age reality couldn't be ignored. She tried to get him help. She tried.

Helen opened the door to the passenger side and settled herself in.

"You have to let it go Mom," Tom said. "I know it's hard, but we have to believe that they are all in a better place."

Helen forced a reassuring smile. "Of course."

How could Tom know that I'll never be able to let it all go because for me there will always be the lingering question of what exactly was the truth? There is something more after physical life, but the only truth I know is that I'll never understand what happened to Steve during those last months of his life.

Tom turned the key in the ignition, but faced his mother. "Hey, here's something you'll find interesting. Lisa was telling me that her former boss at the newspaper is a writer. From what she was saying, it sounds as if this lady is a distant cousin to Nana. Her maiden name was Waldron."

"Really. I wonder how she's related?" Helen asked casually.

Tom grinned. "This is the part you'll like. This woman is researching the Waldron family tree straight back to Dutch Manhattan, and she plans to write a book series that will span four hundred years of the clan and the connecting families that were rooted in New York."

Strangely, Helen found herself chuckling. "Oh, Tom, how you put things. The Carey's were a clan, and I loved just about everyone I met, but I doubt my grandfather would be pleased to hear his Waldron ancestors described quite that way. He was more the solitary type. I remember him as being tall and very handsome. Actually, come to think of it, in some ways you remind me of him."

"You think so? I'll still buy dinner, but you can butter me up all you like."

Helen smiled, "I'm serious. Anyway, I'm glad you and Lisa made up."

"Seems to me that I remember that both of my grandmothers regarded their maiden names as sacred."

Helen reached for a notebook and pen in her purse. "What was the writer's name again?"

"Tena something, but you'll get to meet her because she's going to the lunch they're having for Mrs. Mann this afternoon. That's why Lisa was so anxious to have a few words. She knew you'd want to meet her and so was double-checking that we planned to go. Pretty cool, right?"

"I'll say," Helen whispered, half to herself.

"Well, we'd better get rolling." Tom was convinced that he had put a dent in the doom and gloom that had a hold of his mother. "If MapQuest is right, it's about twenty minutes up the road to the restaurant."

Helen buckled her seat belt. Tom clearly wanted to help with the sadness of final good-byes, and she loved him all the more for his consideration. It would be interesting to hear what this aspiring author proposed.

CHAPTER 4

Albany, New York -
As the 18th Century began....

There were many reasons that might have contributed to Peter Waldron's decision to leave his father and mother's comfortable home located on Broad Street in lower Manhattan, but the main catalyst for change undoubtedly was his wife's family connections in Albany. More than anything else, after two years married, and with him, his wife, and their infant daughter still residing under his parent's crowded roof, Peter dearly wanted to be his own man. Because of his Cate, the northern frontier city had offered a blank canvass where he could paint a bright future. So along with his budding family, twenty-five-year-old Peter had departed Manhattan during the summer of 1700.

In Albany, the Quackenbush family dominated the business of supplying and laying brick. The founder's son, Walter Quackenbush, who was married to Cate's aunt, Neeltje, managed the enterprise.

A trained mason, once in his adopted city, Peter Waldron soon found himself working beside several of his wife's Quackenbush cousins ... often with Walter's brother, Adrian. From the beginning Peter liked the brawny, good-natured Adrian.

Peter Waldron always believed that the Almighty had smiled upon him when Cate had put her soft little hand into his own. Before meeting Catherine Vandenbergh he had been seriously in love and seriously rejected thrice. The fathers of those maidens to whom Peter had previously presented himself had negotiated what they undoubtedly considered a far better match than he would be for their daughters. These romantic disappointments had been hard for Peter to swallow, and finding a good wife was an uphill struggle that he'd all but given up on.

Surely he understood that his countenance was not that of a man whom a desirable young maiden living in the bustling late 17th Century city of New York would find so appealing. His nose was long, and his reddened ears protruded wing-like through thin brown hair that hung freely to his shoulders. His elder married sister, Rebecca, trying to sooth his hurt and boost his spirits, had openly encouraged him. To her mind he had one fine facial quality ... the dimple in his right cheek. Unfortunately, the dimple appeared only when he smiled or when he laughed.

Often he'd thought that an angel sent from God must have been in the room that day long ago when he'd been formally introduced to sixteen-year-old Miss Vandenbergh. Catherine had spent her childhood growing up between her grandfather's New York City house near the Broadway, which was not far from his own parent's house, and her family farm at Papscanee Island far up-river. The diversity of her unique upbringing, Peter suspected, had provided something captivating in her countenance that was not generally found in girls her age. She had been a delightful surprise.

Certainly, when he had first sat nervously before her, perspiring through to his waistcoat, an angel *might* have intervened. Perhaps Almighty God Himself had set the stage for a jest, for as they spoke politely of all things common, her aunt, who'd been seated properly in the room's corner, had belched, and Cate's soft lips had turned upwards. Peter had liked that Miss Vandenbergh found humor within the seriousness of such an awkward moment. She showed spirt, and so he had smiled back at her. That smile had written the first line of his Albany future.

Cate's cousin, Adrian Quackenbush, like Peter, wanted to make his own mark apart from a successful father, and neither of them wanted to run a personal race in their father-in-law's boots, but as God would have it, their wives' family connections had provided solid stepping stones.

Cate and Adrian's wife, Catherine, soon became close friends as did their husbands. Although Peter was a newcomer, Albany born Adrian and he had much in common, being close in age and newly married. Both men were also consumed by their ambition to improve their status in life, and soon, along with laying brick for the City of Albany and building new homes in the ever expanding Third Ward, the two friends devoted a portion of their Sunday afternoons planning how they could succeed in the lucrative business of trading furs.

To that end Adrian took action in 1701 when he, along with other Albany merchants, petitioned the provincial government for protection and support with regard to the fur trade. Following Adrian's lead, Peter was granted a license soon after to trade within the Albany city limits. But the number of beavers had greatly diminished around Albany. It was apparent that successful trading depended upon dealing with northern Natives and the wild western "far Indians" who were allied with the five tribes that made up the powerful Iroquois League. Though Peter continued to work as a mason in Albany, he was always on the lookout for other opportunities.

In 1702, following the birth of Peter and Cate's second daughter, Cornelia, war was declared on France by Great Britain and Netherland. Albany was the buffer between New York City and New France's hub, Montreal. Albany defenses required bolstering. Shortly after Cornelia's baptism, Peter was made an overseer of workmen in the construction of a five foot masonry wall that replaced the old and rotting wooden stockade that had stood on the hill on the western side of the city for over twenty years.

As the newly fortified Fort Frederick took shape, Peter Waldron, now a member of the Albany militia, let it be known that he was here in Albany to stay and he did so by way of direct action and not idle words.

While still living in Manhattan Peter had joined the Anglican Church as his father, William, had done later in his life. In Albany Peter began attending services at the Anglican Church. However, Adrian soon suggested that it was far more beneficial in establishing good relations in Albany to belong to the Dutch Reformed Church. Although Waldron was a valiant English name, Albany and New York were very different types of cities. Powerful Dutch families with deep roots controlled the frontier city.

Still wavering about church allegiance, Peter had further reassessed his church affiliation upon meeting the dynamic Peter Schuyler, the most prominent man in Albany. Soon, Peter thought better of worshiping at the English church and had joined the Dutch Reformed Church. Thereafter he'd be ever grateful to Almighty God that He had shown him the right path to follow.

In 1705, on the day that their son, Cornelius, was baptized, Cate overheard her husband talking to Uncle Walter about him and Adrian building farmsteads on a parcel of land north of Albany not far from where the North River and the Mohawk River joined.

Cate handed the swaddled, newly christened infant to Peter's Aunt Rebecca visiting from Manhattan, and whispered to her soon to be sister-in-law Maria, "I am sick of hearing about the northern land. I do not want anything to do with that land, and I will never move there."

"Have you said so to your husband?"

"I have told Peter I know about the hardship one must suffer living on the frontier. My brother is up north on land the Van Rensselaers purchased from the Indians. He was lured by promises made by Henry Van Rensselaer. As a boy, the esteemed Van Rensselaer learned to ride a horse on my father's farm at Papscanee. For years Henry had tried to convince my father to move there, but my father so loved the island that he is buried there in the apple orchard beside his first wife."

Accepting a cup of punch, Maria responded, "Above all else, Peter would have you happy, Cate. He has said as much to his brother."

Cate answered pleasantly. "'Tis nice to hear, yet I believe my husband sees the River Road as the road to riches. Recently, Henry Van Rensselaer has been elected as representative for Rensselaerswyck in the New York General Assembly. My husband regards him in the highest manner."

The slender, blue-eyed Maria answered wistfully, "A wife should be able to trust her husband for what is best."

Cate sighed. "Surely, that is true. Oh, Maria … you are a dear innocent. All men are adventurous. They cannot help their nature."

"Goodness, Cate, do you not love your husband?"

"Of course I love my husband. He is a good man. And …" Cate added as Peter's younger brother strolled toward them with a cookie in hand, "Hendrick will make you a fine husband, and you will be a beautiful bride in only a few months. Go to him now and enjoy the food."

Cate watched the young couple stroll off, but she couldn't dispel ominous thoughts. Only months before Cornelius was born, 80 miles away from Albany in the Massachusetts Colony, another small settlement, Deerfield, had been viciously attacked by the French and Canada Indians. They had killed forty-seven of the settlers there and marched their captives over 250 miles to Montreal. Many of the hostages died along the way. Spearheaded by Col. Schuyler, many of the people of Albany had shown their solidarity by donating money to be added to the ransom funds collected in Massachusetts. Attempts to buy back captives had continued, aided by Albany's Indian agents.

Cate quickly wiped away a tear. What good did it do fretting over that which she had no control. Better to ignore her husband and cousin's land speculation proposal. Taking the baby back from Rebecca, she carried him to his cradle. *All the men have drunk too much rum punch celebrating Cornelius's baptism.*

Years passed and the Waldron family grew secure in Albany, but Peter's dream for expansion lived on. In the spring of 1719 Peter and Adrian petitioned the Albany council to lease land up north where they had often traded with the Natives for furs. Throughout that summer, with the help of fourteen-year-old Cornelius and their Negro carpenters, a barn and log house were constructed at each property site. Crops were planted the following spring. Over time, Peter slowly came to the realization that his desire to invest outside of Albany had indeed altered the course of his life.

Adrian's plan was not Peter's initial vision. When he had moved to Albany he had anticipated the life of a mason and not that of a fur trader or a farmer in the wilderness. Certainly he had not planned on maintaining a second house outside of the city.

But, Peter also came to understand that though new beginnings are indeed possible with help from one's relatives and friends, one cannot run from past associations. In Peter's case, it seemed that the misunderstood choices of his uncle, Johannes Vermilye, had followed him to Albany.

In the time of what came to be known as England's Glorious Revolution in 1689, his Aunt Aeltie s husband, Johannes, had aligned himself with the then popular revolutionary Manhattan immigrant, Jacob Leisler. Believing in Leisler's cause for Manhattan dominance, Uncle Johannes had signed himself as Commander in Chief of the Province after James II had been removed from the throne by the King's daughter, Mary, and her Dutch husband, William of Orange. Though a dozen years had passed by the time Peter Waldron had moved his family to Albany, there were those living in the frontier city who still passionately recalled how they felt when Peter Schuyler had adamantly resisted Jacob Melborne, Leisler's son-in-law, and his five hundred Manhattan Militia soldiers, who came to Albany demanding allegiance to Leisler. Although most were delighted to see the Catholic King removed, who was this upstart Leisler to demand anything in Albany?

At every Dutch wedding, baptism or funeral, the story of Schuyler's bravery continued to be told. Valiant, stubborn Schuyler would not, did not, turn over His Majesty's fort to the usurpers. He and his Albany militia, along with friendly Indians, had initially rejected Melborne and his high-minded men, forcing them to return to Manhattan.

But following the horrific Schenectady massacre by the Canada French and their Indians in February of 1690, Schuyler had no choice but to swallow hard and welcome Melborne and his men back. All the same, Schuyler made it known that he felt Leisler was a mutinous person in the wrong; a power seeking Scottish immigrant who, as far as he was concerned, had no right to any position and anyone connected with him should be hanged. In part, Schuyler was prophetic. Leisler and Melborne were hanged. Peter's uncle nearly suffered the same fate, but through the intervention of loyal family friends, Johannes Vermilye was eventually cleared and his properties restored to him.

When Peter Waldron and his family moved to Albany in 1700, it did not help Peter's position as a newcomer that his Uncle Johannes had been a close ally to the man who had turned the New York Province upside down. However, he was determined to make a new life for himself and his family and had not entered Albany empty handed. After his maternal grandfather Peter Stoutenburg's death in Manhattan in 1699, Waldron had inherited enough money to purchase a modest residence in Albany. That inheritance had been a great help in his establishing himself, but what had helped him all the more was his willingness to work as hard as any man... and that he had married Cate Vandenbergh.

As it turned out, Adrian Quackenbush had given Peter Waldron solid advice in many areas and increased his confidence in his own ability to improve his status in life. By 1723, Peter's ten children had been baptized at the Albany Dutch Reformed Church, he had established himself as a respected tradesman in Albany, and he had even increased his landholdings in the outlying areas.

Evidence of his success hung prominently on a wall in his house: a grand portrait of Peter painted by renowned New England artist Neimiah Partridge who also painted many of the Albany Schuylers. At first he'd not cared for the likeness the artist had presented to him and even had refused to pay for the work. Again Adrian had stepped in, advising him that surely the work of the man being called the "Schuyler Portrait Painter" was worthwhile. Adrian believed that all who Partridge had painted would be immortalized for generations yet to be born. Peter found Adrian's perspective intriguing, but then, he often did. And so, for posterity, the portrait was hung in the Albany Waldron home.

CHAPTER 5

Albany, 1724

Sunlight trickled through the thick glass pane beside Peter Waldron's desk this Sunday afternoon as he penned a long letter of reply to his cousin Phillip Ringo who for the past five years had been living on the woodsy frontier of West New Jersey.

Peter enjoyed corresponding with his younger cousin whose letters were always filled with unstoppable optimism. He envisioned Phillip's dark eyes flashing, something that occurred whenever he was excited by the prospect of a new baby or a new business venture, and Phillip's most recent dispatch had been filled with both.

Chuckling now, he matched Phillip's unbridled enthusiasm with his own full-bodied account of the recent comings and goings of his ten children and four grandchildren.

However, as he recalled his joy upon hearing that his daughter-in-law, Elizabeth, was again with child, the pleasantry of the thought was suddenly severed as ten-year-old Eva shrieked. A wooden bowl filled with raw eggs had fallen to the floor.

"Rebecca! You are always underfoot. This is all your fault!" Eva shouted at her younger sister.

"I am not the fault! You are a clumsy goose, Eva!" Rebecca battled back, stomping her foot, her small fists clenched by her side.

Cate sighed, picking up her wailing infant, Garret, who'd been shocked out of a sound afternoon nap. "Enough—the two of you!

Dinah will help you both to clean this up, yet I fear there will be no special cake to bring to Elizabeth tomorrow! Well you know our chickens do not make eggs on command!"

"Mother, she ..." Eva began tearfully.

"Quiet! For shame, Eva, that a big girl like you would point your finger at your little sister!"

At that moment Peter noticed his daughter Catherine standing outside of the closed bottom half of their Dutch door. "

"What is the matter? Catherine asked dramatically. "I was half-way down the street and I could hear all the shouting."

Sheepishly, Eva dropped her eyes to the floor. "The bowl slipped out of my hands and now we will have no cake. I must suppose that I am a clumsy goose. I should have waited for you to come back from William and Elizabeth's house as mother asked me to do."

Catherine closed the bottom half of the door behind herself. Avoiding the wet, slippery portion of the floor, she approached Eva and patted her shoulder. "Here, let me help you. Our sister, Engeltie will be home soon, and we will ask her if she will help us make another cake next Sunday, all of us together."

Briefly, Peter and his wife exchanged glances, both of them pleased by Catherine's compassion.

Peter cleared his throat. He surely did understand the trials and tribulations of a hectic household. After decades of marriage he was accustomed to the tumultuous nature of it all.

As the girls bent beside Dinah, all four quickly cleaning the spilt eggs to keep them from seeping into the cracks between the floorboards, Peter continued writing:

Our William, these days, is a much sought after mason, often laying brick for the City of Albany, whilst Cornelius, who is nineteen, now lives permanently at our farm up north. I must add that William was here earlier this afternoon after church service and asks that I send you his good wishes.

Like Cate's father, Cornelius Vandenbergh, our second eldest son is a born farmer, and I am happy about this as I cannot have him working for me here in Albany. We two butt heads far too often. We do better apart, and I have entrusted him with keeping the farm's account book. He is a capable overseer of the workmen there. Last year's harvest was very good, and we look forward to another good one this year. Although my son has things well in hand, I would like to go with my family up to the farm as soon as it is possible.

I tell you, Phillip, we are overrun in Albany with Indians who many times are drunk and then brawl amongst themselves and local tradesmen. Recently, a fight transpired at the base of my front stoop. I was not at home when the incident happened, but my younger boy, Pete, recklessly put himself into the middle of the skirmish and was pushed to the ground causing him to hit his head against a rock. British soldiers were down the street and ran to his aid. The two troublemakers were carted away to the goal. Poor Pete's head produced a terrible bluish ball, and he had headaches for days.

Again dipping his quill into the ink bottle, Peter had no doubts that he had done right to send both his older sons to Manhattan for their apprenticeships. Because of his Uncle Samuel's influence in the city of New York, both William and Cornelius had also learned how to read, write and cypher. Though his Cate would not like it, she being so partial to little Pete, he planned to do the same with him come next year when he would be nine years old.

He continued:

Whilst I think of the fight, I also recall something else worth mentioning, something quite apart from this sort of unhappy conflict which seems to occur hereabouts more regularly than not.

February last I was glad of the sight of prominent Albany resident Mr. John Lansing standing precariously on my stoop's slippery top step. To my utter astonishment, Mr. Lansing held in his half-frozen hand an invitation to the funeral of Lansing's father-in-law, the renowned General Peter Schuyler.

Pausing, Peter turned and read these last lines meant for Phillip back to his wife as Cate finished changing the quieted but wriggly Garret's diaper. Suddenly, with an onslaught of irrepressible giggles, she rose from the pallet on the floor with the baby in her arms, and stoutly declared, "When I had laid eyes on John Lansing that day, he was more akin to a golden haired angel from God than an ordinary mortal message carrier."

Peter was befuddled. He had never been able to fully understand the feminine sense of humor, yet he gave Cate's amused perception a few moments of thoughtful reflection. Well he knew that neither he nor John Lansing were angels. On more than one occasion the two of them had drunk too much good Quackenbush rum together which had sometimes resulted in a foolish lack of decorum or worse. Although he, and he suspected John, too, had persevered in the pursuit of self-control, nay, neither of them would ever aspire to the divine.

Still, few women did not find the rugged, quick-witted John Lansing appealing. Peter imagined that this had been taken into consideration when selecting a currier. Housewives would have welcomed him in from the cold and would have been quick to set out a warm drink.

However, with Lansing's arrival on that particular day, he believed that Almighty God must have held the reins along with Lansing's carriage driver, and he took the Schuyler family's funeral bidding as a blessing. He had finally, officially, established the Waldron family within the inner circle of his adopted city. Perhaps this was what Cate had had in her mind when she had peered over his shoulder at Mr. Lansing standing in the doorway that blustery day, and what now prompted cackles.

The most recent household disaster righted, with their mother's permission, Eva and Catherine departed the house hand in hand to walk a block over to Elizabeth and William's house for a short visit with their twin infant cousins.

Pete passed them on his way in carrying a small hymnal Cate had asked to borrow from Rev. Van Driessen. Curiously, he eyed Rebecca sulking in the corner, but knew better than to ask questions. He went straightaway to the table in the far corner of the room.

Seemingly oblivious to these comings and goings, his thoughts of Schuyler and the past still on his mind, to himself Peter pondered thoughtfully, *is it not interesting how the simple gesture of one man could validate another's life? Over three thousand call themselves residents of Albany, yet I was one of the chosen few. A hand-delivered invite to General Schuyler's funeral feast was indeed an unexpected honor, and undoubtedly one which Cate would think a sign from heaven, so what are these outbursts of cackling from my wife, especially on the Sabbath day?*

Still wondering, offhandedly Peter remarked, "Cate, you should not jest about Mr. Lansing, And I suspect that Cousin Phillip understands how such a solicitation could be construed as a signal of significance. Phillip has also forged a new life in an area that is far different from the world either of us experienced growing up on Broad Street in lower New York City. I am the son of a cooper, and Phillip is the son of a shopkeeper, and we both know well the difficulties of elevating one's self amongst more strangers than friends."

Dinah took the baby from her mistress and silence filled the room while Peter completed his letter by wishing God's blessing as Phillip and his wife awaited the birth of their second child. Closing and sealing his dispatch with a few drops of sealing wax, he believed that both his grandfathers Waldron and Stoutenburg would have been pleased that sons of their offspring had carried forward the pioneering spirt of their ancestors.

Raising his head he saw Cate had resumed her Sunday mending, and Garret, in his cradle, chewed contentedly on his teething coral.

Ah, yes, his immigrant grandfathers would be pleased, but Cate would admonish sternly that he could add pride to the list of the sins for which he must atone. And he would take her criticism in this regard as quietly as any man could do, for such silence within a marriage, he had learned, was an attribute.

Recalling the beguiling young maiden he had wed, their difficult move to Albany, and the infant children that they had buried in the Albany churchyard, he saw that these years taught that it made no difference that he and Cate did not always agree. He accepted that he could not have become the man he was without Cate beside him. If any man was to be successful he must have the support of a good woman and to think otherwise was foolish. He had said as much to his son, William, when his eldest boy had considered proposing marriage to the comely Elizabeth Beekman to her father. Beauty was unimportant. A maid should be both tender and stout of heart in order to be a proper wife, he had counseled. A woman who would put her husband and the children first was most important. Praises be to God. His son had chosen well.

Five year old Rebecca again skipped past, interrupting his innermost thoughts. With her white, Sabbath ribbons tied into neat little bows at the end of two honey-yellow braids and her blank-faced cloth doll tucked safely within the crevice of her arm she was determined to catch the eye of her father.

Distracted, Cate called to her youngest daughter. "Come here to me, Rebecca, and I will show you a special stitch that my mother taught to me when I was a little girl."

Meandering toward her mother, Rebecca's eyes widened curiously as Cate reached to pull out a ball of blue thread from her sewing basket.

Peter's thoughts returned to John Lansing and all that had ensued from the moment the funeral invitation had been placed in his hand.

Although the prominent Schuler family had many servants, Albany women were naturally inclined to understand that the deceased General's children, especially, his eldest daughter, Margarita Livingston, were overcome with their duties. A devoted daughter burdened with the task of feeding and accommodating scores of visitors required neighborly assistance. Hence, many Albany women, both of high station and of more modest means, had stepped forward to the task of preparing funeral foods. Cate, with her servant,

Dinah, at her side, had baked plenty of caraway seeded, dead cakes for the Schuyler family. His heart swelled as he recalled the sweet aroma that had floated throughout their house and how his wife had impressed each small cookie with the sign of the resurrection—the rooster, and then carefully wrapped each one in black crepe paper. She had personally taken them to Mrs. Livingston; tokens of remembrance that the deceased's family gave to mourners who had come to call.

Cate's heart must have ached beyond measure as she worked her kindness. She had used the same wooden rooster mold many years before when they had received mourners after they had buried their small, first born daughter in the Albany Dutch Reformed churchyard.

Along with his wife's gift, Peter had given a barrel of Dutch brandewijn—a special burnt wine that his cousin Sam had shipped on his yacht from Manhattan for the purpose of celebrating the baptismal feast of Garret last spring. One unused barrel had been saved, and Peter now believed the Lord had meant the brandewijn for the exact purpose of toasting a good and faithful servant—the departed Schuyler.

Of course, the Schuyler and Livingston houses would have had plenty of beer and Madeira, but to be sure, nothing as good as his cousin's fine burnt wine. After the funeral service he had enjoyed a tankard of his gift to the Livingstons, which the English officers who attended called brandy. As a token of gratitude for his and Cate's kind generosity, Mrs. Livingston had gifted him with a finely crafted silver funeral spoon monogramed with the letter S. Later he had written to his cousin of how the brandy was appreciated and that he did not know of anyone outside of the Schuyler family who had received such a prize as the gifted spoon.

Peter rested his eyes upon his wife and daughter. Patiently, Cate guided Rebecca's small anxious hands while the child made her first stitch.

"Ah, I see you want to do good work, daughter. Soon you will do as well, or I dare say, even better with the work than your sisters. I am pleased to see you begin to learn."

Rebecca beamed and giggled, leaning closer to her mother.

"So, did you finish your letter to Cousin Phillip?" Cate asked.

"Yes, I have. I felt it my duty to warn him about the continued chaos here in Albany brought on by the influx of so many Indians since General Schuyler's death."

"Yes," Cate answered quietly. "All the tribal people wish to offer customary condolences now that the snows have melted and the river flows free again. The Indians loved their Quidor, and they, like us, know that we will never see another like him."

Peter nodded in agreement as he lit his pipe. The various tribes of the Six Indian Nations—the Sinnekees, Onnodages, Cayauges, Oneydes, Mohawk, and Tuscarora (recently having joined the league in 1722) as well as those from the Half Moon lands who called themselves "children of the mingling waters", or Schaghticoke River Indians, roamed their muddied streets. Proof of the Indians' respect for the deceased family came with the number of chiefs who had brought gifts of handfuls of wampum and the furs that had been stockpiled at the entrances to Peter Schuyler's house and the Albany Dutch Reformed Church. At the church, the Dutch Minister continued to record each Indian's name and respective clan that was making the offer of condolence. Yet, despite what appeared genuine good intentions, the deluge of so many outsiders upon the small frontier city had been a costly burden to residents.

Several families, including his own, had given Indian friends quarter while they visited. Those who had slept under his roof were from the west and were of the Wolf clan. They asked who would be chosen to replace Quidor? Who could they love as they had loved him? Peter could not answer, and months later he still had no answer. He suspected that all Indians continued to ponder the future of their country. The Indians stayed in Albany waiting for a sign that would persuade them to remain loyal to England and her colonists.

Phillip would read Peter's news of Albany with great interest, for success in New York or in New Jersey, nay the entirety of the English colonies, relied upon good relations with the Six Nations.

The friendship of their Native brethren had been nurtured by the Schuyler family for decades.

Cate said, "Do you remember when years ago Peter Schuyler and others traveled with the five chiefs to England? Do you remember how we celebrated?"

Peter chuckled. "I do remember. We welcomed Catherine into this world thereafter."

"The womenfolk spoke of nothing else for months but how lavishly the chiefs were entertained while in London and what good Queen Anne must have thought to herself when she saw them."

"Those were great times for Albany," Peter replied. "And of course, Phillip kept copies of the English newspapers sent to him by a friend living in London. He took the papers to Frances Tavern in Manhattan where the news was read to the populace." Glancing toward where Pete sat thumbing through the book lent to him by their Dominie, Peter said, "A time will come when our boy yonder will read the London papers to us."

Cate smiled as she took the precious book from her son and placed it safely high on a shelf. Carefully she inserted it between the books that his great-uncle, Joseph Waldron, had bequeathed to Peter's father, William. "Yes, our Pete has been blessed with a good mind. I thank God for this."

Cate and Peter often talked about the voyage that had been made to show their Queen the importance of retaining Iroquois allies. It had been a great success and had resulted in more funding for the colony of New York. British forts along the pathway keeping open the corridor to the far west's fur trade had been built. The encouraged Iroquois remained British allies against the French, and Albany was celebrated as a buffer between Montreal and New York City.

Peter sighed. Although the Native peoples' friendship with Schuyler never wavered, fourteen years had passed since the famous London visit, and yet French Montreal still remained strong. Canada had not been conquered, and Schuyler, the *Great Communicator*, had departed this life leaving behind numerous uncertainties.

Though it had been months since Schuyler's death, indecision remained, and the whole of the situation with the Indians worried Peter. He had not shared in his letter with Phillip the violent confrontations between the Natives and several of Albany's people of servitude in recent months. Peter suspected that some of these disruptions were promoted by drunken, unsavory overseers.

A boyish loud groan disrupted his thoughts as Rebecca threw down her doll beside her brother, Pete. She squatted on the floor beside him, her tiny face set with a firm resolve. She pointed to a cloth bag hanging on a wall peg, suggesting a game of marbles. Apparently she'd become bored with her sewing lesson.

Peter offered her a stern scowl. Gaming of any sort on Sabbath day was frowned upon by the Dutch Reformed Church, as well his children knew. He looked to his wife, but it appeared that Cate had no intention of intervening further while the baby remained asleep in his cradle.

Pete groaned again, he also glancing longingly toward his mother, a ploy that often evoked sympathy but not now. His mother's eyes were clamped on her work.

The boy studied his sister. "Rebecca, shall I show you how to make the first letter of your name? Would you like that?"

Peter hoped that he would not have to open his door to anyone this afternoon. He was quite tired and would like a short nap before his two chattering girls returned and Engeltie came back from helping Widow Myers. He stood, and with his pipe in his mouth headed toward his soft feathered bed.

CHAPTER 6

2014

Following Christine Mann's graveside service Helen and Tom arrived at the restaurant sooner than anticipated, and looking around the near empty parking lot Tom was concerned that he'd misunderstood the time schedule Lisa had given him. Entering, they were relieved to see Chris's daughter already standing in the foyer, chatting with one of the uniformed staff. Beside Chris stood a slender redhead dressed conservatively in a black linen suit. *Thankfully, we aren't the only early birds.*

"Seating," Lisa announced gesturing them forward, "is open over here in the side dining room."

With a quick nod the staffer disappeared down the hallway, smiling politely as she passed.

"Oh, hey you two, perfect timing!" Lisa exclaimed as they approached.

Nearing, Helen whispered, "I think we might be a bit early."

"Not at all," Lisa insisted. She glanced at the woman next to her. "With the three of you all arriving at the same time, I feel as if the fates are in charge here today. Helen, Tom, I want to introduce you both to Mom's, dear friend, and mine, Tena Waldron Van Ness. Lisa turned to the woman beside her, "Tena, these are the old friends from Arizona I told you about: Helen, and her son, Tommy Carey."

"So nice to meet you, Tena, although I wish it were under better circumstances," Helen said.

Tom extended his hand, smiling broadly. "Tom Carey. Tommy faded away some time ago. It's a pleasure to meet you."

"And please—call me, Tena. Tena Waldron Van Ness is such a mouth full."

As her son and Lisa's friend stood chatting, Helen couldn't help but notice how the tables had been set up in the dining room behind them where they would be lunching. Large round tables covered in white linen tablecloths had been decorated with clear glass vases filled with fresh pink and white tulips.

Lisa caught Helen's audible sigh.

"Yes," she said softly, "they were Mom's favorite. How could we not have tulips on the tables?"

"Of course," Helen responded, giving her a gentle hug. "They're perfect."

Tena added, "I'm sure your mother would have loved them, Lisa." Looking at Helen, she continued, "Lisa and I worked together for quite some time. She introduced me to her mother, and Chris and I soon became good friends. It was as if we had known each other in another life."

"Co-conspirators who sometimes called themselves 'Chairwomen," Lisa interjected.

Tena laughed. "We co-hosted the annual golf tournament banquet together. Tulips were always Chris's first pick for the tables."

Helen smiled, her thoughts turning inward. *Yes, always tulips, always pure and simple, but exquisite.* While remembering Chris's creativity, she noted Mick Van Schaick's arrival with his wife. It was the first Helen had laid eyes on Judy in decades, and she was stunned by how much Chris's sister-in-law had changed.

"Oh," Lisa exclaimed, "there's my aunt and uncle, and I see some of my husband's cousins walking in behind them. I'd better go say hi. Sorry to have to leave you right off like this; please make yourselves comfortable, and we'll catch up later."

Lisa darted off, and Tena turned to Helen. "Would you two like to join me at a table?"

Awakening to the opportunity to move to any table and rid themselves of the awkward moment, Tom took charge, "That would be great—how about that table right over there?"

Soon Tom was pulling out a chair for his mother and then a second one, "Mrs. Van Ness?"

"Please, Tom, call me Tena," she said as he pushed in her chair. "Mrs. Van Ness is my husband's aunt, and she's ninety-three."

"Yes, Ma'am," Tom chuckled.

Tom sat but almost immediately rose again. "Good God! I don't believe it. That's Buddy Vandenberg over there! Holy cow! Please excuse me ladies, while I go say hello."

Helen leaned toward Tena as she followed Tom across the room. "Buddy—actually George— Vandenberg is an old friend," she explained, hardly recognizing the bald-headed and bearded heavy man who'd been the skinniest of all the boys who came to their house.

But then, she'd hardly recognized Mick's wife either. Other than Mick's remark that Judy was under the weather with a cold and couldn't make it to Chris's wake, he hadn't mentioned her again. Glancing around the room, Helen found the frail, despondent Judy sitting by herself, and she wondered sadly what had happened to the once dazzling 'queen' of the tennis court. A cold, coupled with grief, could knock anybody off the throne, and Judy had been close to her sister-in-law. If they'd kept the same relationship all these years, Judy would miss Chris terribly, and Helen doubted she'd feel the comfort of her husband's arms around her. Mick was a man to cajole but not console.

Helen reached for the water pitcher in front of her, automatically filling her empty glass and Tena's. *Humpty Dumpty fell off the wall and all the king's horses and all the king's men...*

The ice rattled as the cool water touched her lips.

Tena waited until Helen put her glass down before breaking through the awkward silence between them. "I'm glad we have this chance to chat alone for a few minutes," she began.

Helen twisted slightly in her seat, resting her eyes on the attractive woman seated beside her. She welcomed the distraction. "Yes, I am too. Lisa said something to Tom about you working on a book series all about the Waldron family?"

"Actually, I've just finished the first of what I hope will be a series of historical novels that highlights many of the first families who came to live in New York. Several 17th and 18th century Waldrons drive my story, but I've woven in many first families—most just ordinary people who happened to live in extraordinary times. I've begun working with an editor on my manuscript for the first book."

"Oh, how exciting for you."

Tena smiled wanly, "More nerve wracking than exciting is how I'd describe the editorial process, but I was very lucky that this experienced editorial team took an interest in a newbie writer like me. It was a miracle, really. A mutual friend from my newspaper days told this husband and wife who'd been editors for a large publishing house about the Manhattan novel I was writing, and they called me out of the blue.

"For years, other than my husband, I resisted letting anyone so much as take a peek at what I'd written, let alone show it to an editor. I have another friend who wrote a novel, and her editor slashed the heck out of her manuscript. She was so discouraged she says she'll never write another one. But so far, for me, it's not been that way. They both are, of course, very professional, and they've been considerate with their suggestions. They've connected me with a publisher who seems interested. Still, it's no vacation."

"I'm an avid reader," Helen stated matter-of-factly. "I'll give you my email so you can contact me when your book is available. I'll definitely want to read it."

"How nice; I will let you know, and I appreciate your interest. I'm keeping my fingers crossed."

"I hope your friend changes her mind, too, about the writing that is," Helen added thoughtfully. "Our world today is such a mess. Who doesn't want to sit curled up with a good book and escape into another place? What happened to your friend is terrible. Writers should be encouraged."

"Amen to that." Tena sighed. "I think you'll enjoy the Manhattan story. Some of the characters may well be mutual ancestors."

Helen studied Tena intently. "Do you really think so?"

"Well, it seems possible. A couple of years ago Chris was the first to read my bare-bones manuscript, and we discovered that we share Van Schaick ancestors, and I understand your Waldrons were in Albany early in the 1700s. I have Waldron lineage, too, that goes back to early Albany and beyond."

"Yes," Helen replied thoughtfully. "I think I remember some of that old family lore. One of my grandmothers was a Waldron, and my husband's aunt had traced their family roots back to the first Waldron who came from Holland during the 1600s. Steve, my late husband, and I used to kid one another about being kissing cousins." Helen picked up her glass and took another sip of water.

"Wow, how fascinating! My idea for another book is for an 18th century focus on the Capital District and also Saratoga County. Several families that first immigrated to Manhattan from Europe later moved up the Hudson River to Albany. The fur trade was going like gangbusters up there. And to the west of Albany around Oneida. Those pioneers provide me with a broad platform for another great story, but that's well into the future."

Tena paused, and the two sat silently watching Tom laugh with his old friend across the room.

It was obvious to Helen that Tena was optimistic about getting her first novel published, and though Helen knew nothing about such things, she could see that this lady had the passion to see it through. If Helen had learned anything throughout her life it was that stamina and perseverance made things happen.

Softly Helen said, "I remember my grandmother taking me to *Jack's Oyster House* in downtown Albany for my fourteenth birthday. It was a very big deal. Sweet memories."

Tena nodded, "I'll bet that *was* special. When I was working, a bunch of us from the office would go to *Jack's* for lunch every so often. One day a couple of years ago, Chris and I got to talking about how things used to be in Albany and the history of the Albany Dutch. It was around the time that the newspaper did a piece on 48 Hudson Avenue which historians have decided is the oldest house in Albany. It was quite a discovery for history buffs. The house, now known as the Van Ostrande or Radliff house, dates back to 1728, if my memory serves me right. Nobody had known the building was so old because over the years a more modern façade was constructed. It had been a storefront business for years. The original modest structure was a one-and-a-half story house and is still there hidden inside this other structure."

"No kidding," Helen responded, wide eyed. "I had always heard that the Quackenbush house was the oldest surviving house in Albany."

"Well, it was believed to be until quite recently," Tena replied. "The Quackenbush house has long fascinated me for many reasons. We've traced my father's roots back to the Waldron family of early Manhattan and Albany and in my case eventually to North Creek. I also traced them back to the Albany Quackenbush family who, you might know, were in the brick business in Albany in the 17th century."

"No, honestly, I don't know very much at all," Helen answered quietly. "My grandmother was the genealogist. You know ... official keeper of the flame. Chris, like my grandmother, had a lot more interest in the family roots and tramping through ancient cemeteries than I did. Although my husband, Steve, well he had….." Helen's voice trailed off.

"I know what you mean about the grave hunting," Tena inserted reflectively. "I've tramped through dozens of cemeteries myself, but I was always more interested in them living than after they were dead. I imagined what their daily lives must have been like, and then the discovery of the hidden older house really peaked my interest."

"Why so?"

"It's a stretch, but I'm always thinking of possibilities. Many of the Waldrons were masons back in the 1700s which made me wonder if our ancestors had anything to do with building the house at

48 Hudson. My Waldrons, and I'd guess yours as well, trace back to Resolved Waldron, the original immigrant from Holland, and then through his eldest son, William, and William's son, Peter, who was a mason trained in Manhattan and the first Waldron to move from Manhattan to Albany. I suspect thousands of us can claim Peter."

Suddenly Tena paused and began apologizing, "I hope going into all of this right now about my book and all doesn't make me come off as insensitive—irreverent to Chris."

"No, of course not," Helen soothed. "This is so interesting, and I think Chris would have been tickled that you're moving on with your book."

"I agree. I feel as if Chris is elbowing me along. I can't explain it, but I know she's with us."

Thoughtfully, Helen said, "I wish I had paid more attention to my grandmother when she talked about our ancestors living in early Albany. And, to be honest, when my husband and his Aunt were into all this genealogy stuff I wasn't in a good place in my life and didn't pay much attention to them either. Now I wish that I had."

Tena continued chatting about a trip she'd made to old St. Mark's Church in lower Manhattan, and Helen was intrigued to learn that the church was located on the site of Peter Stuyvesant's 17th century farm and that Resolved Waldron had worked as a sheriff under Stuyvesant, the then Director General of New Netherland Colony. Although stern in his rule, apparently he had the heart of a pious man, and he'd built a chapel where St. Mark's would later be built which was not far from his grand house. When he died, he was interred catacomb style underneath his chapel where St. Mark's now stands. His wife, Judith, as well as many other dignitaries are also buried there.

Tena Van Ness had researched all over New York and beyond, and Helen was even more astonished to hear that she had recently visited the Abby Aldrich Rockefeller Folk Art Museum in Williamsburg, Virginia, where she'd found an original oil portrait of Peter Waldron, the grandson of Resolved. From documentation that the museum shared she had learned that Peter's portrait was painted in the forty-sixth year of his life, 1721, and was discovered in the 1930s in Rensselaer, New York. Her description of the man in the portrait, who could be their mutual ancestral grandfather, was mesmerizing, and Helen made a mental note to one day visit Williamsburg.

But it was when Tena mentioned the murder of another Waldron in Half Moon, New York during the French and Indian War, documented within a New York City newspaper that the hair stood up on Helen's arms. Because Half Moon in those times was a far larger area than the Halfmoon of today, it could be possible that the murder happened someplace near their old house in Milltown.

Spellbound, Helen wanted to hear more, but before she could ask another question, Tom returned to the table, his arm clamped around the brawny shoulders of George Vandenberg. "And here's Buddy," he announced.

"Hi there, Mrs. Carey," Buddy offered shyly.

Helen smiled. "Oh, gosh. I've not been called Mrs. Carey in a very long time. How nice to see you."

"Very nice to see you, too. Still, I sure wish it wasn't like this."

"I know," Helen replied. "I'm sure everyone feels the same way. Even so, it's so lovely to see so many here for Chris."

"She was a nice lady," Buddy replied.

"Why don't you come sit with us?" Helen suggested.

"I'd love to stay and chat longer," Buddy apologized, "but I see my dad has arrived. My dad and Mrs. Mann's husband worked together at GE back in the day. Come to think of it, the last time me and my dad saw Mrs. Mann was at her husband's funeral. Anyway, Dad doesn't usually come to these things, or for that matter get out much at all anymore. I'd better go sit with him, but I'll give you a call, Tommy. As I said, my uncle moved out there to Phoenix awhile back, and my wife and I are going out for a visit this fall. I'll definitely look you up."

Buddy waved to his father who seemed relieved that his son had spotted him. He then turned back to Tom, "Again, I *will* be in touch."

"Please." Tom encouraged. "Hey man, it was great seeing you!"

Tom grabbed Buddy's hand for one last shake. When Buddy strolled away, Tom pulled out a chair and sat with his mother. "Ya know, I don't think I ever met Buddy's dad, not once. Sort of weird."

Abruptly, Helen leaned over to Tom and whispered "I want one last look at our old country house. I know we agreed to steer clear of the place, but I do have a good reason. I'll explain later."

Tom nodded, but he was confused to his core. *This has been one hell of a trip.*

Seeing Buddy had triggered memories of them shooting hoops in his driveway, but Tom didn't know how he'd feel about going back to their old place again. His grandmother had once told him that her mother believed that all the houses in his neighborhood sat on the site of what had once been an Indian village. As boys he and Buddy had collected dozens of Indian arrows and he'd always thought it must be true. However, he was also sure his grandmother loved to bedazzle him with family lore, telling tales as if his ancestors knew the old village chief personally. It was an enthralling legend for a little boy holding something that could have been shot from the bow of a buckskin-clad hunter.

As he grew older though, Indians and the dead didn't excite him much at all, except on Halloween when he, Buddy, and a couple other guys sat drinking beer in the cemetery on the old fallen headstones.

After his grandmother passed away, when he was in the service, his mom had gone down to Florida to visit with cousins and clean out her mother's apartment in the retirement community. Helen returned to Phoenix with several old photo albums as well as a couple of shoeboxes full of mementos, and she'd stuck the boxes up on a closet shelf in his room. As far as he knew they were still up there, but he doubted she'd looked at that stuff for years. She probably took comfort knowing everything was in safe keeping. Now, after today and what seemed to be a huge history conversation with the woman writing the book, he suspected there would be a resurrection of that memorabilia.

He had to admit he was somewhat curious about how their old house would look after all these years. Although he didn't think his dad had ever been able to find the original documentation, he'd always believed the center portion of their farmhouse had been built sometime in the seventeen hundreds. He also believed in the rumor about the Indian village, and Tom guessed that therein was the root of all his father's problems. If it were true that the house was close to three hundred years old, it made Tena's story about local Waldrons all the more interesting, especially since her maiden name was Waldron. Curious, too, that her husband was a Van Ness. He distinctly remembered that they had had Van Ness neighbors.

As intriguing as all of this was, Tom still felt that pushing back the hands of time wasn't a good idea for either him or his mother. It had been hell making the move out west, and he had no interest in revisiting the pain of his Dad's sudden death which he assumed would happen the minute they set eyes on the place. But, he knew how his mom could be when she got something into her mind. She probably thought meeting this woman who'd been friends with Chris and was writing a book about their ancestors was some sort of a sign from heaven. He didn't believe in signs, but that didn't matter; he'd go with the flow.

Before they said their good-byes at the restaurant, Tom stepped out to make a few quick calls, switching around prior hotel and air reservations. He called his office and his wife. He and his mother would stay another night in Saratoga Springs. The following day they would revisit their old house where one more time he just might run into that buckskin-clad Indian who played one of the title roles in his boyhood dreams. What the hell. The Indian always smiled at him.

CHAPTER 7

Exhausted, Helen and Tom sat in silence waiting for the traffic light at the Clifton Park intersection to change. It had been a good and interesting day honoring a terrific woman who'd touched so many, but they had stayed far longer than anticipated at the luncheon.

Tom's thoughts about what was piling up at the office back home were overshadowed by the mini metropolis that had been carved out of the rural residential area of the Saratoga County he remembered, as well as by the faces, both old and new, he'd encountered during these past few days.

During lunch he'd had an interesting and informative conversation with an innovative Albany business man, David Mahoney, who'd grown his Albany based business selling industrial gases and equipment into a dynamic company serving the eastern part of New York State. Mahoney, a native of Waterford, enthusiastically described how his and Tom's old stomping grounds had become the gateway to one of the most rapidly growing communities in Upstate New York, thanks, in large part, to sprawl generated by a technology company with links to Germany and Singapore.

In 2009 Global Foundries had claimed Malta, a hamlet slightly north of Clifton Park, as bull's eye for their US computer-chip manufacturing business, leading to thousands of new jobs and a promising future. A housing boom along with the growth in services needed to support incoming families had sprouted all along the main corridor from Albany to Saratoga Springs. Saratoga County would never be the same. That was evident.

"Tom, did you hear me?" his mother asked.

"Sorry mom I was thinking about other things."

"That's okay." Helen pointed to a complex across the road. "As I said, your grandmother used to have her hair done over there once a week. Back then the only thing on that corner was a tiny strip mall, and her hairdresser had a shop there. The Star Market was next door, and she did all her grocery shopping there. Good heavens, Mom would never believe all of this!"

"I remember," Tom responded, perusing the string of buildings including office space, a furniture store and huge supermarket. "I used to drive her over sometimes. She was one of the few people brave enough to ride with me when I first got my license. Remember?"

"I do," Helen replied with a smile. "But she would have let you pilot her to Mars if you wanted."

"I don't know about Mars, but I was pretty good at schmoozing her."

Helen sighed impatiently while staring at the hodgepodge that surrounded the corner she barely recognized. "I think this damn light is stuck."

"As Nana would say, 'you'll just have to hold your horses.'"

"I think the only horses we might find around here these days, Tom, are at the racetrack. This nutsy conglomeration is a far cry from the peace and tranquility of those old, Dutch farms Tena talked about today. If only the dead could speak like your father insisted they could. The Knickerbockers and the rest wouldn't know what to make of it all."

"Neither would Dad."

"No, he wouldn't," Helen whispered. She remained quiet.

Tom considered that *conglomeration* was far too soft a term to describe what had happened to the rustic area of tall pines. He followed his mother's line of sight through an endless stream of traffic toward the historic Ephraim Stevens Clifton Park Hotel. A long-standing, white clapboard building, the hotel had once been a stagecoach stop between Albany and Saratoga. The stalwart structure, with its distinctive second floor front porch, had stood the challenges of time and weather. It was a testimony to another era when the hinterlands fringing the Adirondacks had provided escape from steamy hot summers for Manhattan urbanites and also provided supportive wages for locals.

"Well, the ancient place still stands," Helen observed. "And I'm relieved to see that it does."

"Astonishing, isn't it?" Tom noted. "Carpenters in those days sure built them to last. I remember Nana telling me that she kicked up her heels there plenty of times back in her day."

"Yes, she sure did. She loved to dance. From what I've heard that place was quite the hotspot after World War II. I remember my mother saying that she and her girlfriends would meet beaus there. My grandmother thought the notion of meeting strangers—guys without a proper introduction by a family member or friend—just scandalous. Imagine what she'd say about internet dating!"

Tom glanced over at his mother. "Ridiculous, I would imagine."

"Absolutely ridiculous."

"I still think of her once in a while, and of course, I've told Kyle all about her. Kyle loves hearing these family *golden-oldie* stories, but, as you've guessed, he's more of a futuristic man. He tells his mother that he plans to fly a spaceship and help build a new colony on another planet. Alison calls him our little 'rocket-man.'"

With twilight settling in they continued northward toward Saratoga Springs where rooms at one of the city's established mainstays, the *Gideon Putnam Hotel*, had been reserved. It was too late to stop by his dad's grave, and so they agreed to visit the cemetery right after breakfast the next morning.

Tom shook off thoughts of his father's bones six feet under the ground. It was all wrong. That wasn't Dad. He'd rather remember him as he'd been before his mind had gotten all torn up. As they passed Round Lake he could almost see the two of them side by side, quietly baiting a hook at the break of day.

Across the seat his mother was obviously dealing with her own memories. Tom doubted she'd ever touched a worm, but he was sure his parents had their own special moments.

"What ya thinkin'?"

"Nothing—just tired," Helen said. "Like you, I suppose I'm going to be happy to get home."

"Yeah, it's been a rough couple of days for you."

"And you."

"It's not all been as bad as I thought it would be," Tom said. "Actually, it's been satisfying in some aspects—like clearing the air with Lisa. Sad for everyone, but there were a couple of nice surprises."

"Well, as for me, yes, and no," Helen said, leaning back against the headrest. "It was nice to see old friends, and it's exciting to hear that some long forgotten souls who lived hundreds of years ago will have their stories told, but you know me; I'm the compulsive worrier. I'm ready to go home. I left my house in such a hurry…"

"It will be okay. It's only a few days. I think we're both feeling the effects of jet lag."

"I'll just rest my eyes," Helen murmured.

Tom's thoughts returned to his dad, the parent often absent from parenting long before his untimely death. He really was an enigmatic person, a puzzle never to be solved.

It was different with his mother, or so he'd always thought. They had always had a special bond. They seemed to be able to talk about anything. After they'd moved to Phoenix, and after the death of his grandmother, she had been his sole family connection.

The Marine Corps had become his family for a decade. The Corps would always remain family, but it was his mother who had been his primary support while he struggled through rehabilitation and learned to walk again with his foot prosthesis. Without her, and Alison's can-dos, he probably wouldn't have gone to Law School.

However, during the past few days he had begun to realize that he knew a lot less about Helen Carey than he'd thought. It really wasn't any of his business who his mother had known or knew, or how she had spent her time when he was a boy, or what she did now, for that matter, yet how could he have grown up living under the same roof without recognizing some of the strangers she had hugged at the wake? And after all Mick Van Schaick had done to pull his dad down, he didn't get how she could speak civilly to that high-horsed control freak.

He'd tilted the truth when he'd said the trip back hadn't been so bad. He could feel his guts turning inside out from the moment they entered the funeral chapel. As a result, he'd gone through a half bottle of antacids in a couple of days.

Before leaving Phoenix he and his mother had promised each other they wouldn't suffer through an Auld Lang Sine, but for his mother, from his perspective, the chorus commemorating the by-gone had picked up where it had left off decades ago. Helen seemed resolved and maybe even eager to sing along, and that was a big surprise.

Charlene's pendant had been a tender remembrance. Yet for him, it was one of the few comfortable familiarities he had found.

The following morning, seated beside scenic country murals in the hotel's lavish dining room, Tom and Helen breakfasted on fresh croissants, orange juice and coffee. Soon after they checked out and headed south toward the old neighborhood and the house that kept secrets only they knew. Helen had dozed off.

Before long Tom drove by the Clute's place, one of the families he had been close to until his father's death. He, Buddy Vandenberg and Sid Clute had played high school basketball together, and Tom was surprised to see that the basketball hoop was still standing straight. The Clute house, he remembered, had been layered over with light blue aluminum siding back when they lived in the neighborhood. It looked the same. The brass doorknocker that Mr. Clute complained Tom always banged way too hard was still on the front door. As he breezed by he remembered Mrs. Clute and her apple pies. Second helpings were anticipated by the three boys who camped out in her kitchen, so usually Mrs. Clute baked two or three at a time. Another good lady like Mrs. Mann.

Now though, the property looked abandoned. Gone was Mrs. Clute's front rose garden, yet Tom could still smell those pies and envision the pink and yellow blooms alongside of Sid's dad's vintage 1967, turquoise GTO parked in the driveway.

He swung the car onto River Road—the county road leading to the white clapboard house where he'd grown up. He was happy to see that there hadn't been many changes. Many of the centuries-old family homesteads had somehow survived the developer's demolition crews, and it lifted him up seeing the number of American flags posted. He also noticed that, just as it had always been, some of the accompanying antiquated carriage houses had become catch-alls for junk rather than garages for cars. Most everything here had a familiar look to it.

Since arriving at Albany International Airport—called "International" he'd been told, because a couple of flights flew back and forth to Canada every day—all he'd witnessed was change: new industries, Walmart Super Stores, new office buildings and retail space. Even a large casino-like gambling hall called a 'racino' had been built next to the Saratoga trotter horse track.

Yet here in the old neighborhood time had stood still. Here was preservation, or perhaps more correctly, here was sheer stubborn survival.

Tom pulled over to the side of the road and turned off the ignition.

"Hey, Mom, wake up."

Helen sat up abruptly. "I wasn't sleeping, really."

"Right." Tom chuckled then asked, "What do you think? Interesting—the old place hasn't fallen into the underworld. Our neighbor Charlie Van Ness would have been pleased. It was Charlie, right?"

"Yes, and he was a wonderful neighbor. He told some great stories about the history of our home. He would have been so pleased to see that so many of these houses have endured. Ours, too, and whatever do you mean underworld?"

"Glad you weren't sleeping, Mom."

Helen put her window down and pulled her jacket around her shoulders. She wasn't used to the cool, New York spring mornings anymore, "You know, on one hand, it's been a lifetime since I first opened the front door to that house with your dad, and yet, now, suddenly, it feels like only yesterday. I can even remember where we celebrated buying the place. It was down at a little Italian eatery near the old Quackenbush house in Albany. And the Italian place disappeared long, long ago."

"Yeah, Dad always liked Italian food."

Helen stared at the barn. "So strange to think somebody other than your father could be using the workshop in the barn."

"It's a little eerie."

"Well, the house looks good. Seems like the Dutch door your Dad repaired was replaced with something modern. Oh, that's a shame. Just so foreign now. Hard to be here, Tom. Maybe we should have stayed away."

"I know what you mean, Mom."

But you don't. You know nothing and much better that way.

"Tom, I think we should go before somebody starts wondering about a strange car parked in front of their house. They might call the State Police on us. Besides, I've seen enough." Helen looked at her son and noticed for the umpteenth time how much he looked like Steve at his age. Tom had his father's strong, square jaw, the same searching deep-blue eyes that had made her feel as if she were the only other person on the planet. Suddenly it struck her that Tom was nearly the age that Steve had been when he died.

Helen shivered and said, "I'm glad you remember Mr. Van Ness, dear."

Tom started the car. "Do you suppose the Albany State Museum still has the bayonet Dad dug out of the barn floor?"

Startled, Helen responded nervously, "I don't know. I've not thought about any of that for years. I would imagine so, but I can tell you this," she said stiffening, "there are many things I'd just as soon forget."

"Sorry Mom, I'm an ass. I shouldn't have mentioned it. Guess it just comes naturally."

"Being an ass?" Helen asked. A thin smile played along her lips.

"I think that might be a correct description of me right about now. You know my need to know every detail. It's an attorney curiosity thing. Really, I'm sorry. "

Helen nodded. "I remember something my father once told me about the fears that sometimes kept me awake at night. 'Facing down demons is the only way to put an end to the bastards'."

Tom grinned. "You know, Mom, there just might be something to all this DNA genealogy stuff after all."

"Maybe." Helen's voice sounded flat.

"Tell you what," Tom said, putting the car in gear. "Let's go pay our respects to Dad, and then get the hell out of New York."

CHAPTER 8

Albany, 1724

Wet and thirsty, John Collins, a prominent solicitor and member of the Board of Indian Affairs, stood patiently in the cold while the Red Rooster's dark servant, who had been posted outside the entrance, pushed against the tavern's door. It was obviously blocked by patrons enjoying the fruits of the establishment. Finally, after a good amount of struggle, enough of an opening was made, and the portly Collins squeezed through. As the door closed behind him, he removed his water-soaked brown felt hat and mostly dry woolen cloak. Acknowledging no man though he knew many, he made his way across the packed room to the warmth of the blazing hearth. In this part of the country the first of May had arrived feeling more akin to a wet, windy March day. Even the weather was against the peoples of New York. With his backside to the flame, Collins anxiously combed through the tavern's boisterous mix.

Earlier in the day he'd sent his Negro servant, Jimmy, to the home of Peter Waldron on lower Broadway with an urgent note. Waldron generally made rounds to his various jobsites around the city seeing to his bricklaying crews during the mornings, and was most always at home, at his desk, by mid-afternoon. John Collins counted on Mr. Waldron keeping to his schedule. He'd asked to meet him here at the tavern at 4 o'clock. He was compelled to warn his old friend of yet another dangerous situation developing in Albany.

"John! John! Lieutenant Collins! Over here in the corner!"

Collins swung around. Sighting Waldron, he excused himself as he pushed through the crowd. He smiled—the first after a long, grueling day. Few these days addressed him as Lieutenant Collins although he'd kept his title. He was rarely called out of Albany anymore for soldiering.

"Ah, excellent, Peter. You received my message."

Peter grinned and shouted over the din, "How long do we know one another?"

John stepped closer. "We knew each other when we were young and carefree roaming the streets long into the night in Manhattan, and as newcomers here; both of us newly married men."

Merrily, Peter interjected, "Our wives taught us a few things."

"Indeed the ladies did so."

"As I say so often—"

"A man is a failure without a routine!" Collins finished Peter's sentence. "Yes, I remembered as I wrote the note to you this afternoon."

As they exchanged discourse, John Collins noted that they were not alone. A muscular young man seated next to Waldron rose. "Sir, I take my leave, please sit here."

"I hope I have not interrupted," John said, glancing at Peter.

Peter explained, "This is one of my overseers—Henry Van Wie."

Turning, John smiled amicably. "'Tis good to make your acquaintance, Mr. Van Wie, and again I hope that I did not interrupt."

"Not at all."

Henry looked from one man to the other, waiting for the signal that he was dismissed. "I will be on my way then, and bid you both good eve, and Mr. Waldron, I *will* take care of the problem."

Peter grunted. "Do so."

Taking his seat, John observed the newly introduced Henry as he wrangled his way through the crowd. He liked the man's resolve. He sensed this was an up and coming young man who would make his mark in time.

His assessment was interrupted as Peter shouted to the thin, droopy-eyed serving girl as she passed, juggling two pitchers of beer. "Wench! Lieutenant Collins requires attention!"

The frazzled girl glanced back over her shoulder, but scurried away.

Red-faced, Peter mumbled something and then, in a voice brash enough to be heard across the length of the room, bellowed, "The Widow who now owns this establishment should bring on more help! Terrible service is an insult to her good patrons!"

Several turned to see who was causing the ruckus.

John rolled his eyes. "Calm yourself man, or you shall frighten the maid such that she will never return. I am satisfied to wait my turn to be served."

"You are a kind-tempered gentleman, John, but I assure you a quiet man will not prevail in this establishment."

John laughed. "You never change. Truthfully, I am full up with more pork and cake and rum than is good for any man. I would be better with a hot cup of good English tea than strong drink."

Peter growled. "English tea!"

John picked up one of the clay pipes left behind on the table for patrons wishing a smoke. He broke off the tip of the long stem that the pipe be fresh for his lips and tossed it on the floor. Pulling out his tobacco pouch, he filled the pipe and lit it. Peter continued to search the room for their server like a hound upon the fox's scent. His impatience shrouded the original urgency of their meeting, and John leaned across the table. "Though you would not remember her, you have met the frightened little rabbit before."

"I surrender," Peter mumbled looking down into his empty tankard. "How is it that I have met this servant girl? I only know her working here at the tavern, and she cannot be more than twelve. How would I know her?"

John answered soberly. "You met this girl, Hannelore, as a babe in her mother's arms years ago."

Refocusing his attention, Peter studied him sternly. "This is a curious jest you throw at me, John. And I am in no good mood today for jesting. What is the answer? Who is she?"

John shrugged. "Back in 1711 when we traveled southward to Livingston Manor where we put down the rebellious Palatines?"

"I remember the Palatines and more. How could any of us forget that terrible year of brutality? You followed Henry Holland's orders, and I mine, but not one of us was glad to do so."

"Our duty was harsh," John replied earnestly.

"Harsh!?" Peter yelled across the table. "These Germans are good Christians of the true faith, and I did not blame them for bonding together against authority after they were given one contract back in England and another contract to go by when they arrived here."

"It was difficult for our good Queen to decide what to do with such an onslaught of thousands of Germans anxious to leave their homeland. Unfortunately," John pleaded, "mistakes were made when so many of them were sent to New York."

"They deserved better," Peter replied morosely, "better than what they received. Those families came over on English ships, eager for work producing hemp, tar and pitch for our Royal Navy. Instead of work, the poor souls found starvation, and as it came to pass, many found their graves."

"As soldiers and citizens, Peter, we all did what we had to do in those times, and remember we had our hands full with the brutal, nay savage, Indian attacks near Fort Schaghticoke. Livingston and the other commissioners did as best as they could do with rationing out food and supplies," John replied defensively.

Thoughtfully, Peter observed his friend, remembering that John's wife and Robert Livingston's wife were devoted Schuyler sisters, sisters as well to the recently deceased Peter Schuyler. He immediately sobered. "Of course, and I mean no disrespect to Robert Livingston or Mrs. Livingston nor to any in your dear wife's family," he apologized, pausing to let out a long sigh. "But what does resurrecting pitiful by-gone times have to do with the girl?"

John said, "It occurred to me that your bark might soften toward her if you knew of the hard trail the maid had traveled before she arrived at Albany."

Peter adjusted his waistcoat and sat quietly waiting for further explanation.

"Not long ago," John began, "I dined here with a friend whose name shall remain undisclosed. The same girl waited upon us that evening, and it was then that I learned that one of the leaders of the Palatine rebellion had been her father. Sick and starving, this immigrant who had come to America full of hope with his family had died shortly after we had done our duty at the refugee camps on both the west and the east sides of the river. This Rhinesman left behind his wife and twelve minor children. Although rations of bread and beer and meat were given out, as you have indicated, the food came up short." John paused to stifle a rattling cough. "Excuse me. The winter troubles linger within my chest, I am afraid."

Peter waited for John's coughing spasm to subside before he spoke. "I am certain the loss of her husband was a great blow to the girl's poor mother."

"I can only imagine her burden," John returned. "And, of course, the passage for her entire family including her dead husband had to be worked off. Her elder children were all indentured to members of the Lansing family, and the younger children to wealthier farmers all over New York."

John followed Peter's gaze to a table where the German servant girl and a young Negro boy plunked down bowls of hot fish stew in front of a ferryman and his crewman.

"It seems," John resumed, "our servant girl, Hannelore, stayed with her mother who had found work in the kitchen of a prosperous Dutch farmer whose land was near to Livingston's. However, the flux that took so many during that bitter winter also claimed both the farmer and his wife as well as Hannelore's mother. I do not know how she survived, but perhaps another of the German families took her in.

"Years later she was found by the then owner of this tavern whilst he visited with his cousin who had been made an overseer at Livingston's Manor. When he saw her she was dressed in deer hides and begging for her bread in one of the east bank Palatine refugee camps. His heart directed him to bring her to his wife here in Albany for mothering. His wife, not having been blessed by children, was happy to have her in their house. Now it is the widow who needs the child's help."

Peter stared ahead thoughtfully. "She reminds me of my Cornelia at that age." After a moment, he added tenderly, "Now Cornelia is herself a wife and mother."

John answered matter-of-factly, "My prayer is that in time a match can be made for the girl. Ever since I heard the sad tale, though she can be most trying, I have held my tongue around her and have done the same at home with my own daughter, for who of us knows the future or how we shall be parted? I have spoken to my wife about finding a match for her, but for now the widow needs the help of her adopted daughter."

Peter nodded his understanding, now feeling embarrassed by his earlier outburst. After a period of silent reflection, he said, "I have been meaning to make an appointment with you for writing my last will and testament."

"Are you not well, Peter?"

"I am as good as any man our age, but, as you point out, it is best to think of these things."

John nodded. "We shall find an agreeable mutual date for the appointment."

"Good."

"But today," John continued, "I am afraid that I have some troublesome news ... 'tis the reason I summoned you here. I am wondering if you can help me?"

"Of course. "I am, as always, at your service."

"To speak bluntly," John said, "we have Abenaki savages in Albany."

Peter jolted backwards, questioning what he had heard. "Abenaki?!"

"Yes, sources tell us they have come to the city with condolence gifts for the Schuyler family. I suppose that none should be surprised that the Abenaki would not want to be overshadowed by the Mohawk."

Peter's concern was obvious as he replied. "I am sorry to hear of this."

John put aside his pipe and folded his hands in front of him. "Albany council members are indeed concerned. The subject of the Abenaki dominated our agenda today. Many fear they are aligned with the Canada French."

"As well they could be," Peter added.

"These particular Abenaki are a small band and have been questioned extensively. They claim that they are not from Canada, as suspected, nor that they are aligned in any way with the Canada French as most are, but that they come from the wilderness lands north of your farm. Their homeland, so they say, is not a far distance from the Schaghticoke village, and so I thought that you might know of them?"

Peter leaned forward, "As you know, many of the Schaghticoke Indians have Abenaki kinsmen in Canada, and the furs that the Schaghticoke often bring to us for trade at John Knickerbocker's place are probably trapped in Canada.

"White traders look away from this activity between Native kinsmen, and the result of this indifference is a handsome profit for all parties. Having said this, I am suspicious of any Abenaki who say they call Half Moon territory home. More likely they are guests of their Schaghticoke cousins. These smugglers have a place in the line of bargain, and if one wishes to continue the trade we must be civil, but surely we do not need them lurking around Albany."

Finally the German servant girl reappeared at their table and the two men drew apart as she set a full pitcher of beer in front of them.

Addressing the timid girl, John queried, "You go by the name of Lore?"

Surprised that any patron would care what her given name was, or even that a man of such stature would take the time to ask such a question, Hannelore's eyes widened, "Yes Sir, I be Lore."

"Well then, Lore, do you think that you could ask your Mistress to find me a hot pot of English tea? And a cup, of course, would also do well."

The young girl fixated on the pitcher she'd just brought to the table.

"Leave it!" Peter barked, and then, remembering the girl's tragic history, he softened his tone with a smile.

Lore curtsied, and then glanced shyly at John Collins. "I will go to my mistress right away, Sir, and ask her." She lowered her eyes, curtseying again before leaving.

Peter started. "John, I have had no knowledge of any Abenaki hereabouts, though I should think that my son, Cornelius, might, and I will soon see him up at the farm."

John sighed in disappointment. "I thought that I would ask you about them, but I should hope they will be gone before you have the opportunity to speak with your son."

Peter grimaced. "You know the history of the migration of the Indians in our part of our country as well as I do. Hundreds who originally came from Massachusetts settled in a portion of that area of Half Moon which back in those times belonged to Van Schaick. The land was offered by Governor Andros to a large number of Indians including some Abenaki. But all of this migration and placement took place long ago. I've been told that the grandchildren of these Abenaki now live north on the shores of the big French lake, *Lac du Saint Sacrement.*"

"I understand," John said. "Today, as the committee readied to vote on the matter, a new development arose. One of the Schaghticoke chiefs suddenly claimed one of the Abenaki to be a kinsman and that the family had lived by him for years. After an amount of commotion it was then decided that the foreigners would be allowed to remain a few days longer so that they could present their gifts properly."

Perplexed, Peter asked, "Who is it claiming the Abenaki as family?"

John rubbed his eyes. "Forgive me. I am weary after a day of meetings. I do not recall the Schaghticoke's name or if a name was given, but British soldiers from our fort were assigned to the Abenaki as well as the Schaghticoke who made the claim. We are all united in our opinion that we are against any foreigners blending freely amongst those who are known to us. Over and over the Abenaki pledged their peaceful intent, but we cannot verify who they are, and so, their pledge is not enough for residents of Albany to sleep tight in their beds."

Peter shrugged. "If only I could be of more help."

Coughing again, Collins studied the man across the table with the eye of an interrogator. "I have heard that you have had trouble in front of your house?"

"Yes—a fight occurred weeks ago, but the trouble had not to do with Abenaki. Some local problem, that was all."

Lore approached again, this time carrying a small, Dutch majolica tea pot and small matching cup. Talk suspended while she filled John's cup. Dashing off, she left the pot of tea behind.

Leaning forward, John half-whispered, "These, shall we say, 'fur traders' will be allowed to offer their condolences, but Albany will remain alert."

"We should have sent them away immediately," Peter insisted. "Considering the uncertainty of these times, I would not trust any savage I do not know, should he be full up to his ears with condolences."

"I agree," John replied, "yet the council majority has spoken."

"Unfortunate," Peter muttered.

"Still, I wonder," John deliberated. "How do we legally justify allowing Abenaki, who might be in communication with the enemy, to remain in Albany as our guests? The Iroquois are our brethren who are legally bound to us by treaty, and by that treaty must have no communications with the French. If it turns out that the guests are not truthful, and if they do have an affiliation with the Canada French, how will our Iroquois friends look at the English?"

"John, you know the answer. Our friends will see us as unworthy to negotiate any future terms. Plainly, the Six Nations profess their loyalty by the terms of the Albany Treaty in which it is written and agreed that the Iroquois will not have any correspondence with the Canada French. It is our covenant."

"Amen," John replied between most satisfying sips of his warm, English drink, and he thought of his aged mother at home in London.

CHAPTER 9

The tavern began to thin out, and Peter nestled back into his chair. As it sometimes is between close friends who have known each other many years, and together experienced much, no words were necessary between him and John Collins, allowing both of them space for reflection.

Peter thought of home. His curly haired, red-headed toddler would be awakening from his nap on the pallet near the parlor hearth about now. Cate would drop her work and rush to his outstretched meaty little arms as he wobbled toward her. She would gather him up to her breast and rock him and sooth him to smiles.

Peter's chest tightened. He must keep his family safe. When he returned home later he would hold Garret and promise before God to protect him and all of his children always.

With Peter Schuyler at the helm, Albany citizens had enjoyed a decade or more of peace, but now, with him gone...*Every man must be on guard. We must not grow lazy in mind and heart, dulled by false security. Foreigners have to be taken seriously. Everyone must be reminded of the massacre of the Kittle family near Schaghticoke village, to avoid suffering the same fate.*

Who of them who had lived through those terrible times would not understand that it was still foolhardy to trust anyone who could be kinsman to one of the demons who struck down the Kittle settlers? How could they forget the mutilated bodies brought back to Albany when the militia men went up to the Kittle place the day after the attack? One of the women, who was large with child, was discovered with her head nearly severed from her body.

Gruesome details had been learned from an old local Indian who had run into the woods during the attack. The young mother had been scalped while still alive and then tomahawked to death. The bloodied body of a bludgeoned infant, the child of Mrs. Kittle's sister-in-law, had been discovered hanged in a nearby tree. The Schaghticoke Indians, who swore that they had no part in the murders, said it had been done in front of the babe's mother's eyes. Soldiers, settlers, and a Negro boy had been shot dead, and their bodies mutilated and burnt. Houses and barracks of corn had been burnt to the ground.

During the somber October days that followed the attack, Cate, too, had heard this barbarous news as their then newly born Catherine suckled at her breast. She had all but collapsed at the thought of any mother seeing her child dead in such a horrifying way.

Filled with terror that these murderous savages would come into Albany, she had rushed to see their minister, and she and Peter were grateful to have their Catherine baptized at the Dutch Reformed Church four days after the attack. Peter had recorded October 24, 1711 in his large Dutch Bible. Cate had kept herself and their children housebound for weeks thereafter, comforted by one thought...all of their children had been saved by the holy waters of baptism.

Peter refilled his tankard and drank the beer till he saw the bottom.

The hand of the Almighty had preserved David Kittle, and after the attack, he had assembled a group of Provincials and English soldiers and formed a rescue party. Kittle's wife and other victims were found and brought back to Albany a year later. Resolved to endure, David Kittle had rebuilt his house on the lands near the Schaghticoke village and not far from the location of his first dwelling that had been destroyed by the savages. And then, astonishing everyone, he and his wife had returned with their children.

* * *

It was hard to think that those who brutally murdered the Kittles most likely had been baptized by the Catholic French Jesuit Priests. How dare those savages call themselves Christians! Long ago, his grandfather, Resolved, witnessed a Jesuit priest perform the Catholic baptism when traveling in the North Country with his friend, LaCroix, himself baptized Catholic. The newly baptized Indian was given a new name, and from then forward he was known by the name of one of the Papist's saints. Without baptism the soul could not enter heaven, but where is the location of the French Catholic's heaven? Surely, Peter thought, his children would not share the same heaven with murdering savages or Catholics.

John Collins lifted the lid of the teapot. Peering in, he groaned. "Pity. 'Tis empty."

"Do you know, John, that David Kittle and his wife and family have been guests at my farm many times over these years past?" Peter asked.

"I did not." John replied.

"Cornelius hunts with David, and our families share in a harvest feast together. I wonder what David Kittle would feel about the decision of the gentlemen on the Council with regard to the Abenaki in Albany as guests?"

John Collins responded swiftly. "There are few men as determined as David Kittle living in the North Country. Yet, not a one who chooses the pioneer's life is ordinary. I should think that Mr. Kittle would trust in the authorities, as should you, my friend."

"Trust? How should I trust? John, these past weeks have seen many fights between servants and drunken Indians, each accusing the other of starting the trouble. This afternoon, from my overseer, Henry, I have heard about threats to burn down the city, and now you have brought me more worries. I will say what I think about 'trust.' Today you have convinced me to move my family out of Albany to my farm where it is only a short walking distance from Fort Schaghticoke. I would rather stand by David Kittle and the soldiers up there than linger here in Albany while the authorities host savages."

"That is your decision and probably for the best," John agreed. "The fort at Schaghticoke is well garrisoned, and British soldiers regularly patrol the roadways between Albany and there. We think the same. I am sending my wife and children down to relatives in Manhattan and would go myself if I did not have pressing matters in the court."

"I shall deliver mine upriver to my farm, but with all that is happening, I dare not leave Albany unattended for long," Peter said, rising. "Well, Sir, I take my leave and wish you and your family safe travels. Give my regards to your wife, Margarita."

Rising himself, John clasped Peter's arm. "And I the same for you and your family," John said as they embraced. "Let us pray for safe journeys. And I shall take care of what is owed to our tavern keeper today."

Peter spoke his thanks and departed.

An hour later at home, Peter Waldron ate a late supper of ham and bread and butter that his wife had put before him, while Cate sat bouncing their youngest child on her lap.

Several times Catherine attempted to retrieve her baby brother, but Garret was reluctant to leave his mother, so busy was he twisting around the ring on her middle finger.

"I think that the sparkle in the crystal stone has captured him," Cate mused.

Catherine giggled while Garret squealed with delight. "Perhaps he sees the angel who tossed the bigger part of the mother rock out of heaven like 'Still Water' told us when we were children and she visited."

Cate smiled, remembering the Papscanee Native and her family. She was pleased that the old woman's story lived on within her Catherine.

Peter ate his fill, ignoring their womanish prattle, but his eyes rested on his wife's ring. He was surprised to see that Cate was already wearing it, as he had not yet mentioned they would be leaving for the farm earlier than usual this year. She wore her ring only when attending a wedding or baptismal feast or when they traveled to outlying places beyond the city. She must have discovered his plans.

How was it possible that his wife could see the future and he could not, or so it seemed?

Peter prayed that Cate had not come to believe the *voices that spoke to her alone,* but he also had to admit that strange happenings often surrounded his wife, such as the spectacle that occurred just before they had departed for the farm last year.

He and Cate had been sitting on the garden bench behind the house, both of them enjoying their clay pipes as they often did when the children were settled in for the evening. Between smokes he went over the particulars of their ensuing trip. His wife had responded half-heartedly, and he determined that her thoughts were with Cornelius, and not with him. Like a mother bird indisposed to pushing her chicks from the nest, from the start Cate objected to Cornelius taking on running and living at the farm year-round, even though two of his best men went with him to replace the log cabin with a new frame structure. And, Cate had sent along her well-trained cook—thirteen year old Minnie, Dinah's girl.

Peter sighed. He had not had a good piece of cornbread since Minnie went up there, but he would not say a word about missing Minnie's cooking, or utter a thought that might be taken as criticism. He, too, had enjoyed a close loving relationship with his own mother, until well after he had married Cate. In retrospect though, it was best that he and Cate had left Manhattan and relocated to Albany when they did.

He had sat beside her on the bench, growing more and more pensive, when suddenly out of the dusk, appeared a white, angel-like, winged lunar moth. They had both stared at it in stunned silence as the beautiful creature landed upon a nearby bush, beckoning their attention. All his frustration, and he suspected Cate's worries, had dissolved. Only once had he seen such an exceptional moth and that was the night of Cornelius's birth, a sign that the Almighty smiled upon their infant.

Last year in the garden, after their visitor fluttered away, he had noticed Cate wearing the silver ring that he had had one of the best silversmiths in Manhattan—Peter Feurt—fashion for her in commemoration of their twentieth year of marriage.

Cate considered Peter's gift precious, and especially endearing as her grandmother had bequeathed her several sacred crystal rocks from the Vandenbergh farm at Papscanee Island. The shimmering small stone that the silversmith had set was but a chip off of one of the larger sacred crystals. She often said the stone in her ring twinkled not unlike the stars in the heavens from whence it truly came.

Finishing his supper Peter thought upon his good fortune to be blessed by a fine, healthy family. He abolished all thought of his Albany house burning to the ground as such treacheries were beyond his control. He could only do what he could do, and the rest was in God's hands.

His overseer, Henry, would put an end to the men fighting on the job, and the workers would complete the building on time. He must remain confident that all would be well by the time he returned from upcountry.

Cate should not worry. Cornelius had things well in hand, and he looked forward to seeing how the new smoke house was coming along and also to devouring Minnie's fried chicken.

Peter belched, signaling that he'd finished his supper.

Cate handed Garret to his father, and as she passed the baby he noticed that the crystal stone on her middle finger reflected the candlelit room to him, perhaps foretelling Cate's willingness to journey north. Of course, the world and everything on it was created by Almighty God, but Cate also held fast to the Native lore that Abram's daughter Still Water, taught. Armed by her prayer book, and God's heavenly stone, dearest Cate held fast to her faith that God would protect all of them along the journey.

CHAPTER 10

An hour past sun-up, with the sky promising to remain blue, Peter Waldron guided the wagon carrying Cate, Garret, and their Negro servant woman, Dinah, over the rutted, dung laden and already busy streets of Albany's Third Ward district. Nudging Albert, his big brown horse forward, Peter, his neck wet with sweat, held the leather reins tight. Flanked by Dinah's boys and his older children running alongside, out of the corner of his eye he noticed Rebecca's yellow braids bobbing about her shoulders, as her elder brother, Pete, playfully poked at her with a branch. Eva came to her younger sister's rescue, pushing their brother away.

Cursing as three men ran in front of him across the road, Peter navigated a populous of Indians, local tradesmen and colorfully dressed gentry. Not one of them cared how they disrupted him! Neither did the Schuyler hounds barking furiously at the wagon's wheels.

Jittery, Albert balked and the wagon jolted. "Whoa Albert!" Peter hollered. Albert neighed an angry response, letting his driver know that he was doing his best not to run any foolhardy human or the impetuous small barking beasts into the ground. Above all came a whistle's sharp call, and reluctantly the dogs retreated. *A Samaritan has harkened to my plight!*

Willie, the mulatto Waldron driver, followed behind at a reasonable distance in a second wagon laden with household goods—the response to Cornelius's last extensive list of required replenishments. In addition to the household needs for his master's farm, Willie also hauled gunpowder, blankets, a barrel of Madeira wine, and pots—all for trading. Willie kept a keen eye on the returning hounds, nodding to the Schuyler servant as he passed.

Peter wished that he would have been blessed with extra eyes. An eye for each side of his head would have been an excellent asset today, but he dared not take the time to look back again at his wife. Above the problematic chaos, he heard Cate fervently calling out the sacred Psalm 91. *"I will say of the Lord, He is my refuge and my fortress: My God; in Him I will trust!"*

Despite being encouraged by the appearance of the lunar moth the previous year, his wife had dreaded this day. She did not wish to leave her snug, comfortable nest in Albany, especially with her expectant daughter-in-law so close to giving birth. Reluctantly, she had come round only when Peter shared that John Collins was sending his family to relatives in Manhattan. They would remain away from Albany until things there had settled.

William would take good care of his Elizabeth. Her sister was with her, and the midwife lived close.

Still, budging Cate had taken coaxing. Beneath her grandmother's quilt, Peter had whispered of happy reunions—Cornelius longing, of course, to see his mother, and the pleasure of witnessing Dinah's joy when she would see her Minnie. *Would a good Christian woman deny another mother the comfort of her child's voice?*

Rounding the corner, two British soldiers emptied out of Beekman's Inn, and, hearing a woman's Godly plea, attentively craned their necks in the direction of Peter's wagon. Though Cate continued her prayer, Peter nodded in their direction a confident *all is well*, thinking if the streets were empty and the roadway paved smoothly with gold, Cate would still recite the Holy Psalms.

At the same time he tried to ignore the painful spasms running across his chest. The trouble was occurring more often of late, but he attributed his condition to overwork and had ignored Cate's demands to summon the physician. That was nonsense. He was simply weary from laying brick himself after sending two good men up with Cornelius and then suffering the unexpected loss of another of his remaining workmen to the winter sickness. It had been a long time since he was required to do construction himself.

Van Wie had been a God-send, but leaving a young and freshly made overseer in charge of his workers at one of his jobsites worried Waldron. William, of course, would complete their contract with the City for two small houses outside the city walls meant for the Indians when they came in to trade with Albany merchants, but the Ostrander house was another story. He'd' have to leave his family at the farm to periodically check with Henry. Though Peter often attempted handing his worries to The Almighty, he still worried. It seemed as if his world was falling apart these days. Nothing went right since the death of Colonel Peter Schuyler last February.

Last night as he'd dropped into bed beside his sleeping wife, he'd prayed for safe travels...and the strength to endure. He'd finally drifted off with thoughts of the spring-fed pond behind his farm reclaiming life, cattails, and flowering wet grasslands.

As the wagons jostled along this morning, Peter suspected that when Schuyler's soul had passed into the hands of his Savior, countless persons he'd left behind were touched whether they had loved him or not. It was estimated that hundreds of city residents had braved February's blustery winds when the bell had tolled, and now the Native peoples continued to arrive to pay homage to the one who truly understood Iroquois diplomacy.

Schuyler could not be replaced and therein was the troubling of minds. A successor had been sought, and none doubted that Jon Van Dyke would do his best, but even Van Dyke would most likely agree that filling the past Indian Commissioner's boots would take intercession from Almighty God. Lively discussions in every Albany tavern over the repercussions of political change had helped the shrouded days of winter pass. Every man had his own opinion of what might be better or worse, as well as what was to be expected, but Peter chose to remain silent on the subject of politics. As a former Manhattanite whose family had lived through the Leisler Rebellion he was well acquainted with the ramifications of leaning in any direction during a time of political upheaval.

All in Albany was not complete despair. Peter Schuyler's cousin, Abraham Schuyler, would soon return to the capital of the Indian Confederacy, Onondaga, where he would meet and smoke the pipe with several old Indian friends, area leaders, and members of the Bear, Wolf and Turtle clans. Upon hearing this, Peter had been encouraged as he knew Abraham Schuyler personally. Along with Adrian Quackenbush, it was Abraham Schuyler who had put in a word for him with Abraham's younger brother, Mayor Myndert Schuyler, and because of Abraham's high praise within the right circles, Peter had been appointed Fire Master of the Third Ward. Not long thereafter Abraham Schuyler had spoken for him again, securing him a position as assistant alderman in the same ward. His primary concern now was that Abraham Schuyler was a man well advanced in his years. It would not do well for the country to see Albany attending another Schuyler funeral in the near future.

Peter glanced over his shoulder into the back of the wagon where Cate finally rested peacefully with Garret in her arms beside her servant, the three cozy on a pile of blankets that he planned to trade with the Schaghticoke Indians. He turned away, smiling, and snapped the reins.

At forty, Cate was still a fine-looking woman, but she could be hard-hearted, his Cate, when something or someone displeased her. He did not like it at all when she had climbed up onto her Vandenbergh high horse like she did when she made little of his Uncle Johannes. That man, God rest his soul, had been more of a father to him than his own during his boyhood in Harlem. She knew nothing of Johannes's strong loving heart, his courage, and all that he had endured for love of his country, although Cate would tell anyone who would listen to her that she did.

As a husband it was his duty to admonish his wife that it was a sin to speak disrespectfully against the dead. His reproach did him no good. At an early age, sitting by the knee of her father at Papscanee Island, Cate had learned how to argue from a man who was well acquainted with the courts. *Ah, well, my uncle and father-in-law have lived their earthly lives. I and my fiery tongued Cate must live our own.*

Still, Peter resented being put in the position of defending his uncle since it was unfair that the deeds of one man should affect another who was little more than a boy during the tumultuous years of England's Glorious Revolution. Undoubtedly, he was not privy to all of the secrets locked within the hearts of his elders, but he did know this much—his father and some of his Waldron kinsman believed that the whole painful ordeal surrounding Leisler, and his Uncle Johannes, had killed his grandfather, Resolved Waldron.

His father and uncles had broken with each other because of the Leisler trouble, and they had remained estranged until Grandfather's death. Later, his grandfather's properties had to be sold to pay off his debts incurred, in part, trying to secure a pardon for his accused son-in-law, and Uncle Johannes's misguided decisions ultimately separated his own children from the homestead where every one of them had been born. The year Peter left Manhattan to take up residency in Albany, his Aunt Aeltie could no longer abide living at Harlem, and she sold her Vermilye property and moved to Yonkers with her younger children.

Recently, Aunt Aeltie had written him a letter, addressing her correspondence affectionately, as she always did, *"favorite nephew"*. Aunt professed that she had finally found a harmonious life.

Even now her words filled him. She had suffered through a terrible ordeal and deserved peace.

A familiar clanging interrupted his thoughts.

Tied to the back of Willie's wagon was Sally, the black and white three year old family cow usually kept down at the common grassy pasture during the day. By night she bedded down in front of their house in the street. Poor Sally, Peter thought, listening to the bell as she plodded along; such a long journey for their animal.

Although *the wilderness farm*, as Cate referred to their northern plantation, was home to six milking cows, as far as Cate was concerned Sally was the family's only trusted source of milk, butter and cheese. The family would be away from the city for months, and Cate, like last year, had been adamant that Sally wasn't to be left behind. Eva had milked her this morning and would tend to milking Sally twice each day. And while at the farm, she would help Minnie with milking the other six as well. So had declared Cate, and so it would be.

Peter imagined his ten-year-old daughter's sullen, resigned face, as she no doubt thought about her endless chores while walking beside her charge behind Willie's wagon.

Willie, the senior of all their servants was deep in his own thought.

I wish the master not be so worried. We all gonna get there. I is a better driver than any driver, free or slave, dark or white, in or around Albany. I is a prized wagon master. Master Peter tell me just last night how important Willlie be to him. It sure a good feeling for me knowin' that master think so. Sure enough, the master paid a big price for me. He haggled with old Master Barent Waldron, down at the Harlem farm at Gloudie's Point. Master Barent sure not happy to give over one of his bestus servants to his nephew, but Master Peter say that I be all he wanted for him and his new wife's weddin' gift. Willie chuckled. *Mr. Barent Waldron growled like an old bear when he signed the paper makin' me Master Peter's property.*

Willie sharply observed the wagon's mare struggle. "You go on Bess," he ordered, sternly cracking the reins. "You go on old girl."

That be almost twenty years ago. Long before I got me a wife and the Lord blessed me with five good, strong boys and Minnie. Master Peter sure be happy with all those extra hands for up at the farm. My boys, or my Minnie neither, never have no worries about being sold away. Master say we all belong with him forever. Master Barent never swear no oath like Master Peter.

* * *

Peter turned around, calling out over the street noise, "Willie, watch that wheel; mind you. Take her steady!"

Willie hollered back, "Master, the wheel be good. I pay that wheel mind when we loaded this morn'. It be this fussy mare. I be steady, but she the most trouble I ever handled. Master, this here Bess gonna do like I tell her to do. Mr. Sam Doxie up by the Schaghticoke will have his borrowed wagon and his fitful Bess back in no time."

Peter grinned. "If you say it be so, then it be so, Willie."

Reaching the summit of the hill, Bess, tired from the long uphill haul, snorted and then made an awful sound as if she were about to drop...but she didn't. Obviously relieved and satisfied, Willie commenced to singing one of his favorite spirituals; a simple verse repeated.

"Lord, Lord, oh my Lord, shine on me, Lord, Lord, shine on me."

Dinah awakened from the ruckus. She leaned against her Mistress Cate, and whispered disgustedly, "That big headed man, him crowin' like the Master's prideful rooster." Pointing an arthritic finger toward Willie she hissed "You be right to beg the Lord to shine on you old man. Shine, shine."

Cate's lids lifted, and she laughed, adjusting Garret on her lap. "Oh, let your husband be. Willie is happy bossing Mr. Doxie's mare, and I see no wrong in a man who is happy with his duties."

"Amen," Peter called back. "I would have you hold fast to your sentiments, woman. I will expect you to be as happy whilst we are at the farm."

"I am not your Willie!" Cate retorted in a huff. "I will not be singing praise in that wilderness kitchen up yonder. I will be lonesome for my daughters and the company of the neighboring women folk in the city, and you know this is so. Who will I talk to all day?"

Peter laughed. "You can talk to me, and talk to your sons when we come to the house hungry from the fields. You can talk to your daughters."

"Which of our daughters do you speak of, Peter? Rebecca playing yonder, or Eva who will talk to Sally but wishes not to hear a word I speak? And Cornelia said when she last visited that she and Derek will not journey up with their babes and our Catherine for weeks."

Peter moaned, "Oh Cate, I understand you missing Engeltie, Cornelia, and Catherine, but the time will pass swiftly, I promise, and all our daughters will come up, as will my brothers and their families from Manhattan when they can do so. Do not fret about your lonesome hours."

Cate glanced over the side of the wagon at her exuberant, freckled-faced son and his sisters, frolicking beside the wagon. Eva had again abandoned Sally, again allying herself with Rebecca against her brother. Pete quacked tauntingly at both of them, and the two girls screamed retaliatory quacks.

Again Cate contemplated how few accomplished hands, other than Dinah and Minnie, there would be in her farmhouse kitchen, especially without her elder unmarried daughters, Engeltie and Catherine. She did not look forward to the prospect of preparing meals for nine youngsters and a dozen men with only the help of thirteen-year-old Minnie and her stiffly-moving mother.

Watching Pete mischievously aggravate his sisters, Cate knew her husband was right when he admonished her for her favoritism of his namesake. Still, the tender side of a mother's heart made chastisement difficult where Pete was concerned. Bringing their third son into the world had nearly cost both of them their lives. After three days of traveling through "the valley of death" her boy had come into the world fighting for his life. The hard birth made her want no more seeds to grow in her tired body, but the Lord wished otherwise. Two years after Pete came Rebecca, and then last year, Garret.

Ah well, the comfort of proper womanish talk that I enjoy at home with my elder daughters and my daughter-in-law, Elizabeth, when we visit, should be the least of my complaints. Indeed, Peter is right, I will have little time for discourse up on the farm even if I do have neighbor women close by.

Rebecca had begun to cry and Cate had had enough. "Pete hush! Be still and leave your sister alone!" Pete complied by running ahead. "And you two girls, mind your own person!"

Eva took Rebecca's hand and headed back to Sally at the rear of Willie's wagon.

Cate was annoyed with herself for not having insisted upon Catherine coming up with them. Catherine, at fourteen, had surpassed her elder sister, Engeltie, for cookery and was her best help in the kitchen. But what could she say when her Cornelia had rested imploring, doleful eyes upon her person?

Cornelia and Catherine had put forth a strong argument, giving the excuse that Cornelia's in-laws, the visiting Bradts, had brought along two elder cousins from Schenectady. Cornelia hated her mother-in-law and had complained that they were a burden more than she could endure, and as a mother with a toddler herself, Cate had understood. Cornelia had not been well since the birth of her babe, and she had begged for Catherine's help. She had permitted Engeltie to stay with Elizabeth and William so she had to do the same for Cornelia and let Catherine go.

Cate sighed. So she would be lonesome, but surely blessed in the eyes of Almighty God for her generous spirit as well as her obedience in abiding by her husband's wishes. All the same, *she did not have to be happy about doing so.*

She recalled when she first met Peter in New York City at the home of her aunt whilst tending to sickly Grandfather Van der Poel. A tall, gangly, young man had come to call. She did not think him at all handsome, but she soon found herself flattered by his attentiveness. He wanted to know all about her life in the north, sharing that his father had told him the most astonishing stories of visiting the "Island of the Crystals" during a great fire. Though only a small child during one of the worst disasters her family had ever endured, the terror of the day was renewed every time she looked upon her mother's scarred face. As a seventeen-year-old girl sitting by her ailing grandfather's side, listening to Peter recount her family's tale as told to him by his father, she had begun to feel that this was the man sent by God to be her spouse.

Her parents and all her relatives had liked him well enough, all agreeing that Peter Waldron was both intelligent and ambitious, qualities most valued. He had been accepted as a mason in New York City and surely could provide a comfortable life for a family. In addition to a secure trade, Peter spoke both Dutch and English as well as some Mohawk which was a great benefit for any man. After but a few encounters Peter had won her heart and her hand.

Barely eighteen with her newborn infant in her arms, she had come with Peter to Albany after her grandfather's death. Although she had spent her girlhood at Papscanee Island, she had wondered how she would survive on the frontier after living two comfortable years in Manhattan. Knowing nothing of housewifery, she had found that prayer, and not her female cousins, had been her constant companion during those early Albany days.

Yet it was Peter who held her tight, and Peter who reassured that together all would be well. And so it had been. Thinking about their life together now, she came to the conclusion that she had done well to marry the determined Peter Waldron.

As the wagon rolled along, she pulled her sleeping youngest child close, grateful that Almighty God had not taken her foolish pleas to heart. She had born ten children over the past twenty-four years and praised God for every one of them.

Cate called up to Peter, "Do you think we will be at our farm before sundown?"

"I think it possible; we set out early enough, but I have in mind to accept Madame Schuyler's kind invitation and to stop for a rest at Schuyler Flats. Would that please you?" Peter asked over his shoulder.

In response to this unexpected surprise, Cate's answer was immediate. "I would be most pleased."

Peter smiled broadly, "I thought the visit would do you good."

Pushing loose damp wisps of auburn hair back under her cap, Cate said to Dinah, "It will be a relief to get down out of this wagon, and Madame Schuyler will most assuredly insist that we stay through the night. She so loves the little ones. 'Tis a shame that she and her husband had none of their own."

Dinah smiled and patted her Mistress's hand.

Suddenly nervous, Cate asked, "Do you remember which

trunk you put the good shoes in? We must stop afore and surely change to our better shoes before we make ourselves known at the Schuyler house."

As if Peter also thought of how they would all look presenting themselves, he pulled the wagon to the side of the road and turned around in his seat. Willie followed his Master's example and halted.

"Cate, I will pull aside at de Forest's Tavern where we can refresh ourselves and the children. It is not far from here. And, what think you of giving Mrs. Schuyler a gift of the Madeira I had in mind to keep for trading with the Indians? When we stop at the Schuyler Farm, Willie and the Schuylers' man can pull the barrel off the wagon."

Cate appreciated how much the Madeira was prized as a tool for trade, but she looked with distain upon the trade of any drink that encouraged drunkenness amongst the savages. And she thought that her husband should, too, with all of his complaints about drunk heathens in Albany. Indeed, the Natives had acquired a great liking for spirits. Disgustedly, she'd muttered a silent prayer whenever Peter asserted an opinion held by many that the Indians did not tolerate strong drink as well as white men. With a sigh of relief she called out, "The Madeira will be most appreciated at Mrs. Schuyler's house, I am certain."

As Peter started up the wagon, Dinah whispered to her Mistress that she knew where the shoes had been stored. Anxiously, the servant wondered out loud how long they would stay on at the Flats, and if it would be long enough, it would be good to see the other dark folk she'd not talked with since the week of May Pinkster celebrations in Albany.

Suddenly revitalized, Cate wondered too. She had been to Phillip and Margaret Schuyler's farm a few miles north of Albany only once. Longingly, Cate recalled the cool breezes that swept up over the expansive lawn from the river. "Willie! We shall stop at the Flats!"

"Yes, Mistress, I do hear." Willie turned his attention to the wagon's wheel which had begun to give him cause for alarm. He had spoken the truth about looking it over before they started out, but the packing and the checking was done long before dawn. His eyes were not what they had once been, and his master most likely was right in his concern about the wheel. Willie was glad that they would stop first at de Forest's.

Up ahead, Pete was jumping up and down, jubilantly waving to sailors aboard Captain Winn's sloop in the North River which paralleled their route. Cate found herself again thinking of the boyhood stories her husband had told.

With their Mohawk guide, Peter—then about the age of their own Pete—and his father and grandfather had traveled up river from Manhattan to explore wilderness lands north of Albany owned by Van Schaick. Peter's elders were especially impressed by the great falls and beyond the falls the fertile lands at the intersection of the two rivers where the whites had traded with the Indians for decades. The Europeans called the place Half Moon while the Indians called their village at this spot Nachtenack, which translated meant "excellent land". Their Mohawk guide said the land was blessed by the *Great Spirit*.

Resolved Waldron had felt the Half Moon ground hallowed for trade, but also significant for the richness of the soil where he believed most any crop could grow in abundance. It was then that Peter's aged grandfather had planted seeds of the possibility of a northern Waldron farm. But the seeds would not germinate for many years after their journey and long after an announcement by Governor Dongan in 1686 allowed the City of Albany permission to purchase those lands from the Schaghticoke Natives— lands that would be divided into lots of fifty acres each.

As they had packed for the journey north, Peter reminisced with his wife that he had no doubt his grandfather, Resolved Waldron, wished he were again a young man when he'd put his large, strong hand on his shoulder and prophesied, *"You will be the one to settle the frontier."* Before the old man passed into the hands of the Almighty, Peter had made him a solemn promise. He would carry the Waldron name north to Albany and beyond. And so, here they were traveling to their Waldron farm.

* * *

After what turned into a two day stopover at the Schuyler's farm at the Flats, the wagons, passengers, and cargo finally reached Waldron Farm. At sunset, the evening of their arrival, Cate and Peter walked hand in hand by themselves down to the pond. As they turned back toward the house, Peter envisioned a magnificent future for his farm with Cornelius at the helm. Although he and his second born son did not often agree, they both decided that wheat crops produced in this fertile valley would replace peltry as the "new gold". His one hundred acres were a fine new beginning to contemplate as he approached his fiftieth birthday. His Cate had also promised to have Minnie make him the biggest cake ever to celebrate.

Peter could see himself on his wilderness farm as his pioneering grandfathers, Resolved Waldron and Peter Stoutenburg, had seen themselves in old Manhattan. Although he would never give up his city rights allowing him to partake in trading with the Indians, rights guaranteed by maintaining a residency in Albany, he and Cornelius, like his grandfathers, would soon be overseeing a generously productive farm. He envisioned pastoral fields surrounded by vast woodlands producing a variety of vegetables, good medicinal herbs, barracks of corn, and enough white winter wheat to ultimately fill the ovens of every manor house along the North River.

Looking down at his handsome, petite wife, Peter grinned, impulsively picking her up and twirling her around. "In time, Cate. In time—" he sang out merrily.

Cate thought, *there are no clocks in heaven. The Prophecy would become a truth according to the schedule of Almighty God.*

CHAPTER 11

Summer 1967

Helen and Patrick had played a furious final game of volleyball with friends on Lake George's beach before dropping breathlessly to their knees in the warm, gritty, brown sand. Slowly the twosome meandered back toward their blanket and towels. Laughing triumphantly, they'd shared their champions' thumbs-up with kids they knew along the way. The last of the sandwiches, chips, and chocolate chip cookies Helen had packed in her mother's picnic basket early this morning had been eaten. Their last Saturday off from their summer jobs in Albany had evaporated rapidly today in the fullness of August's heat.

Helen looked at the watch she had stashed safely inside her loafer and sighed. Already it was past three o'clock, and they should start thinking about the hour long drive home, but instead she parked herself on the blanket and didn't stir. Like a cup of Maxwell House coffee, today had to be 'good till the last drop'. She just had to have another dip in the lake before they folded up the blanket signaling the end of their last little get-away of the season.

Lake George's 'Million Dollar Beach' felt to her every bit as luxurious as she imagined Palm Beach, Florida must be, and it sure was more gorgeous here than it was at the Jersey shore. Leaning back on her elbows, she already regretted that they probably wouldn't see the silhouette of sails against the Adirondack Mountains again until next summer. Sighing, she lay back completely and stretched out face-up next to the boy she loved. She studied what she imagined to be a floating family of cumulous clouds moving slowly across a flawless blue sky, and she knew her mother had been right. Everything did fall into place according to God's perfect order. Today, she thought dreamily, had to be one of the most perfect days of her entire life.

Beside her, Patrick looked up into the same sky, and feeling a sharp twinge in his chest he wondered what the sky over Saigon looked like on a hot summer day like this one. He'd heard Vietnam had some really nice beaches at one time, but he couldn't imagine any of the thousands of American boys over there laying on a beach anyplace today. And certainly those guys in that hellhole weren't watching chicks in bikinis bounce by.

He sat up abruptly and pushed his damp, long dark hair behind his ears. He glanced at Helen in her two-piece red, white and blue bathing suit. Throughout the summer her freckles had seemingly melted together into one deep tan. Patrick exhaled. She was no casual bikini girl. Helen was the real deal. God, what was he going to do about her? He'd been agonizing for weeks over how he would tell her that he had changed his mind about attending Rensselaer Polytechnic Institute in September. He just couldn't go to college... not now. The problem was that Helen wasn't just his special girl: she was his *very* special girl. They had known each other since parochial school kindergarten. They'd dated since sophomore year in high school, and although he had never said so, after their first real date, he thought he might love her. Patrick suspected that she felt the same way.

In his senior year his uncle had given him his old Ford so he could go back and forth to his part-time job afternoons and Saturdays at the paper mill. Car ownership had provided more than transportation though. The Ford offered privacy and had upped his confidence level. Soon the long lingering kisses he and Helen shared in the isolated quarters of the Ford grew more intense.

After graduation she'd allowed his hand to explore her breast over her blouse, but she'd always stopped him before he'd been able to get to forbidden skin. They both felt awkward when they'd cooled down. Without a whole lot of discussion he figured that maintaining self-control was the right thing to do. But control was hard because, as far as Patrick was concerned, Helen Brown was drop dead gorgeous; both sweet and smart with those amazing legs that went up to heaven.

Looking out over the water so Helen wouldn't notice, he grinned, thinking about one such night when Helen warned they should remember what Sister Mary Agnes had taught them about their bodies being temples of the Holy Ghost. Patrick didn't believe that any self-respecting dove was resting in his body. But he did sometimes have a foreboding vision of Jesus standing over him with his hands on his hips, shaking his head in disapproval.

As they'd said good-night on her parent's porch after the Senior Ball he'd almost blurted out his undying love, but something inside made him hold back. Now he realized it was better that he hadn't made any promises. Things had to happen before he could make that sort of commitment.

Patrick leaned over toward her on his elbow.

Without moving Helen spoke. "What's up? I know you, and something is churning up there in that head of yours."

Taking her hand he pulled her up. "Sit up. There is something I've got to talk to you about."

Helen faced him. "What's going on? Is there anything wrong?"

"Well, I think it's more right than wrong, but you probably won't like what I have to tell you." Patrick knew what he must sound like with his words tumbling out of his mouth.

"What?"

"I've joined the Air Force," he blurted out. An awkward silence followed. "Oh, boy, I can see you're shocked."

"Well, yeah, I'm shocked. Where did this come from? I mean, what about college?"

"Helen, you must know how I feel about my brother. Joe finished college last year, and he's got a really good job, but he owes my uncle for helping my dad out with his college tuition. He owes for a student loan, too, and he was afraid of being drafted, not because he's a coward, but because he wants to pay his debts. He and Betty wanted to get married, but they can't because her dad doesn't want her to be a young widow if he gets called up."

"What an awful thing for him to say," Helen mumbled.

Patrick continued nervously. "Well, they can't afford an apartment and don't want to live with her folks or mine. So Joe went last month and signed up at the Reserve office for a six year commitment. He's going next week for five months of basic training. He'll have his job when he gets back, and then he has to put in sixteen hours a month on weekends and go away two weeks in the summer, but Betty won't be a widow, hopefully. Of course, he could be called up anyway sometime in the future so there's no guarantees, but they've still decided to get married after Basic. You get paid a little in the Reserves, and they can use that money toward rent."

Helen couldn't help the tears welling up in her eyes. "But what does all this have to do with you? I thought you were looking forward to college. I was so proud of you being accepted at RPI."

Patrick put his arm around her, and pulling her close he kissed her on the cheek. "I know, and at first I was all set to go, but then, ya know, Jimmy came home in a body bag. Jimmy being killed over there in Da Nang early this year really messed us all up. And the truth is, Helen, I don't know if I want to be an engineer like my dad or my uncle. I just think there's something else in me. I don't know how to put it."

"Then what about liberal arts like me?" Helen asked. "You don't have to know what you want to study right away. Maybe you can tell them at the recruiting office that you made a mistake. Maybe you get a grace period when you sign up and you can get out of it."

"I don't need you to be mad at me, too, Helen. My folks are already upset that I joined the Air Force. My dad hates President Johnson and keeps ranting on how the hell we ever got into the damned war anyway. The war is a mess and ...."

"Get up!—I need to fold the blanket," Helen said. She was so angry. So you're telling me you are okay going over there and killing innocent women and children? That's news to me because I always thought you were against this war. You're the one all about peace and how the government should take care of the street people. Or maybe you think you need to take Jimmy's place? We both think the war is all wrong, and now I think you're stupid to go."

Patrick stood and put both his hands on Helen's shoulders. "Drop the blanket and listen to me, will you? I still think being in Vietnam is all wrong, but it's happening, and I just have to do something to help the people over there. I joined the Air Force because I want to train to operate a helicopter and be a part of a rescue team. I want to save lives. That's what I told them when I signed up. Maybe I can airlift the wounded guys out. I just feel that I have to do something. And, no, I'm not okay with killing anyone."

After a long, awkward pause, Helen asked, "When do you leave?"

"I leave for training in Texas in two weeks, and I'll be in training out there for months. After training I'll get to come home.... I think for a week before I'm assigned."

"Two weeks!!"

Patrick struggled to keep back his own tears. He knew it would be hard, but he hadn't expected it would be this hard. "I'm sorry I didn't tell you before, but I wanted us to have some days like this so that while I'm away we could have some good memories."

Helen shook herself free of Patrick's grip. "You have to do what you feel you have to do, but honestly Patrick, I don't get it. You have a student deferment if you go to college, and maybe four years from now the war will be over. You go there and you could get yourself killed."

Patrick stood aside as Helen scooped up the blanket, shaking out the sand.

"I'm not going to get myself killed."

Helen threw the blanket over her shoulder and wrapped her arms around Patrick's bare waist. Pulling his body to her she pressed her cheek against his chest. "Don't go. Please don't go, Patrick."

A young couple who had been sitting close to them on the beach wandered off toward the shoreline of the lake, obviously wanting to give the arguing twosome time by themselves. Patrick gently kissed the top of Helen's head. "I won't be killed. I will come home. I had a dream and heard God's voice. He said, *go and have no fear*. I know this is probably wacky. I'm nobody that God should talk to, but I did hear Him."

"I'll write to you every single day," Helen whispered. She was defeated. How could she go against the voice of God?

Patrick held his girl close. He didn't think anyone could write to him for the first few weeks, but he'd keep that to himself for now. Maybe he really was crazy. Maybe he was making the biggest mistake of his life, but it was done.

"And I'll look for every letter," he replied, forcing down the lump in his throat. "Hey, come on, let's not go home just yet. There's Mick over there." Patrick pointed down the beach to where the volleyball net was set up. "We'll go say hi and then go back for another dip in the lake before we head home."

Holding hands, their fingers locked, the pair headed toward Mick, leaving their towels and blanket behind in a heap on the beach.

CHAPTER 12

Helen Brown grew up in a small factory town situated along the northern bank of Upstate New York's Mohawk River, the single offspring of blue collar parents who were strong Roman Catholics. Her dad, an ironworker who had walked the steel as a foreman during the time Albany's South Mall was being built, claimed his dad had told him that he was a full-blooded Mohawk Indian. That was how Helen's father got his job since everybody in that business knew Mohawk Indians were celebrated in the trades as great climbers.

Brown Family lore had it that the Browns had been Catholic ever since Father Isaac Jogues baptized one of their Indian ancestors hundreds of years ago someplace in New York. Helen's mother took her father-in-law at his word. The idea was, after all, a beautiful thought. Who didn't know the harrowing, but inspirational story of the martyred French Jesuit priest who was worshiped as a saint? Helen, of course, attended Catholic elementary school—kindergarten through eighth grade—followed by four years of Catholic high school.

As a threesome the Brown family regularly attended 9 o'clock mass every Sunday at St. Mary's church where participation during mass in the children's choir wasn't optional for young Helen, whose voice often oscillated between soprano and alto. Sister Mary Margaret, the parochial school's choir directress, oozed that Helen's voice was a wonderful blessing. God had given her a gift.

She was unique. But then, in the optimistic Sister's eyes, all children had very special talents bestowed upon them so that each
could share his or her personal gifts with the world.

As a precocious young teenager filled with curiosity and uninvited opinions, Helen spent her fair share of after school hours during
both seventh and eighth grade at St. Mary's School scrubbing many
of the nun's white bibs as well as writing penitential essays, generally
on the meaning of faith and humility. After graduating with high
honors from St. Mary's, Helen continued to receive the same guidance from the Sisters at Catholic High.

In high school, supervised socialization with Catholic boys was
encouraged; dating outside *the* faith was frowned upon. As a fresh-
man, Helen had had a huge crush on her next door neighbor, Billy
Harris, and when he'd asked her out to a dance at Knickerbocker
Hall she was on cloud nine, but her euphoria was short-lived. Billy
wasn't a Catholic. *He's a likeable enough young fellow,* her dad had
agreed, *but Browns don't date Protestants. That's just how it is.*

Helen didn't get it because her dad and Mr. Harris bowled on
the same team sponsored by McGrath's tavern. Mr. Harris was one
of the men playing poker in their basement every other Friday night,
not to mention that her mother and Mrs. Harris were good friends
who volunteered once a month at the Dutch Reformed Church soup
kitchen. Helen had felt pretty awful about it all until her sophomore
year when she started dating Patrick.

The Sisters who taught at Catholic High were excellent teachers
who, Helen came to believe, could anticipate any question by looking a student straight in the eye before the words formed on his or
her lips. By the time she graduated what she came to understand
about her Catholicism was that acceptance of the unexplainable was
paramount. Acceptance just made life easier.

Helen went away to college, and as promised wrote Patrick faith-
fully. At first he'd done the same, but then his letters thinned out and
those that she did receive seemed almost distant. When they were
both home for Christmas, while standing in the cold on her parent's
front porch, Patrick announced that he was going to Vietnam. He

wasn't afraid and she shouldn't worry. He'd write to her whenever he could, but he wouldn't be upset either if she dated someone else. He didn't want her sitting alone in her dorm when everyone else was out having a good time, and he didn't want to be on the other side of the earth thinking of her in tears. Facing Vietnam, he couldn't make any promises and neither should she. Helen was devastated and couldn't hold back her tears.

Three very brief letters had arrived for her during the winter of 1968. Torn by uncertainty, Helen couldn't concentrate, and after Spring break she dropped out of college and found a job in the household department of a local department store. Robotically, she went to work, attended church with her parents, and occasionally went to a movie with girlfriends. Throughout it all—she waited.

Later, when Patrick returned from Vietnam filled with a vocational passion for the priesthood (rather than the passion for her that Helen had dreamed about for years) she had accepted the will of God. She had lost her one true love. She would never marry. She would never have children. She'd gotten it, but that was when she began to wonder what God had in mind for her if she wasn't going to have a life with Patrick as his wife. She continued in her mundane job.

And then, after being on a barren shelf for over a year and a half, refusing to even consider a date with anyone, Helen had returned to school at the local community college. There she had met Steve Carey in one of her classes. He was nothing at all like the steady, gentle-spoken Patrick. She'd often ask herself why she had agreed to have coffee with such a brash guy, one who often argued with their sociology professor. She had no answer other than divine guidance, which really made no sense at all.

On their first official date Steve talked about the similarity of humans to apes and the resemblance of giraffes to runway models. Helen was mesmerized. Before the evening was over, he quizzed her on what she thought about the possibility of life on another planet. Steve wasn't just different from Patrick; he was different from anyone else she'd ever met, and from that evening on he had her attention.

The Carey family were what her mother called "wayward Catholics", the sort who went to mass only on Christmas and Easter. Her father had said he could understand it since he had heard from someone living in the parish that Mrs. Carey wasn't a Catholic at all. Mr. Carey was the Catholic. As her father understood it, Mrs. Carey had come from a long line of Protestants. Everybody knew what happened with those types of mixed marriages.

Helen suspected that the informer was probably their neighbor, but by this time Helen didn't care if Mrs. Carey had spun off from a long line of Martians. She was wonderfully, lustfully in love with Steve. Of course, there were a few bumps along their blissful road. One night after they had seen Stanley Kubrick's "A Clockwork Orange", Steve suddenly turned to her and confessed that he really didn't think God existed. His atheistic declaration jolted Helen, but the young man to whom she was now committed both in body and soul had been raised a believer, and his mother was a strong Christian lady, a Bible reading Protestant who in Helen's estimation was a better Catholic than many Catholics kneeling at the rail every Sunday. All Steve needed, Helen thought, was the right partner who would bring him around and back to Sunday mass.

Their engagement shocked her parents. Her mother tried to talk her out of going forward with the marriage. They were not suited, she'd warned, and she suspected that Steve's mother felt the same way, being a Protestant and all. Helen rebutted that Mary Jane had welcomed her with open arms. "Mary Jane? You call Steve's mother by her first name?" Helen wondered if her own mother had learned anything at all about acceptance. What about what Jesus said about loving one another?

Her mother wanted to know what she saw in Steve Carey other than his obvious good looks. All Helen could think to reply as a defense against further bombardment was, "He always wants to know my opinion and he's brilliant." She could have said more, but not to her mother. Surely her mother wouldn't care to hear about how his thick curly dark hair felt between her fingers, or how his eyes studied the contours of her face before he kissed her forehead, eyebrows, and eyelids, finally finding her willing lips. Her mother would never know that three weeks after they'd met in class, abandoning all buried thoughts of the dire consequences of committing mortal sin, she and Steve had had sex. After tasting the forbidden fruit she could understand Eve's stalking Adam in the Garden of Eden.

They'd married the following October.

CHAPTER 13

March 1979

Steve stood quietly in front of his wife who was curled up on their plaid, living-room sofa under a warm crocheted afghan reading "The Egyptian"—Finish writer Mika Waltari's complex, five-hundred page historical novel. "How's the book?"

Helen responded, "Well...I've just started, but I think it's going to be a good read. It's kind of neat, too, because of the way it was translated into English by a woman named Naomi Walford. It was written in 1949. Culturally-seasoned. I think you'd like it."

"Maybe. Egyptology? I'll put it on my 'to-read' list. Hey lady, listen, I stirred the stew, and Tommy is out in the kitchen with Crusty and that new kid from down the road playing a hot game of Monopoly."

Helen lifted her head. "Right after we came home from church he asked me if that would be okay, and if his friends could eat with us, and I said it would be fine. I've made plenty. I think it's supposed to snow pretty hard all day." Returning to the book and without looking up, she added abstractly, "Egyptology? No. This is a novel, Steve. You know, fiction."

Steve stepped toward the picture window. "Six inches already... probably get a foot. We should be seeing the plow come through soon. Hell, I heard that the Coast Guard was chopping through twelve inches of ice on the Hudson River last week. Guess Murray Fuels will have oil to deliver."

Helen turned a page. "Supper needs to cook in that crockpot for another three hours, so Monopoly works for now. When the snow stops, if we haven't eaten yet, we'll put them all to work shoveling."

Steve grinned. "I figured that would be the plan, so I'm headed out to the barn. I have a couple of things to do before I'm promoted to Captain of the shoveling team. I plugged in the electric heater out there this morning before we went to mass, and I'd guess it's plenty warm enough by now."

"Okay," Helen mumbled.

Steve left the room, and without missing one word of translated text Helen called out, "You can pour the boys a glass of milk to go with the chocolate chip cookies I made yesterday. There's just a few left...a few bites of cookie won't spoil their appetites."

Helen heard the refrigerator door open and close. Crusty was first to call out, "Thanks, Mrs. Carey." The new neighbor boy, whose name Helen couldn't recall, followed suit, and then came Tommy's disappointed, "None left, Mom." Every morsel had been devoured in less than thirty seconds.

Minutes later the back door closed, and the Irish bells Helen had hung on the back doorknob weeks ago jingled, signaling Steve's departure and reminding her that she was long overdue in taking down the St. Patrick's Day decorations.

In the barn Steve went straight to the large, timeworn, wooden cupboard that he'd picked up last fall at a Saturday estate sale down along the Hudson River in Rensselaer, near historic Fort Crailo. He'd been surprised that nobody else had grabbed it. Although in rough shape, it was a super storage place for his small woodworking tools, jars of nails, and screws. It was darn heavy, too. The seller had to help hoist it up into his pickup, and once home, one of his neighbors had helped him get it into the barn.

Steve felt he'd made out pretty well with the extras: a very old teacup, some large hand-hewed nails taped to the back, and surprisingly, something totally out of context—a Ouija board still in its original box propped up in the back of a shorted shelf. It appeared as if the cabinet shelf board had been cut out on purpose to make a special place for the board game. He'd offered less than what was ticketed, and bingo, it was a done deal. Obviously, the owner was in an "everything goes" frame of mind. Steve had whistled "Yankee Doodle" all the way home.

He thought about Helen inside the house immersed in her Egyptian book. She hadn't been so keen on his historical acquisition when he'd brought it home months ago. After he'd gotten the cupboard into the barn he'd brought his discoveries into the house and laid all of it out on the table for her inspection, thinking she'd appreciate the antiquity of his find. Helen saw the Ouija board and had freaked out as if live snakes crawled around her tabletop, squealing that she wanted no part of what she'd labeled an *evil thing* in her house. She'd insisted that he just get rid of the damn Ouija game. He promised that he would, but he hadn't.

Pulling a rag out of his tool box, Steve wiped the dust off the box cover. Opening it, he was pleased to see that the heart-shaped planchette was still there with the board, but seeing it all intact like this suddenly brought back memories that threatened to put a damper on his afternoon plans.

During college he and some of the guys he shared an apartment with had fooled around with a Ouija board. Nothing unusual had happened during their various drunken attempts at contacting the dead. But one morning after a night of partying he remembered a lofty speech he'd made to his buddies. It seemed to his way of thinking sort of disrespectful to souls who at one point had been living beings. Only a jerk would push his way into a room where he wasn't invited. He had definitely looked at it that way and remembered calling them all a bunch of assholes. Every one of them had laughed.

All the same, he continued to find the paranormal interesting. The possibility of piercing the 'veil' between two worlds had stuck in his mind.

Steve stared down at the board. Finding it, especially after just having read about the experiments of paranormal-phenomena writer Jane Roberts, and knowing she claimed she first made contact with the other side through a Ouija, well, this gave him pause, or more aptly, maybe his finding this board was a permission slip from beyond. He had to try it.

He pulled up a stool, half believing that this was no game, and he sure wanted nothing to do with anything evil. To that end he leveled the field by saying a short prayer, asking God to allow only good spirits to approach him and for the intervention of angels placing their hands over his own. With his Amen, he barely touched the planchette. Almost immediately he thought there was movement. Then the pointer began to slide across the board toward the letter 'k', then, jerking toward the letter 'e', and then over to the letter 'y', spelling out 'key'.

Steve's heart was racing. As much as he'd like to think that some spirit was communicating with him, things like this just didn't happen in the real world. *So if I don't believe it's possible, then what am I doing?* Taking his hands away from the board he sat back on his stool and again, stared at the game board. This probably wasn't a good idea—doing it alone. Normally there would be one or two others present, and one person would be the recorder of what happened. Forget recording. Forget evidence. He wouldn't be able to tell anyone about this. Who would believe him? He put the board and the pointer back in the box and closed the lid.

After a couple of minutes he thought he heard *"your move"*.

Okay, bring it on. Reopening the box, he began again. Amazingly, the pointer gradually repeated the letters of the earlier attempt, again spelling out the word 'key.' Then over several more minutes the pointer moved to other letters that all together spelled out two more words: 'stone' and 'fire'.

Steve tried to think about what keys were near stones. Right away he thought about the house key that was always hidden in a fake grey stone with a false bottom. They kept it outside the front door in one of the flower pots. What was the connection? *Holy shit! The spirit is telling me that the house is going to catch on fire!*

Steve jumped up, completely forgetting that he'd read that one of the most important Ouija rules was that one should always say good-bye to the spirits invited in. Throwing open the barn door, he ran, slipping through the falling snow to the house. Bursting through the kitchen door, he yelled to Helen. "Is anything burning in here?!" Tommy was in the middle of buying *Park Place.* "What's wrong, Dad?"

Steve dashed into the living room.

Helen seemed frozen in front of the television set, mesmerized by what was playing out on the screen. "It's 5 o'clock," she said, "and I just turned the news on to see what the weatherman might be saying about the snow. My God, Steve, look at this news bulletin! There's been a horrible catastrophe—a partial meltdown out near Harrisburg, Pennsylvania, at one of those nuclear power plants. All kinds of radioactive gas is spilling out into the air. The place is called *Three Mile Island.*"

The frightened boys came running into the living room to see what the commotion was all about.

Steve put his hands on top of his throbbing head. "Pennsylvania— the Keystone State," he whispered to himself. Turning abruptly to Helen, he sputtered, "I'll be right back. I forgot to shut off the heater."

CHAPTER 14

The North Country, 1728

Cornelius Waldron sat astride his noble mount, James, the great black stallion that two years prior he'd acquired from Gerardus Stuyvesant's Krom Messie Farm on Manhattan Island. With the wind picking up, Cornelius halted, pulling the red woven Indian blanket that had once belonged to his father snugly around his shoulders. Other than a partial interest in the Waldron farm that he shared with his mother, the blanket that his father had bequeathed was the one tangible piece of property that Peter Waldron had left him. Whenever Cornelius traveled, he took it with him.

At twenty-three he remained unmarried, generally preferring the company of his horse or the farm animals. He answered to no man, or maid, over his whereabouts, and he was content to have it that way. Much to his mother's displeasure, he'd not yet formally joined the Albany Dutch Church, but he, and all he oversaw at the farm, kept holy the Sabbath Day.

Although occasionally Cornelius enjoyed a challenging game of marbles or played cards and drank with the young British soldiers stationed two miles away at Fort Schaghticoke, he would often go for days without so much as a how-do to any person other than Willie. In silence he and Minnie milked his fourteen cows before sun up every morning. He tended James, planted, mended fences, split wood, fished in the river, and alongside of Willie's grown sons he harvested what the rich soil gave up.

Because of his daily workload, and in part because of the distance between farms, he rarely had had the opportunity of any meaningful dialogue with any maid other than his sisters when they came to the country to escape Albany's putrid summer smells.

Words were not necessary between him and Minnie or her brothers. Anything that he needed to say to them he said to Willie, just as his father had done, and Willie took care of letting them know their master's pleasure.

Cornelius placed a hand over the sore, stinging wound on his cheek. Two days ago, as he'd cut timber with Nick Groesbeck for Groesbeck's new house, he'd never seen that sharp broken branch come up at him, but then, they shouldn't have been out past dusk rushing to accomplish the task. Praise God it had not been an eye, and praises, too, that Nick's wife, an able nurse, had been able to pull the bloodied flaps together and sew him up. He would heal, yet, as Nick had put it, he would be uglier than ever.

As he and James traveled in unison on the way to the ferry landing, Cornelius imagined what his mother would say today when she saw his disfigured face. He dreaded that he would be a cause of more burden to her sorrowful heart, but perhaps the terrible look of him would bring her away from the dead. He wanted her *alive* again. He longed for her criticisms. He *should* have a wife who would keep him mindful. A woman should be running his house and not Willie. That was what his mother had said so often when his father was alive. But with his father's passing, and then poor Pete, it had been a long time since his mother cared what her single son did or did not do.

Leaning forward, Cornelius patted James gently, assuring his faithful friend aloud that the hours he'd spent grooming him had been well worthwhile. James was a sight worthy of any king. If he would be late today at the ferryman's landing, his sister, Engeltie, would understand when he'd explain that he wanted James to present himself well.

They were of the same mind, he and Engeltie, when it came to James. And he knew she would be happy when she learned that she would be on James's back when they returned to the farm. Cornelius would bow to her like he had done when they were children and he had been her little prince. "All hail to the good queen," he would chant and she would laugh. Above all else, Cornelius desired to hear his sister laugh again, but he would settle for the smallest smile.

Catherine had written to him that Engeltie's life at home with their dear mother these past months had been exceedingly hard. Since the death of their brother, Pete, last May, their mother was inconsolable. Catherine and her sisters had done everything for her that they could think to do. Cornelia, along with her two small children, had come from Schenectady to stay for a while during the summer with Mother, but of course, Cornelia was busy with her own young family.

Eva went each day to stay with William and his wife Elizabeth and help with their large family.

After a brief visit, Cornelia had taken little Garret and Rebecca back to her own house for fear that her younger siblings were being neglected. Their mother would not cook. She barely looked at either one of her little children. Even though Cornelia and Engeltie had tried to bring Mother out of her darkness, it did no good. All of them worried that Cate Waldron was lost to them forever.

And then in July came word that their father's dear friend, John Collins, had died while on business at Schenectady. Cornelius came to Albany to offer his condolences. After the Collin's funeral, it had been decided that Catherine and Engeltie would bring Mother out to the farm.

After Catherine's beseeching letter, in late August Cornelius had again visited his mother in Albany. While there he saw for himself how far she had declined and the paleness of Engeltie who had confided that ever since the day they had put poor Pete's body into the ground their mother had done nothing else but go to the churchyard and sit by his and their father's graves. The worst of it all was that Mother said the Almighty had shunned all who called themselves

Waldron. Over and over she talked of a curse that made no sense. She ignored her beloved Garret. Their Dutch Minister had suggested, when he had come to call, that perhaps the devil himself had Cate Waldron within his grip.

Cornelius would not accept that his pious mother was possessed. He had thought that if only she could sit at the hemlock grove she and Father had so loved and read the Psalms, she would find consolation. The good country air and quiet would be a tonic for her melancholy.

Catherine, always straightforward, had confessed in her most recent letter that she and the other girls looked to their eldest sister at home for comfort, but Engeltie was too beside herself with her own grief. Even though she had been refreshed by Cornelius's visits and it had been many months since Pete had joined their father in heaven, the tears would not leave her eyes. Catherine worried that soon there would be more freshly dug graves in the churchyard. She then urged that she and their sisters along with Mother and Garret come up to the farm and that he bring along James when he met them at the ferry.

Cornelius thought her idea an excellent one. His *black knight* was the best hope to rekindle everyone's spirit.

He noticed the darkening sky and groaned. From a distance he heard the threatening rumble of thunder. He had at least another half hour ride ahead before reaching cousin Vandenbergh's landing where he was to meet his family. A storm would undoubtedly cause delay in his arrival and certainly muddy up James. It appeared that Almighty God did not support his and Catherine's goodly plan to cheer their grieving mother and sister.

The wind increased, persisting to gust and swirl, causing a sizeable tree branch to break free, startling the stallion as it fell in front of him. James reared up, but Cornelius quickly countered, pulling back on the reins. Leaning forward, he spoke calmly to the apprehensive James, "E...e...easy, easy boy," Cornelius stammered.

Cornelius dismounted and stroked his horse lovingly before clearing the obstruction from the roadway. With the wind blowing against him, he secured his wide brimmed hat, tying the leather straps tight underneath his chin. A downpour seemed imminent, and as he climbed back into the saddle, he reckoned James would probably continue to fuss. "Da...a damn this weather," he cursed.

James felt his master's anger and snorted his personal displeasure. Cornelius nudged against him. "Nay, let us not fear," he whispered. Surely by now his mother, family and Dinah had already arrived at the boat landing and were all enjoying a hot brew, sheltered inside their cousin's comfortable stone dwelling. Cornelius was grateful as he made his way forward. At least the heavy rains held off.

However, shortly before reaching his destination, the downpour began with a vengeance, turning the trail to mud. Soaked through and blinded by the torrent of water, the disheartened Cornelius barely saw Vandenbergh's German manservant running toward him. The stableman reached up for the reins, shouting in Deutsch that he should go straight away to the house where there was a warm fire. Cornelius dismounted, splashing down into the muck, and the German guided the nervous James toward the barn.

At first, thinking that his mother and sisters must be inside, the thought of a warm hearth was indeed welcome, but as Cornelius turned toward the respite of shelter, he was distracted by what sounded to him to be a woman's panicked cry coming from the direction of the river. Alarmed, he turned and ran toward the boat landing with his heart sinking to the bottom of his stomach as the ferry boat became visible through falling sheets of water.

Yonder, halfway across the river, he saw the outline of the distressed, roped wooden raft carrying a large horse drawn wagon. As the carrier thrashed about, through the downpour Cornelius thought he could make out ten or more persons aboard, and he feared among the passengers were his family. He could hear the horses clopping franticly as the raft swayed, and the women screamed at every crackling lurch.

Standing closer now beside a row of moored Indian canoes, Cornelius recognized the voice of his sister, Engeltie, pleading for help. Utter anguish filled his being, and for a moment he considered swimming out to them. *Why is this happening to me again?* All would depend upon the skill and the strength of the ferryman and his Negro man on board. *I can do nothing.*

Cornelius was beyond despair. Would he see them drown before his very eyes? Could the Lord be so cruel? He'd held Pete's hand, while the boy had slipped away, gone to live with their father in heaven. As he watched the angry river decide between life and death, he remembered how he and his brother had wrestled playfully just days before the boy had suddenly become ill. But, he could do nothing to save his brother.

Holding fast to the soaked blanket around his shoulders, Cornelius again recalled the sudden loss of their father after pulling a new calf out of the pond at the farm. *It should have been me who brought the calf out.* The animals...the calf was his responsibility. He should have been there to do what had to be done, but he was not. He had had a disagreement with his father and gone off to play cards at the fort even knowing his father had not felt well. His father had rescued the calf and thereafter gone to the barn and fallen dead, apparently from exhaustion, or so the physician had pronounced when he came hours later.

Tears welled up in his eyes. Forever more he would blame himself for his father's untimely death. Now, again, as with his father and brother, he was helpless to rescue his loved ones. He did not understand. Why was he always the one who was expected to stand by; to be only a witness to tragedy? Facing upwards toward the fitful sky he begged for deliverance for his family. If they drowned today he would be at fault for he had encouraged his mother to come out of Albany for the harvesting.

As Cornelius paced, completely consumed by anxiety, suddenly the winds calmed as if Almighty God had subdued the waters. The rains, too, weakened. The experienced ferryman and his Negro working their poles together against the shallow riverbed were soon slamming the ferry's edge onto the shore. One of the Indians who had come down to watch put his hand on Cornelius's arm.

"The sky world has heard the cries of Mother Earth's daughters," he announced.

Cate Waldron, her children and servant woman stepped onto solid ground and Cornelius grabbed hold of each in turn and gathered them in. They clung to one other. "Pra...praise God," he said looking them over, and then, from a voice he hardly recognized as his own, a second, more fervent, "Praise God!"

Cate threw her arms around her son's chest. "We are saved by the Lord's heavenly crystal!"

Engeltie and Catherine, as well as their still recovering servant woman, looked at her strangely.

Cornelius also tried to make sense of his mother's mutterings. "Wha...what say you? Do you...you mean that you wear the ring that our father gave to you?"

Eagerly with an air of triumph, Cate untied the cloth satchel that had hung from her arm. "Look what I have!"

Cornelius looked inside of the bag and saw his grandfather's Papscanee crystal that his mother believed had fallen from heaven the night of the terrible fire when she was a child.

"Yes," she said extending her hand, "As always I wear the ring your dear father gave to me. As you see, here 'tis upon my finger, but I bring another of God's gifts to you, Son, to keep always with you at the farm. My prayers have been answered. I wondered how I might go on and prayed for a sign. In a dream God spoke to me saying that our little Pete was chosen to be with the angels."

"Mother," Catherine pleaded. "Let us go in!"

"Cate answered her sharply. "Wait Catherine!" Looking up at her son Cate continued anxiously, "I thought that had this heavenly stone been at our farm with you when the calf fell into the pond, perhaps your father would today still be with us in this world. I will wear your father's ring into eternity, but I would have it that you keep the crystal here at the farm."

Cornelius could say nothing more. He felt his mother's love, but he knew who was really at fault for his father's death. A time of reckoning would come.

Tears streamed down his mother's small face. Cornelius let out a long breath and then took the bag containing the crystal rock from her. Together the family walked toward the warmth of their cousin's house.

CHAPTER 15

Near Schaghticoke,
September 1732

Seated at the table of honor amongst three of his sisters and across from his close friend, the handsome, dark haired Stephen Van Rensselaer, and Van Rensselaer's soft-spoken wife, Elizabeth, Cornelius Waldron was thoroughly enjoying the unabashed ruckus of his and his new wife's marriage feast.

Giggling, his buxom, fair-haired bride, the former Miss Van Ness, and her 'best woman', her seventeen-year-old sister, Marratie, hiked up their pale blue silk skirts, allowing their feet to freely fly across the crowded tavern floor. Arms clasped, the two wove in, out, and into guests and servants alike, twirling round and around in wild abandonment. The Dutch minister along with the Waldron women hooted and hollered their approval. Eva and Rebecca, with brother, Garret, wedged between them, pounded their fists harder and harder against the table whilst keeping time with the fiddler.

Clapping along enthusiastically, Cornelius matched their frenzy, lost in his joy, and while roaring with laughter, he'd not noticed that the lit candelabra in front of him had begun to wobble precariously.

Joe, one of the Van Ness servants who'd been refilling the pitchers on the eight tables with beer and Mrs. Van Ness's deliciously intoxicating rum punch, saw the impending calamity. Dashing forward without time for an 'excuse me, Sir', he reached one ample, dark hand across the honorable Stephen Van Rensselaer to grip the candelabra. Although he was successful in rescuing Mr. Waldron and Mr. Van Rensselaer, as well as the ladies, from the possibility of being burned, regrettably, in the process, Joe had knocked over a half-filled pitcher of punch, some of which made its way into the luxurious brown velvet lap of Mr. Van Rensselaer.

The frenzy didn't miss a beat while Joe stood frozen in place holding the candelabra high in the air, candles flickering as the hot wax dripped down over his hand. Van Rensselaer jumped up out of his seat, and Joe's eyes dropped to the floor. He readied himself for a good reprimand. His heart beat like a Mohawk drum. Like an angel, out of nowhere one of the Negro kitchen wenches appeared, snorted haughtily at Joe, and offered Mr. Van Rensselaer a cloth to clean himself off.

Mr. Van Rensselaer took the small piece of cloth, but seemingly the injury to his attire as well as to his person was minor, for the good gentleman bade Joe put down the light from whence he retrieved it, tend quickly to his hand, and return to his duties. No fuss was to be made that would spoil the happy occasion.

Relieved, Joe did as he was told, and as the Waldron women took to the floor, it appeared that not one of the wedding guests noticed Mr. Van Rensselaer's damp breeches or Joe's hand wrapped in a rag.

Cornelius never saw any of this; no doubt the bridegroom's thoughts were too full of the prospect of pleasures to come. He had never thought he would marry, and yet, here he was. He was sure his scarred face and stutter worked against him. He knew that he was fortunate to win such a beauty, but then, Miss Van Ness accepting him had not come easy. But he liked her, and his persistence had won over his disabilities. Before others might ask for her hand, he decided to be forthright and summoned his courage to put himself before her. Strangely enough, Janet had said she would be pleased to be his wife. Only then had Cornelius presented himself to her father who knew the last few years had been good ones for Cornelius. He was known far and wide, even in Manhattan, as a prosperous farmer. With her father's approval, promises were made between them, and the banns of intent were announced at church.

Cornelius reached for the familiarity of the felt hat in front of him. He'd begun to perspire. *Strong drink and too much cake do not fare well in a man's innards.*

Recovered from the 'incident', Van Rensselaer patted Cornelius amicably on his back. "You have married a good handful there. Not once did I think I should see such a day as this merry occasion."

Cornelius stammered, "I did not think to see such… such a day myself. What can I say? Mother off…off…offered her daily prayer up to Almighty God that I should be…saved from a lonely life of solitude."

Van Rensselaer grinned, returning, "You will come to understand that a man's solitude is a blessing lost after marriage. Hopefully, it is a void replenished by the laughter of children."

"I will do my…my best," Cornelius replied sheepishly.

Van Rensselaer laughed. "I suspect you are right. Your good mother's prayer had all to do with this day. I had believed within my heart that you would stay married only to your cows and the fat hens clucking around your barn, yet, you fooled all of us. Good for you!"

"I am indeed happy, and 'tis good to…to…see my mother pleased and content—at long last.

"You have made a good match for yourself, Cornelius. Your father, God rest his soul, would have been pleased, too."

Reaching for his tankard, Stephen Van Rensselaer, the man whom all recognized as destined to one day become the esteemed head of the Colony of Rensselaerswyck, stood ready to offer his toast. The attending musician, who had kept a keen eye on Van Ness's most revered guest, immediately stopped playing, sharply signaling all present that apparently His Honor was about to pay homage to the bride and groom. A respectful pause in the merriment was required. Van Rensselaer's damp breeches were tactfully ignored.

The happy, nineteen-year-old bride and her sister slowed, both of them half dazed by the pace of their feverish dance. Janet raced toward her new husband, and the two clung to one another for support while their exhausted, frantic mothers rushed toward them with two glasses filled with sweet rum punch.

Van Rensselaer waited patiently while the room hushed to silent reverence, and then proceeded to deliver his robust proclamation. "I give to thee all a toast, to Cornelius Waldron and his goodly bride, Janet Van Ness, now Mrs. Waldron. Long life, continued prosperity, and many children!"

With that everyone shouted back, "To Cornelius Waldron and Mrs. Waldron!", then all drained their tankards and glasses.

Barely had seats been reclaimed when Cornelius's brother, William Waldron, stood ready to deliver another offering. "Aye, all of you keep your place, and have your vessels full again. I, too, should like to give a toast."

The room spilled over with laughter as servants dashed from one table to another refilling the cup of every person. William shouted merrily, "God save the King, and God save our Country!" A few moments passed before a strong male voice from far across the room returned heartily, "God save the King, and God save our Country!" Most returned the salute, but no one mistook the uneasiness that followed William Waldron's toast.

The bride's father, seeing the dampening of spirits amongst his guests who had hitherto been so joyous, ordered the musician to strike lively his fiddle. "Come now," Van Ness shouted, "eat of the cake and cookies the women have baked, drink up, and let us have a good and merry time!"

Elizabeth, William's wife, took the bride's hand and the two led a dozen young people to form a line, making ready for the popular "Country Dance" in which one couple would dance down the line, pairing with each person as they passed until they reached the other end of the line.

Mr. Van Ness, pleased that the festivities were moving along once again, picked up a plate of cookies in passing, and went to sit by his new son-in-law and Mr. Van Rensselaer.

Addressing Cornelius, he complained, "Your brother means well enough, but truly, what man here has it in his heart to give a toast to our Sovereign King on the heels of the English 'Hat Act'? This new English law puts a burden upon everyone within the colonies. Just another law that holds us back."

Cornelius eyed his hat on the table. It was a broad-brimmed, beaver skin hat he'd purchased from a local Dutch trader who'd told him it had been fashioned by one of the finest French hatters in all of Montreal.

"And too bad that we will do no more business of that kind with our kinsmen and friends hereabouts," Van Ness snapped, nodding toward the hat.

"Aye," Van Rensselaer replied, "yet we have long lived here with the 'Wool Act' restricting us from exporting our yarn or wool cloth outside of the colony wherein our sheep are raised. New York, like all other colonies, exists at the pleasure of Britain. We, as loyal subjects to the Crown, will learn to live with this new 'Hat Act' for it is much the same in kind. No man must put himself above the law."

Van Ness shouted over the noise of the festivities, "This new 'Act' is set to ruin many merchants, especially here in New York and New England where hatters have long made a prosperous living making hats and selling them wherever they please. I tell you that it is preposterous that a hat maker now must serve an apprenticeship of seven years in England afore he makes one hat here. And now, in addition to the wool, the Lords of Trade have forbidden any colony to engage in the business of hats. Taxes upon taxes are England's gift to her subjects. What comes next? Shall they advise us whom our precious daughters should marry?"

Van Rensselaer leaned close, "It is not that I disagree with you, Sir, but we should be still or suffer consequences."

Van Ness toned down but would not be silenced. "Like you, Sir, I was born in this country as was my mother and my father. Most here are American born and good English subjects, but without the least of rights that are naturally bestowed upon, and guaranteed to, the lowest born Englishman living in England. What freedoms do we call our own? The English Lords take away a man's trade, and now I hear that despite all endeavors made we have been shunned in our request to be able to elect our own Mayor and city officials. Few changes have been made to these old laws that have prevailed for most fifty years. And what of the latest decree that the hops grown in our fields can no longer be exported to Ireland? They say we are undercutting the farmers in the mother country. More money withheld from the purse of the hard-working farmer!"

Cornelius rose. He had no desire to listen to talk of politics on his wedding night. "My...my...my beautiful bride beckons. Please excuse me."

"Of course, of course," Van Ness replied, appearing somewhat chagrinned. "I apologize for my rantings. Go to your wife. Go to her, my son!"

With a slight bow Cornelius took his leave, preferring to stumble awkwardly around the dance floor than sit listening to the dismal worries of his new father-in-law. After leaving the table, he took a slight detour to where his exhausted mother and sister, Catherine, had fallen into their chairs next to Catherine's betrothed, Henry Van Wie.

Leaning down to kiss his mother on her cheek, she smiled up at him, and he wished that the Dutch of old New Amsterdam had never lost New York to English rule. If the industrious Dutch had held on to this land there would be no talk of such taxes. His grandfathers had always agreed that though Waldron was an English name from olden times, once in America they were all of Dutch constitution.

With his hand resting gently on his mother's shoulder Cornelius observed his wife chatting with the minister. Last spring when he had returned to Albany to visit with his mother and sisters, they had attended the baptism feast of William and Elizabeth's sixth baby. Janet had attended the baptism along with her family. Cornelius was embarrassed when at first, not having seen the girl for several years, he had not recognized the woman before him. The troublesome skinny little thing had evolved into a quick witted, most comely woman who insisted he call her Janet rather than her given name, Jannetie. Janet was how her Anglicized friends addressed her, and she understood that Waldron was an English name.

Not long after, Cornelius joined the Dutch Reformed Church at Albany. Perhaps that was what Van Rensselaer meant when he had remarked that Peter Waldron would have been pleased by his and Janet's marriage. By marrying a Van Ness surely the Dutch line would be preserved should they have children. Van Rensselaer often complained about the Dutch maids who'd married English soldiers.

And he could understand his father-in-law's angry sentiments, Van Ness being deep rooted in this country. Both of their families had called New York home for many generations. While one branch of the Van Ness had since migrated south to New Jersey, Janet's branch had settled in the Greenbush area across the river from Albany. Her grandfather had purchased his northern lands from the Indians for thirty beaver skins. The land was passed from father to son, and like Cornelius, Evert Van Ness had prospered on his inherited farm. Since 1720, Van Ness had been listed as a Freeholder at Half Moon.

Suddenly, like never before, Cornelius clearly understood that he was not a Dutchman nor an Englishman. He was an American. And so it aggravated him that even on his wedding night powerful men living in another country could mar his good future. Van Ness was right. The distance was growing between them and Mother England. Surely this was not the prosperous and secure road he wished for his future children.

Finding his bride, his heart quickened as Janet stood on the tips of her toes and brushed her full, soft lips against his scarred cheek. Plainly, the new Mrs. Waldron, her ample breasts begging to escape a tight bodice, gave evidence that she was no longer a twig.

He took her hand, and she laughed all the harder as he attempted to pirouette beside her down the line. Their 'dance' had begun.

CHAPTER 16

May 1741

Two small, yellow-haired boys followed excitedly behind Janet as she collected eggs from around the barnyard, each running to his mother triumphantly with his find. Under her watchful eye, her eldest, Peter, placed his egg into the reed basket that she had bedded with fresh straw. Little Evert, barely two, followed his brother's lead, carefully putting his egg in. Spotting another one, Peter ran to retrieve it. But Evert had been distracted by one of the mama chickens nearby who was clucking and pecking at the seed Janet had scattered about. Evert made a good show of trying to catch the elusive bird. Laughing, Janet stopped to enjoy her child's persistent chase, thinking that already her younger boy was much like his father.

Cornelius was a stubborn one. Ever since Dinah went to be with the Lord and Minnie and old Willie went back to live at the Waldron house in Albany with Janet's mother-in-law, he'd taken to milking all the cows each morning and afternoon by himself. Since the cows must be milked every twelve hours, this was an awful burden for only one man, and she wanted to help, but he forbade her. They had lost one unborn child before their Garret was born, and he could not bear to bury another infant that had not the chance of a first breath. Cornelius had told her that no burden could ever be as great as carrying the small wooden box holding one's dead infant. He would do what needed to be done, and she should not worry.

Janet rubbed her large belly and wondered if this child she carried was another son for Cornelius or a daughter? After three boys, she would be grateful for a safe delivery either way, but a girl would be good this time.

Standing in the nave of the barn she watched Cornelius work, but she thought of the dream she'd had last night. Again she'd dreamt of Dinah holding her white apron open, outstretched. They were here, in the nave, where she was now, and Dinah bade her to come closer and to take what she offered from the apron's fold. It seemed to be something sharp and pointed. Every dream it was the same. As she approached, Dinah would look away from her into the distance. In the shadows was the figure of a man shaking his head no, and Dinah turned away. In her dream, she seemed so close. *Where are you Dinah? Why do you call to me?*

"Damn!" Cornelius growled, hunched over the wood staves.

Janet saw him rub the back of his neck and sighed. *He is exhausted. Minnie should have stayed with us after Dinah died. It was just too bad that Eva married Mr. Witbeck and moved to the Greenbush. And what is wrong with my young brother-in-law Garret that he cannot milk Sally and drive his mother's wagon? Why, he is old enough and surely big enough for the task. Why does Willie have to squire them around Albany?* Janet didn't understand any of her husband's family nonsense and decided that she would talk to Cornelius again about Engeltie coming to live with them for a time. She had no husband and no perspective suitor. She was wonderful company, and Janet thought her sister-in-law a better cook than Minnie. And Engeltie loved their stallion, James, as much as Cornelius and the boys did.

"Mama, Mama," Peter called out. "Mama look—the ribbon." Janet snapped to the present, turning to a pudgy outstretched hand and dirty fingers clasping a blue piece of cloth that obviously had fallen away from the long, unraveled braid hanging down her back.

"Thanking ye, son," she said. Accepting the ribbon, she wiped it against her apron and then tied it tight around her braid. "Now you and your brother run back to the house to see your Grandmother. Go on, now. Play with your baby brother."

Full of giggles, the two headed toward the Dutch door of the house where their grandmother awaited with the top section open. After the boys were safely inside Janet saw her mother wave the all-secure sign. Picking up the basket of eggs, she wished she had the heart of a child, without dreams that robbed her of sleep and daily worries over the terrible troubles that raged all over their country; the fires that burnt in New York City; slave uprisings. She'd been horrified to learn about thirteen Negroes and some poor whites who were burned at the stake in Manhattan.

Cornelius had warned her to be cautious because he had heard that many in Albany believed some of the troublemakers were on the run. Officials were suspicious that they could be on their way north to seek safe harbor in the French territory. Her husband cautioned her to keep vigil, yet in the same breath, he was thankful of how fortunate they were to be raising their youngsters on the farm and not in the city. Janet wished that she knew nothing of these atrocities.

But, with Garret's baptism this week, she had trouble enough right here on the farm with her husband, and she was determined to soldier-on with an unresolved argument they had had the night before.

She approached him softly, "My mother sent me to fetch more eggs," she began. She waited for him to look at her. "Cornelius, I am sorry that you think me cross. I do not like us to disagree, and I know that you are tired, but you must promise me that you will behave yourself when Reverend Sergent arrives tomorrow."

Cornelius frowned as he continued to work, "Wha...what is it that you want from me, Janet?" he stammered in frustration.

"I desire you to sit, and to make pleasant discourse with our Dominie, and not drag him all over the farm boasting over your cows, fattened lambs, or the hens, as you take such pleasure in doing. Mostly though, I desire you not fill yourself with so much drink that you forget the names of your children."

Cornelius reddened. Perspiration dripped from his face. "I do not forget my children's names!"

"You do when you have too much drink."

Facing his wife, he obstinately folded his arms and began to speak slowly and deliberately, concentrating on every word, a practice he had recently learned from Nick Groesbeck's wife. Her brother had had a speech problem, and a physician up from Manhattan one summer had helped him with the "procedure of patience". Cornelius practiced the procedure every morning here in the barn by talking to James. He was a good listener and Cornelius was determined to overcome his stutter.

"Only once," he began, "did I forget the names of my children, although my memory was not so good that day, it is true. If my wits serve me well, and by God they do, I had no bed, giving it over to your cousins, who came up from the city for your sister's wedding feast. Be good enough to remember that I had no sleep for days whilst you and your folk nestled tight. I did not forget the names of my children because I had drunk too much strong drink, but because of a lack of sleep."

Janet sighed, conceding that she could not win this dispute. Besides, her husband, to some degree, spoke the truth. She doubted that any of the men who celebrated through three days of Marratie's marriage feast at Fort's Tavern last year would recall their own mother's name. She was herself merrily intoxicated.

Satisfied that she had no more to throw at him, Cornelius turned back to his work.

While Janet searched for a better example of the embarrassing consequences of drunken mischief, the croze cutter he'd been working with slipped from his hand. "Damn this trouble!" Cornelius again erupted. "You are the cause of this, woman," he growled. "I beg of you to go back inside the house to your mother and tend to your own business. Leave me to mine. Do you not see me trying to work?"

"Yes, I do see," Janet replied calmly, "but I only want that our Garret's baptism celebration be blessed with good cheer. Do you see that? I only wish all to be well. You cannot fault a mother for wanting a pleasant gathering for her child."

Straightening, Cornelius looked down into his wife's anxious blue eyes. His words softened. "Why wo... wo... would I not wish our fine boy every... blessing? I do. You worry for no reason. It is just that if this barrel is not tight, the salted fish will spoil in it. We are in terrible need of a new barrel, nay, we should have two new ones. I told you last night the others are old and will do well enough for shipping the grains, but the fish will not fare well."

Janet nodded in defeat. She was alone in her wants. She had said all she could say on the matter of self-control. An infant's baptism was not a wedding feast, something she feared Cornelius did not understand. She could only hope that the minister and his pious new wife would find her husband's drunken tour of their property entertaining. She paused, but thought better of saying anything else. She would ask him about bringing up Engeltie from Albany another time. "My mother awaits the eggs, and I dare not leave her any longer with our boys," she said. Picking up the basket, she left the barn.

Running powerful hands through his long brown hair, Cornelius wiped the sweat from his face with his shirtsleeve. He followed the swing of her full hips as she headed back toward the house. When she was out of sight he examined the staves in front of him, wishing he was as good at the task as his grandfather. As a small boy he had spent summers with Grandfather Waldron at Manhattan and he remembered watching him at his craft. Grandfather had been formally trained for the coopering trade, whilst he had learned by necessity. He would like to be better at this task and others.

Cornelius was sure his wife thought him a troublesome husband and a bad father. He would have it different. He would have it that they loved each other as passionately as once they had on moonlit nights, caressing one another upon a bed of soft grasses behind the tall cattails down by the edge of the river.

Now, a decade later, they pecked at each other as harshly as the English and the Spaniards. Only when they were tight under their coverlet, yet with children sleeping soundly in the next room, did they fulfill their lust wordlessly and swiftly. He wondered if this was how it was with every man who took the sacred vow. Were they all as unsatisfied? Did every wife see only the faults of her husband and none of the good?

He didn't remember his father as being unhappy, nor his mother nagging her husband over his faults. His parents strolled hand in hand around the pond, and they laughed while enjoying their pipes.

Why did Janet not like him? Surely he had done all in his power to make her a better house. The year they had wed, he had plastered all four rooms with fine, white lime putty made from thousands of burnt oyster shells brought up in barrels from Manhattan. What a laborious task it had been with his brother William taking precious time away from his own work in Albany to come up to the farm and act as overseer of the plastering. Janet had been so pleased. She had loved him then.

Why did she fret so over *this* baptism? At the other two, she had drunk her share of burnt wine. Cornelius supposed she would act the same way about every baptism that would come, God save him.

He would have to talk to her again and reassure her. And…he would apologize for his angry words. *The humble man is the happy man,* his father would say.

He would hold his hat in his hand before her and he would make her laugh. He would tell her that what his father had foreseen for their farm was all, and more, than Peter Waldron had imagined decades ago, and it was all so because of her. She had made this house a home. He would take her in his arms and tell her that she was what was most precious to him, even above all the cows, sheep, hens and yes, James, too. He would make her laugh as she used to do.

Cornelius groaned as he picked up his tools and turned back toward the staves. *It is foolish to waste time. She will either love me or not. I must get back to work.*

CHAPTER 17

Rensselaer County, New York - The Late 1970s

Not long after Steve and Helen Carey had purchased their fixer-upper along with the dilapidated barn out back, Steve had become obsessed with learning all that he could about the history of the abandoned property they'd bought from the bank. Answers came far easier than he or Helen had anticipated. A search that went back to the early 1800s revealed the names of four previous titleholders, and it looked as if the house had been modernized sometime in the 1920s, but Steve wondered if there could have been even more owners.

While poking around at the county library looking through three file cabinets packed full with manila folders containing years of information on historical houses in the area, he'd struck gold. He'd found an aged drawing that sketched properties dotting the River Road—his road. The map, dated 1780, included the outline of a mill, a church and churchyard, as well as several residences, many of which were either no longer standing or their facades had been redone. But the biggest surprise was that despite centuries of use, the old Protestant church structure had endured. After locating the church and thoroughly scrutinizing the diagram, in Steve's mind, there was no question that his and Helen's fixer-upper was one of the survivors from that post Revolutionary War period. It might even reach back further.

But the conclusive evidence that the base age of their house, or at least the center core of it and most assuredly the barn, was well over two hundred years old came a couple of years later. While digging the postholes for a new fence, Steve accidently dug up what appeared to be pieces of broken gravestone slabs that were several inches beneath the ground's surface. They were far to the back of his property along the edge of his tree line within sight of the Hudson River. The fragments had propelled him back to the library. Something about that old map stuck in the corner of his mind.

At the library, Steve made a beeline to the file cabinet he remembered. He pulled out a drawer, and within a few minutes he was revisiting the 1780s sketch. There it was. How could he have missed the small family plot detailed behind one of the houses? Now he realized that since that burial ground had existed at the time the sketch was drawn in 1780, he could assume that the fractured stone pieces he had held in his hands earlier were the remnants of the graves belonging to the colonial people who had been interred. It seemed logical to think there was a possibility that they could have been original settlers. He had only found a few vestiges of a stone, yet the map clearly showed half a dozen gravestones clustered together.

The remnants of the past he'd found had made the local newspaper when several area historians agreed that obviously there was indeed a burial yard that predated 1780 on Mr. and Mrs. Stephen Carey's property. The public announcement, for a time, had been a royal pain for Steve and Helen who were suddenly inundated with uninvited genealogists and photographers; some coming from as far away as Los Angeles.

When Steve and Helen bought their *money pit* (as they eventually came to call their "new" home) there had been no evidence of a family plot in their backyard, which was probably a good thing because Steve was fairly sure that Helen would never have signed her name next to his on the dotted line if she had known a graveyard was a part of the package. As they had surveyed the property during those pre-ownership days, all that could be seen beyond the patch of an unkempt yard was land covered by a small forest of hemlock and pine. Helen had loved the idea of keeping it wild.

Tommy was conceived soon after they moved in. Helen jokingly blamed the well water for her surprise pregnancy. Becoming parents, as expected, had changed everything. Not long after Tommy was born, Steve decided that the yard had to be bigger so he and his boy could toss a ball around. Steve and his dad had felled half of the trees. A short time later he began encircling the new open space out back with ranch fencing. He'd made his big discovery while digging the post holes. He'd always believed that finding those fragments was no mistake. *They* wanted to be found.

Steve had questioned his neighbor down the road about the graves shown on the map. Mr. Van Ness had told him that he'd lived on that street most of his life, grew up on a farm about four miles away, and he'd never heard about any cemetery other than the one up by the church. He did remember from his grandfather's storytelling that the street had originally housed a lot of Dutch families who had come up from Albany to settle, and that the ferry crossing was supposed to have been down behind his place.

Van Ness had also suggested that the fragments Steve had unearthed might be leftovers from the stone slabs that had been taken away and used for door steps. If true, then the big pieces of the tombstones, however, wouldn't be found in the immediate area. It made no sense to search the neighborhood. Van Ness had checked around and been shocked to hear that in the '40s and '50s one could get good money for an old tombstone, especially one with legible script. He'd agreed that it sure did sound damn disrespectful for anyone to do such a thing like selling something as sacred as a burial marker, but some folks just didn't give a damn. It was his understanding that some markers from plots in Upstate New York and Vermont had found new homes as far away as Beverly Hills, California. Might be interesting, Van Ness proposed, to dig farther down to see if any old coffins could be found, but after all these years he imagined that not much more than dust would remain. He thought it strange that no records seemed to exist for folks supposed to be buried there, but then, from what he knew, the church record books were missing too. Evidently this sort of thing often happened when a Minister moved on and took the record books along with him.

Helen had been horrified at the unholy suggestion of disturbing the old bones buried in her yard. She immediately called her parish priest who eventually came over and sprinkled holy water over the soil where Steve's newly-planted grass sprouted lushly. Father had decided that it would be best to leave the souls to rest, if souls indeed lay beneath the ground, as there was no true proof of interment, and he had assured Helen that she should relax. If all the evidence was as her husband thought, many families had once occupied their home. The yard was now a blessed, beautiful spot for children to play in as once they might have done centuries ago. The following year Steve built a sandbox in that corner of the yard. He was happy their priest had calmed his wife's fears.

Steve was obsessed by the concept of time, imagining the calloused hands of the generations of the original Dutch farmers who'd swung the barn's stall gate open in the morning getting ready for their day, and closed it behind their animals as the evening dusk rolled in.

The image of that by-gone life spoke hugely to Steve. He had no doubt that something of all those men still remained behind. Steve swore he could feel their sweat on the split rails. Theirs was a marked presence, an imprint that the passing of time only enhanced. Theirs was the aura that Steve hoped to someday capture with his Nikon. The solitude he found in his barn was priceless, and yet he was never alone, of that he was absolutely certain.

Helen didn't like it when he talked about auras and images. She complained that all that dark, free-thinking supernatural stuff gave her the creeps. Her fear of the unseen and unknown was a bit confusing to Steve since they'd met in a class on the study of the paranormal while in college. Back then, after breaking up with her boyfriend, he'd supposed that Helen Brown was searching for reasons or maybe a place where she would eventually fit in. That was okay by him. He was a believer, and just like Helen he was looking for reasons. He never had stopped looking for them. Unfortunately for Steve, Helen had stopped, and he didn't understand her closed mind, or more accurately, Steve just didn't understand Helen anymore. At one time he had thought his openness to the universe and the possibility of other worlds was what had attracted her to him. Now it seemed they were hardly on the same page at all, and he didn't know what to do about it. However, he had an idea.

Steve's hobby was making something new out of antiquated, reclaimed wood, and he had long had his eye on the old horse stalls in the back corner of his barn. He'd told Helen he thought that with the stall gate material he'd salvage he could build a small wooden chest for Tommy's collection of arrowheads and coins. What he'd make use of was perfect, he'd determined, because that wood was original to the barn and was well-seasoned with a phenomenal aura.

Helen didn't know what she felt about old wood soaked with the perspiration of the dead, but she very much liked that Steve was focusing in on a venture for their son. She gave her husband a big bear hug as he went off to begin the project of tearing out the stall in the area where he planned to build a new workbench.

Steve had been in the barn for hours working like a bull. He carefully dug into the ground around the base of the posts. Suddenly his shovel hit something that sounded metallic. He got down on his knees and brushed away the dirt, staring in sheer wonder at the corroded gadget in his hand. He couldn't be sure, but he thought that it was an 18th century split socket, the kind of thing that would have been used hundreds of years ago for attaching a bayonet to a musket.

He remembered how he and Helen used to joke to friends that they hadn't bought a house but an expensive, totally gorgeous, two acre parcel of land with an old broken down, two-story stone farmhouse thrown in to sweeten the pot. At first they thought that after a few years they'd tear most of it down and build new, but remodel the kitchen so that Helen would have a picture window facing the back where the birds nested. But Tommy had come along, and building the window was as far as they had gotten with the house. The idea of removing the exposed first-floor beams seemed sacrilegious. However, years later they had added a two car garage to the side of the house, and during the construction excavation had made another discovery when the contractor found the ruins of what was most likely a stone, colonial summer kitchen. The following year Steve utilized the stone when he added a small office on the side of the barn. The barn was his sanctuary, an escape from the massive pressures of his job as a union arbitrator.

It wasn't as if some damned interesting artifacts, other than the gravestone remains, hadn't turned up every so often through the years. During the first couple of years he and Helen found a myriad of 'treasures': buried old bottles and hand hewn nails, a circus hoop tucked away in the far corner of the attic, and even what appeared to be a child's chair. (They learned later from locals that the chair might have belonged to the midget wife of a circus ring master who'd rented the then fifty acre property back in the late 1800s.)

A few years ago when Helen decided she'd plant an herb garden Steve had invested in a metal detector. He, Helen, and Tommy got into scanning all over the property, but it was Tommy who was elated when he had found two silver dollars dated 1803. This had become the motivation for Steve's plan to build Tommy a "treasure chest" of his own. Maybe he could get Tommy to put it together with him. It had been a long time since they'd shared anything together, and, like his wife, he could feel his son drifting away from him. Other than occasional dinners at the kitchen table they barely spoke. He didn't know how he and Helen were going to get it together again, but building something like this just might help him and his disengaged boy break the ice and reconnect.

Putting aside the socket, Steve dug deeper. Within minutes something else emerged—a rusty bayonet. His suspicion about the socket was confirmed.

Clutching his unearthed discoveries, Steve returned to the house, rushed past Helen and dialed his mother's number. As a genealogist and town historian who seemed to be constantly working on projects with the Daughters of the American Revolution, Mary Jane Beekman Carey was a woman with deep New York roots. She would eat this up.

CHAPTER 18

Saratoga Springs, 1987

As he'd been instructed, Steve Carey used the harp-shaped, brass doorknocker, knocking in code— one knock, a pause, and then a quick double knock. Shortly, the grandiose oak front door of the 19th century redbrick Victorian a few blocks from Skidmore College opened, and he was greeted by one of the most gorgeous women he'd ever seen. "Welcome to SORE," she whispered, outstretching a hand. "We're so glad that you decided to join us. Come in."

"Thank you," Steve answered. Somewhat confused, he stepped over the threshold and took her hand. He was surprised by the familiarity of the greeting which seemed to imply that he'd been expected, but the invite he'd had a few weeks back in a downtown Albany bookstore was more of a casual suggestion, a 'why don't you drop by' sort of thing. Nothing definite. What he was hearing now suggested something else, and that made him just a little bit uncomfortable.

His greeter, who Steve thought was dressed pretty snazzy in matching beige slacks and sweater, closed the massive entrance door behind him. Without introducing herself, she smiled warmly and then turned to head down the wide hallway toward a set of closed pocket doors on the left. Glancing back, she urged, "Follow me. You're just in time. We're about to begin."

Steve trailed obediently as if he'd been waved on by one of the patrol ladies who stood at the crosswalk during his grammar school days. He'd never done anything quite like this before, not even in his crazy college days, but his curiosity had gotten the best of him, and he wouldn't be a pansy and cave to cold feet now.

The double doors slid apart, and Steve saw that although he had thought he was arriving right on time, there were already a half dozen others in the parlor: three women including the black woman who'd welcomed him in, and three older men. He relaxed somewhat when he recognized Joe Bennett's familiar face. He'd been the one who had suggested that he come tonight. At the bookstore, Joe had told him he belonged to a group of professionals who explored the supernatural. Although he and Joe had shared some wild conversations through the years, belonging to something like this struck Steve as strange, for Joe, that is.

Joe approached quickly. "Hey there. I see you found us and you and 'Four' have said hello."

Steve reciprocated Joe's reach and shook his hand. *"Four?"*

"Yes, this lovely lady," Joe explained, pointing to Steve's guide, "for this evening she is the number '4' since she was fourth to arrive, and you, my friend, for tonight's purpose, we'll address as 'Seven.' That's how we do it here at our SORE meetings, as I explained last week; as best we can manage, everyone is incognito. Numbers are assigned as each person arrives, and we've had as many as twelve."

A heavyset man with a beard approached Steve. "Call me 'Two.'"

"Glad to meet you, 'Two,'" Steve responded, as one by one each person in attendance held up a hand, stating their assigned number and offering a few words of welcome.

Joe sobered. Addressing Steve again he said, "For individual private reasons, we've all agreed that we would like to keep our SORE participation low profile. I wouldn't say we're secretive, but definitely under the radar. You might remember that SORE stands for *Searching Other Reality Extensions.*

"I do remember, I wrote it down after I left the bookstore that day."

Joe nodded. "Some of us might know each other outside of

SORE, but like Vegas, anything that happens here tonight stays here. We don't discuss any of this with anyone—no pillow talk with a partner—nothing. " Turning toward the others, Joe explained, "'Seven' and I ran into each other in Albany at a bookstore a number of times, and the last time I saw him he was reading 'Edgar'. I thought that he might be a right fit for our little discussion group."

He contemplated that Joe Bennett was definitely going 'lite' in clarifying how well they were acquainted. He'd been flabbergasted when he approached him that day. Joe Bennett was a paradox; that was for sure. Nobody would take the articulate, business-minded Bennett as the type of guy you'd imagine had an interest in Edgar Cayce, mysticism, or hosting a séance.

Suddenly Steve's feet iced up again. *It wouldn't go good for me down at the labor hall if any of the guys got wind that I had a part in anything like this. And Helen—she'd go ballistic.*

Joe clapped his hands together. "Okay folks, what do you say? Let's clear back some of this furniture and make some space here."

Looking at Steve, Joe explained, "What we're going to do is to form a circle, but most importantly nobody touches anyone. That's a major rule. Clear your mind of everything, be at peace, and focus on the center of the circle."

Feeling awkward, Steve moved in between the two middle-aged women he thought looked like sisters. "This okay with you ladies?"

"Not a problem. Happy to have you."

Facing Steve from across the circle, Joe said, "We're searching for something amazing to transpire. We've been exploring levitation which takes tremendous concentration."

"Oh, I see." Steve nervously responded.

"Yes, oh...a big oh", the woman next to him whispered with her eyes already closed.

At that point the black woman who'd escorted him in earlier stepped to the center of the circle. Steve supposed she would act as a medium of some sort. Levitation, from what he knew through reading various books and articles, had been witnessed down through the ages by many people in various cultures. When he and

Helen had studied the paranormal in college their professor had told them about a case in Pennsylvania in the '60s where a young guy belonging to a Transcendental Meditation organization had supposedly levitated in front of twenty people at a party. Everybody there that day had claimed he was floating up in the air six or seven feet off the floor and they could feel the 'cosmic energy'. When the man brushed the ceiling though, he'd fallen…fortunately into the waiting arms of friends. Back then, he and Helen had agreed that it sounded like pretty weird crap. Nobody could power-up over gravity. It was a party. Helen was sure that they all must have been drunk or on something.

After calling upon all 'souls' that might be present to assist, 'Four', her arms hanging listlessly by her side, appeared to be in a trance. Her eyes had teared up and remained fixed open. What raised the hair on Steve's arms was that 'Four' had planted her eerie gaze on him. He got the definite impression that she was signaling him out.

Steve scanned the others who fixated peacefully on the core of the experiment, most appearing to pray silently. Steve stared into Four's emotionless dark eyes. Within a short time he couldn't believe what was happening. Their medium's feet departed the room's Oriental rug, and she floated upward to what he estimated was a good six inches. She remained there, suspended in the air for several seconds before gently regaining ground. Steve thought he could faintly see the image of two angels who had helped her regain solid footing.

Everyone exhaled. Joe was the first to go to her. "Are you all right?"

Still looking at Steve, "Yes, I never lost consciousness," 'Four' replied weakly, but clearly she was shaken.

"How do you feel?" Steve asked.

"I feel a little weird. How do you feel?"

Steve could only manage a feeble, "Okay".

Joe said, "Well, not much happened tonight, but it was a very good exercise in meditation."

Steve couldn't say anything more. His throat was dry. Something had happened to him. Something had passed between them. They'd witnessed an incredible phenomenon. What did Joe mean by *"not tonight"?*

Abruptly, Joe suggested that they all pour themselves a glass of water from the pitcher that had been placed earlier on the table. One of the women said she'd go to the kitchen for some ice.

Fifteen minutes later they'd broken up, and not one person had mentioned anything further about the levitation experience they'd all witnessed. 'Four' walked out the door with him. "This is it for me," she whispered shakily. "I'm never doing this again."

Steve went to a nearby bar and downed two Manhattans. Was he nuts or did he witness something that was beyond belief? He was convinced that something had happened, and 'Four' had meant it to happen, yet he seemed to be the only one who actually saw it happen.

CHAPTER 19

"Hey Babe," Steve greeted, breezing in. "How'd Tommy's basketball game go at school today?" Rounding Helen at the kitchen table, he opened the refrigerator and slithered in two six-packs of Bud. Retrieving the last can of beer from the shelf, he popped it open and leaned against the Formica countertop, waiting for Helen's report.

"They won, 56 to 47. Tommy made a couple of nice shots. He's really very good. And we gals raised over a hundred dollars with our bake sale. Steve, I..."

"Wow that's great. Is Tommy upstairs?"

"No. He's over at Crusty's house. He's been invited for supper. At least that's what Crusty said when we were leaving the auditorium— so I dropped them both off at his house."

"Look, I'm sorry that I couldn't get away from the meeting today down at the hall. I wish I could have seen him make those baskets. I'll make it up. I promise."

"He understands. You have to do what you have to do," Helen sighed.

"Oh, and wait till you hear this: I had the radio on coming home. The big global news is President Reagan is in Germany. I heard part of his speech. He's ordered Mikhail Gorbachev to 'tear down that wall'. Man, this President of ours sure has the Irish grit. Those Ruskies will think twice about screwing around with us while Reagan is Commander-in-Chief."

Helen remained seated at their table, her hands folded. She stared sullenly at the Dutch boy and girl saltshakers in the middle of the turntable. "No, I didn't hear about that."

"The Wall has been up between East and West Berlin since 1961. I'd forgotten how long it's been," Steve said, rummaging through the top cabinet. "Are there any more bags of pretzels left?"

Absently, Helen replied, "I didn't vote for him, but I do agree he's really trying for the positive with the Soviets. Steve, look, can you sit down for a minute? There is something important that you should hear."

Steve pulled out a kitchen chair. "Sure. Geeze, you look so serious. Did somebody die?"

"Well, nobody that I know, but you might."

"What are you talking about? What's this about?"

"I ran into Mick this afternoon at the game."

"Well, that's too bad. So?"

Steve finished off his beer as Helen pushed her long hair behind her ears. He knew that gesture. Something momentous had happened, and a bomb was about to explode.

"Mick accused you of something pretty bad, Steve, and I want you to know that I don't believe a word he said, but you have a right to know about it."

Steve felt his anger rise up into his neck. "What, something worse than accusing me of taking money from our business and worse than the two thousand bucks that it cost us to straighten out that mess?!"

"Don't shout at me!" Helen snapped, trying to control the trembling in her voice. "I want to be honest with you, and you're making this so hard for me."

Steve sighed. "You're right. I'm sorry. Just tell me what he had to say, and we can talk about it."

"Mick says that a couple of days ago someone overdosed in an apartment in Watervliet. Mick heard about the details from his cousin—you know, Bart, the big guy who's a cop. I know you know him. He used to be on the Tri-City wrestling team."

"I remember him. So what does any of this have to do with me?"

"Well, this poor kid was found half dead on the living room couch during a drug bust. He died later at the hospital. When the cops went into the place there were several people there they arrested. All of them though got released."

"Why wasn't any of this on the news if it was such a big thing? Big drug busts and someone dead usually make the local news," Steve remarked sarcastically.

"That's just it, Steve. It's all being covered up because of who was in this strung-out group of people and what besides the drugs was involved. It's some sort of weird witch cult. Joe Bennett as well as some New York City politician seem to be connected. According to Bart, Joe and this New York City guy were with several young, naked, strung-out girls, chanting and dancing around, worshiping Satin." Helen stood up and looked out the back window toward the woods. She whispered, "He says you're one of them."

Suddenly there was a blast of dynamite in Steve's chest. "What-the-hell! Is this the shit that Mick is feeding you? And...Joe Bennett? Really? I wish you would show me some respect and not talk to that man. And where the hell did he say all this stuff—in the bleachers? I know he's Christine's brother and that you and she are tight, and I've respected your friendship, but you know I don't want us to have anything to do with Mick. I think my request has been reasonable. Mick is a liar—short and simple."

"No, we were in the parking lot," Helen retaliated.

"That son-of-a-bitch."

"Well, here it is Steve, Mick says that he knows that you have a connection to this bunch and for me to be careful around you. He promised he wouldn't say anything to Chris, but he wants me to call Father Burns in and have our house blessed."

"Holy shit! He's completely nuts!"

Helen responded quickly. "So this is all Mick trying to do you in? Why would he want to incriminate you in such a terrible thing if there's nothing to it? And why are you always someplace else other than where you should be? Were you really at a meeting to-day, on a Saturday?"

Steve steadied his voice. "Helen, I can't believe that you're swallowing this stuff. Yes, I was at a meeting, and you can call my boss if you want." Steve picked up the wall telephone receiver. "Call Pete right now. I'll give you the number."

"Hang it up," Helen directed. "I believe you."

"I mean it. Go ahead and call Pete."

Helen grabbed the phone and slammed it onto the wall telephone hook. "I believe you, alright?"

"Okay, Helen. I'm going to tell you something about Mick, but you have to keep it quiet. The reason Mick is trying to discredit me and see to it that you don't believe a word I say is because he is having an affair with his secretary."

"Rhonda?" Helen's eyes widened.

"Yes, Rhonda, who as far as I'm concerned can't hold a candle to his wife, but Mick can't keep his hands off of her. I saw them out in a bar about a month ago. I'd had a few beers already when they walked in. When I saw them, I paid up, and then I called him an asshole as I walked out. He's probably sure that, based on all our past troubles, I'm going to rat him out. But I'd never lower myself to his level. I'd never go on the attack and deliberately hurt his family."

Helen studied Steve for a minute. "No, I know you wouldn't," she said.

He reached out to take her hands into both of his. "Everybody but you it seems thinks he's a pompous ass. I'll admit to having hit the bars after work every so often, but I think you know I need to wind down before I come home from the day I put in. That I have a few drinks out before I show up here shouldn't be a surprise."

"Okay. Let's not talk about this anymore." She sighed. "I hope that it's all hogwash. Although I'll tell you this—I'm not sure that I'm going to be able to face Joe over at his Boutique. He's holding a dress for me. I always thought he was such a classy guy. I don't know how I can shop there imagining him dancing around with naked girls and worshiping the Devil."

Steve did his best not to smile. "Listen to yourself. You've known Joe for how many years? A witch's coven?"

Helen mumbled, "I know, but what an out-of-sight-story to make up."

She was trying to make some sense out of Steve's explanation. She knew Steve had a drinking problem, and without his knowing it she'd looked up Alcoholics Anonymous and sent away for information about it. She had hidden the AA pamphlet in her lingerie drawer. But she also knew that Steve swallowed up every kind of book on religion and the occult, and she hated it. Still there was a lot of truth in what he said.

The phone rang and they both jumped. Helen picked it up. "What?—Oh. Okay, we'll see you soon."

"Who was that?"

"Tommy. Looks like I'm cooking for four. Crusty's mom isn't feeling well."

"Are we okay then? Have I dispelled all this bogus voodoo?"

"Yes," Helen said. "But you have to promise me that you won't make a big thing of this to Mick. I don't want anything to come between Chris and me, so please just say nothing—at least for a while. Do promise."

"I promise I'll think it all over. Let's see if anything does come out about it in the papers. I assume that there should be something."

"I told you. Mick said that there wasn't even a police report."

"We'll see, won't we? You know, I think that I need a shower before the boys get here. Hey, tell you what. How about we all go out for pizza? We'll celebrate the kids' victory," Steve said, heading upstairs.

Soon the sound of the shower drifted downstairs.

Helen stood watching the small, black second hand on the large, round wall clock tick off the passing time. *He loves me, he loves me not. He lies, he lies not.*

CHAPTER 20

Not long after Tommy's seventeenth birthday Helen and Steve agreed that he should have his own car, but definitely not the spiffy red mustang Tommy had apparently gone back to see multiple times at the used car lot near the Saratoga Speedway in Malta. They both knew what he had in mind for the coveted mustang and that just wasn't happening. No way would he be blowing out tires drag racing on the dirt track or anyplace else, Steve had thundered.

Tommy didn't like it much either when his parents made it perfectly clear to him that even though he'd saved up five hundred dollars for the car, and would be a part of the final decision, he needed something practical. After that, Tommy's fear of some old Dodge parked in their driveway was overwhelming. Reluctantly, he'd bent to the idea of looking around with his father for something other than the mustang.

One Saturday morning, after making a list of three car lots, Steve and Tommy headed out in the family Volkswagen van. Driving along Route 9, Tommy registered his complaint, "You know, Dad, I don't know why we couldn't have gone out yesterday to do this. I mean, I was off from school all day for those teachers' conferences, and you could have gotten time off. You make your own schedule, Mom says."

His eyes clamped to the road, Steve batted back, "First off, kid, I can't take time off anytime I want. People depend on me. Secondly, I had an important early meeting down at the office yesterday. Besides, yesterday was Friday. It's bad luck to do serious business on a Friday."

Tommy wriggled around in his seat, pulling out a pack of spearmint gum from his jeans pocket. "Do you want a stick?"

Steve shook his head, then added, "No thanks."

Putting the gum in his mouth, Tommy clumped out, "I never heard that before. It would be pretty stupid if nobody ever bought a car or anything else on a Friday."

Steve shrugged. "I guess you're right. It wouldn't be too good if all of everything shut down on a Friday, but for me it makes sense. It's an old Irish thing."

"An old Irish thing. What's that?"

"Well, I remember my father telling me that he and my mother almost walked away from buying the house I grew up in because the lawyers had set up the closing for a Friday. His dad, your great grandfather, who was born in Ireland, had never signed anything on a Friday, and though my mother was in tears thinking they'd lose out on the house, my father just couldn't do it on a Friday. Some things stick with you."

Tommy turned to his father. "But grandpa did buy the house."

Steve grinned. "Sure, but the following Tuesday which was the first day of the month. First day of the month was always considered lucky in the Carey family."

"Holy Cow! I never thought you were that superstitious."

Steve said, "Hey, what do you say we stop at Dunkin Donuts for some jellies and coffee before we hit the lot?"

"Okay, sounds good to me," Tommy answered eagerly. "So, after that if we see something that looks good can we buy it today? I have the cash in my wallet."

Steve swung into the parking lot. "You're carrying around five hundred bucks?"

"It's my five hundred bucks, Dad."

"Yeah, you watch yourself with that kind of money on you. Let's just see what they have available and then maybe we'll talk. We're just supposed to be looking around today."

In the donut shop while standing in line browsing the shelves, Steve thought he recognized the back of someone familiar waiting for his order; someone who he would rather not have met this morning.

Joe Bennett turned around. "Hey there, Steve. Hello Tommy. You remember Ginger?"

Steve replied. "Hello Joe. Ginger, nice to see you."

Tommy glanced over at the well-dressed, middle aged man sporting a silver mustache standing next to a pretty, dark haired, twenty-something, woman. He vaguely remembered Mr. Bennett from one of his dad's union picnics at Saratoga Park last summer. "Hi Mr. Bennett."

"Tommy, I don't think that you know my associate, Ginger. Ginger, this is Steve's son, Tommy."

Extending her hand, Ginger smiled, "Hello."

Tommy swallowed his gum and took her hand. "Nice to meet you."

"Ginger is one of my shop's top sales associates."

Ginger quickly added, "We all make a good team."

"Mr. Bennett's shop is called Joseph's Boutique," Steve clarified. "By the way, Helen loved the leather jacket that you suggested, Ginger."

"Oh, good, I'm so glad. The leather in that line is just so soft."

"I knew that she would look great in it," Joe interrupted, smiling broadly. "Let's face it, Steve, Helen makes you look good."

Steve laughed, but his eyes weren't smiling. Studying Joe thoughtfully, he replied, "You know, you're right. I'm a fortunate man."

Joe Bennett paid for his donuts and coffee. Handing the boxed dozen to Ginger, he picked up the crated hot coffees. "Well, we'd better get rolling, Ginger. Jim's opening up, but I expect a busy day. See you around the circle, Steve."

Seemingly still annoyed by Joe's condescending remark, Steve replied flatly. "You will."

Ginger hesitated at the glass door that Joe was holding open for her and glanced over her shoulder. "Nice seeing you again, Steve, and great to meet you, too, Tommy."

"Same here," Steve called back.

After they'd left Tommy said, "Wow, she's a tall fox. That's the first time I was almost eyeball to eyeball with any girl."

Four big bites and Tommy had finished the first of his two jelly donuts. Slowly nurturing hot coffee, he paused. "Dad, how do you know Mr. Bennett? I remember him from that picnic, but I'm wondering why he'd be at a union shindig if he owns a ladies clothing store."

Brushing powdered sugar off the front of his sweater, Steve answered matter-of-factly. "He was there because his wife used to work for the union. She died a few years ago, but it's a policy to invite the widower or widow of a past employee to the annual picnic. People in the trades are like that. They take good care of workers and their families. But actually, your mom and I met Joe long before he was married. He used to bartend at the Schuyler Country Club, and that's where Joe first met a whole lot of women who've become his customers."

"Really? Wow, that's cool."

Steve, staring out the plate glass window, answered reflectively, "Yeah, Joe always knew how to captivate the female audience."

Tommy said, "I'm trying to get a job at the Country Club. If I get a car I know I'm going to need more money to keep it up. I've been talking to Mom about it. Mrs. Mann knows the lady who is the banquet manager there, and I figure I can make more money bussing tables than working at McDonald's. You know Paul—Crusty's older brother?"

Steve nodded.

"Paul used to work there waiting tables while he was in college. He says that waiters give a share of their tips to help the kids bussing. Everybody gets something on top of the $3.35 an hour, so that's really good."

Steve reluctantly nodded an approval despite not liking that Tommy would probably be running into Mick who had long held a membership there. "Nice to hear you're looking to better yourself; hope it works out for you, if that's what you want."

"Don't get me wrong, Dad. McDonald's is okay, but I just think that the Country Club would be better." Tommy finished his second donut.

"Want another?" Steve asked.

Tommy smiled. "Thanks, but I think I'm full. What did Mr. Bennett mean about seeing you at the circle? Is his store around Latham Circle?"

Steve finished his coffee. "You're sure full of questions this morning. Yeah, it's down around there. I was surprised that you seemed to remember him. It's been a while."

"I did...sort of, but he was right about Ginger. I didn't remember her and sure would have if I'd ever seen her before."

Steve grinned. "She is memorable. Okay, I can see you're itchin' to get at it. So let's do it."

Five hours later the pair trooped into the house.

"Well?" Helen greeted.

"A really cool Ford pickup truck won," Tommy announced. "Wait till you see it, Mom! It's seven years old, but it's been somebody's baby, and man it's great! One owner, the salesman said. I have to call Crusty. Geeze, I didn't know it was that late. We're supposed to pick up the girls."

"Pick up the girls?" Helen asked dully.

"Yeah. We've been studying the French and Indian War and the Revolutionary War at school, and the whole American History class is going to a big bonfire over at Saratoga Battlefield. Paul is driving tonight. He'll be here in fifteen minutes."

Helen put her hands on her hips. "Nice to let me in on all the news, but I ordered pizzas for tonight. I was just about to go out and pick them up when you guys pulled in."

"Sorry, Mom," Tommy called back as he ran upstairs. "You can put my slices in the frig. I'll eat them for breakfast tomorrow."

Helen threw her arms up in the air. "I can't win."

"I'm game for pizza," Steve offered. "But I have a few things I want to re-check on this paperwork for the truck so you'll still have to go get it."

Helen grimaced. "Wait a minute. It's a go on the truck—right? He's over-the-hill excited about this so I hope you don't think there is some sort of problem."

Steve looked up. "No—, it's all good. I just want to check the tire warranty over, and then put it all in a folder, that's all. It won't take me long. Helen, you should have seen Tommy's proud face when he paid the two hundred dollar deposit on it. The sticker was a thousand, and we got them to go for nine hundred. I offered the salesman eight to begin with, but it also has four brand new tires. So I'm loaning Tommy the additional four hundred that he needs.

"Loaning?"

"Yes, loaning. He has to pay us back, but some he can work off staining the deck this summer and the rest through his job at the club, if he gets it. We're picking the truck up Tuesday night. I thought we'd both go down with him to get it."

Helen reached for her brown sweater hanging on the coatrack by the door. "Sounds like a plan to me. That is, if we can keep to a plan." She grabbed her car keys off the counter and opened the door. Half way out she shouted back "Oh gosh, Steve, will you tell Tommy that Paul just pulled in with Crusty? He's waiting out in our driveway."

"Tommy! Your ride is here!" Steve called up the stairs.

Tommy flew past. "I'll be home by midnight."

"You'd better, kiddo."

"Oh, yeah, and Dad,—thanks." Tommy raced past Helen sitting in her car waiting for Paul to back out.

Through the front window Steve watched as the kids and then his wife turned out onto the road. Immediately he went to the living room phone and dialed the number he had memorized.

"Hello," a male voice sang out.

"Joe?"

"Yes, this is Joe."

"It's Steve, Steve Carey. What the hell is with your 'see you around the circle'? Are you nuts? And in front of my kid? My family knows nothing. Got it? So I would appreciate it if you would watch what flows out of your mouth. Good God, I was flabbergasted when you said that."

After a few seconds of silence, Steve wondered if the phone had gone dead, but then came a faint, "Sorry."

Steve lowered his voice. "Well, all right then. I just wanted you to know how I felt. I'll leave it at that."

"It won't happen again, Steve."

Steve banged down the receiver. All of this was too unsettling. All day he'd had a hard time concentrating, and he hoped he hadn't made any mistakes with Tommy's deal. He'd have to rethink some things. *Damn that Joe Bennett!*

CHAPTER 21

1753

Late in the summer of 1753, Cornelius Waldron received a disturbing letter from his cousin, John Waldron, of New York City, the contents of which heightened his deep concern about what he long suspected was inevitable. Although Britain and France had been at war off and on for decades in Europe, a bloody war between these two great powers would soon engage provincials on American soil. Often, smaller skirmishes between England and France had disrupted the colonies. Yet now, as John lamented, *the pot has spilled over and will make what ensued in forty-five seem as nothing more than a boil on one's ass.* Cornelius immediately understood the brash reference.

In 1745, just days following the birth of his son, Henry, a surprise attack of six hundred French and their Indian allies had plundered Fort Lydius, an important trading post located where previously Fort Nicholson had stood and near what the Indians had long called the "great carrying place" north of Albany. Beyond the hamlet begun by John Henry Lydius—a Dutch trader from Albany—navigation northward on the North River was impossible because of rough waters, thus forcing the portage of their canoes across land to French Lake Champlain.

Lydius's trading settlement that had survived since 1731 had been burned to the ground. There, barely an hour's hard ride from

Waldron's front door, more than thirty settlers were murdered, and over fifty taken prisoner and carried away by the French. With the help of Mohawk friends, some of these desperate souls had been rescued by the Albany Militia, but others who had been captured were feared lost forever. Thereafter, the fortification of Albany, as well as the building of new forts, and refortifying the outlying British posts such as Fort Schaghticoke, were of the utmost importance to Americans. Some wilderness settlers had abandoned their outlying farms and moved back to Albany. But not Cornelius Waldron. Despite what had occurred at Fort Lydius and other hamlets along the North River, Cornelius and Janet had decided to stay put in the country with their eight children. Waldron Farm had been home for over twenty years.

Cousin John's greeting had begun with his usual cheerful salutation, *Greetings, Bear,* but his dispatch soon turned sober, launching into news of a surprising communication he'd received from William Johnson, New York's highly revered agent to the Iroquois League, a man with whom Cornelius was fairly well acquainted. Although the Colonel's mainstay house was west of Schenectady, he owned another along the Albany shoreline close to Cornelius's brother, William, and his wife, Elizabeth. Quite often William Johnson had been a guest at William and Elizabeth's table. Waldron Farm was also a familiar stop-over for Johnson when he traveled north.

Cornelius was somewhat surprised by Colonel Johnson's reaching out to his Manhattan cousin, but then, who in New York City, Albany, or those living on the frontier beyond, did not know of the flamboyant, stalwart man whom many compared to the great Quidor of old? The Colonel had been in fact responsible for the Albany Militia since 1748.

However, when in Albany, Cornelius kept his own admiration for William Johnson to himself. Comparing anyone to the great Peter Schuyler, even decades after his death, left several with the surname *Schuyler* with their blood boiling. He visualized some of their faces as he continued to read John's letter and reminded himself that a good rule was to keep eyes and ears open and mouth shut. Johnson being Irish and raised by a Papist mother did not warm the hearts of the old Albany Dutch. Yet, inwardly Cornelius argued that William Johnson, who was just twenty-three years old when he came to America, had long seen the truth. Wisely, Johnson had left his Papist religion behind in Ireland and was now a member of the Protestant Anglican church.

Early on Johnson had visited a fellow Irishman, the Pennsylvania Indian agent, George Croghan, on his thousand acre farm in the Ohio wilderness. There at Croghan's house he had met both white and Native traders and had learned that the frontiersman had packhorses traveling far and wide in every direction. In every Indian village George had set up a trading post. Soon, Johnson used his friend to learn the Mohawk and some of the Delaware languages and to establish a personal relationship with the Natives. By opening up the trade with the western Oswego, William Johnson had made his fortune in a very short time.

Some Albany traders resented Johnson for intercepting trade with the western Indians outside of Schenectady, thereby diminishing their profits. But silently Cornelius admired his cleverness and his tenacity. He was quick-witted and knew how to get along, especially with the Indians. Like his father before him, Cornelius spoke fluent Dutch, English and Mohawk. Like Johnson, his linguistic abilities were a great aid when he dabbled in the trade for furs.

All living in the American colonies knew of the volatility blanketing their homeland. Trouble with the French who controlled much of the rich, fur trading region deep into the western Ohio land was nothing new. The French claimed all the land on one side of the Ohio River and the English on the other side, and more often than not the far Indians sided with the French whom they called "strong-hearted".

By way of Mohawk friends, Cornelius learned that the French had increased their military presence in the wilderness by the thousands. At the Kittle homestead, he'd heard about the western Indian runners who'd come to William Johnson's home at Mount Johnson seeking the help of the British Superintendent of Indian Affairs. One

Ohio Indian had cried that a savage Frenchman had killed and then eaten his father. The Indians living in the west demanded to know where then was their homeland if the French and English own the lands north and south of the Ohio?

The savages' plight had gotten Cornelius to thinking. He could foresee a time when he might ask the same question about his own land. Something had to be done to put a stop to French advancement and protect English and allied Indian rights. In John's letter he read that the English had once again warned the French to keep out of English western territory. Warned them? Cornelius could almost hear the French commanders roar with laughter.

John wrote of a great meeting between the English and the Iroquois that would be held that next summer at Albany, and he supposed, of course, William Johnson would play a large role in such a significant gathering. Seven colonies were to send representatives, and some said that hundreds of tribesmen were also expected at the conference.

Cornelius grunted disgustedly. At last...the long awaited meeting. The English Lords of Trade holding power over all provincial business finally had realized the problem between all parties. These esteemed gentlemen were more than somewhat worried about the Iroquois joining the French in the fight and so the meeting at Albany was encouraged. The fools should be worried. The Six Nations were not happy of late with the various agreements with individual colonies. The Indians urged unification. Joining together with one agreement between the King of England, the Iroquois and other tribes would be far less confusing. Such unification of Americans would be a blessing for the colonies as a whole. Cornelius agreed with all John had said so far, but why had William Johnson written his cousin?

As if John had anticipated the quizzical look upon Cornelius's face, he'd penned the following.

Yes, 'tis Col. William Johnson to whom I refer, the esteemed Irishman who I did meet at your up-country house One October, 1751. He is the same who held our hearts and

minds in the palm of his hand as he spoke of his adventures as
a younger man. I will never forget my last visit up to see your
good family. It was at that time I also met the great Indian,
King Hendrik.
Also present was Patrick Clark, your niece Cornelia's
amicable husband.

Though cordial at the start, John Waldron's letter was more than
a social communication of pleasantries meant to evoke fond memories. According to John, William Johnson, by order of New York's
Acting Governor, his Honor James Delancey, had inquired of him if
he could compose a list of cannon and stores that might be had in
and around the City of New York. Johnson, it seemed, was lining up
details to be included in his report to Delancey.

Cornelius grimaced. Cousin John was an odd, orderly man, a
great one to remember the exact dates of baptisms, marriages and
deaths. Being one who was most impressed by a man's position,
it was understandable that he would remember meeting with the
distinguished Johnson. The Mohawk had made Johnson an honor-
ary chief. Who would forget the man who seemed to be able to accomplish the most impossible and was now one of the wealthiest
in the land?

Cornelius recollected well that particular meeting at his farm.
One of his wife's uncles as a child had been carried away by savages
during an attack, eventually traded by his captors to another tribe.
Ultimately, Janet's Van Ness uncle had married a Mohawk woman
and stayed with his wife's family. Once a year Janet's mixed-blooded
cousins and their Dutch relations enjoyed a week-long visit. The la-
crosse games were great fun, and the kinship offered a blanket of
safety for his family.

During this yearly visit Waldron Farm often served as a meeting
place for traders and Indians who, Cornelius supposed, felt comfortable to drop by whenever they pleased.

So it was that in 1751, just as John arrived—the Manhattanite
tromping in three days before he'd been expected—King Hendrik

Theyanoquin, the auspicious, most powerful Iroquois leader in the country, along with his entourage made an unexpected stopover while returning to Canajoharie Castle, their village along the Mohawk River. It was most unfortunate timing. John Waldron still had no idea of how well acquainted Cornelius was with Johnson, or King Hendrick, or his own wife Janet's bloodline. He had prayed to Almighty God that "Tedious John" never know of the deeply rooted intricacies of his business, his acquisitions, or his family. Unfortunately, Almighty God had not granted his every wish. He was leery of how much John had repeated about his visit.

Sighing impatiently, Cornelius came to the true point to John's post.

Might you, Cornelius, and your kinsman, Patrick Clark, assist in securing good, strong, Albany men, as many as you think would be needed, to transport and install the cannon in fortifications? If able to accomplish this request, you should give the list of names to a member of the Common Council, Sybrant Van Schaick, Esq. He often acts as Recorder during official meetings in Albany. Van Schaick will give this list to Colonel Johnson, who I suspect would, of course, wish to discuss it with him at an appropriate time when Johnson is in Albany prior to the Indian Conference.

Again, Cornelius grunted.

The materials to be produced and then delivered to Albany would be significant. Many tradesmen around the City of New York have already been contacted. Cousin Sam Waldron, a blacksmith, has received a work request from a Mr. John Dies, as has David Provoost and others who would make and find the iron for carriages to carry the cannon. Peter Geraurd is ordered to make ten carriages with limbers timber included and to fix a boom to each carriage along with ten sets of wheels. James Lawrence has been ordered to make seven sets of wheels with spokes included. The carriages and stores must be shipped to Albany in care of Mr. Schuyler and Mr. De Peyster. The latter gentleman, who resides on Yonker Street, is in charge of military supplies.

Right away Cornelius thought of several able bodied men who would be willing to take part in this task. At the top of his list would be his own German manservant, Herman, who had worked for him now several years. Recalling how he had acquired the powerful Herman, he hoped that Colonel Johnson would be amused when he noticed Herman's name on his suggested list of laborers.

CHAPTER 22

Herman

A German manservant joining the Waldron household had not been a foreseen acquisition by any of the parties involved. Although the unexpected addition of Herman's strong, powerful hands proved to be a Godsend after the deaths of Willie and then Willie's eldest son, Tom, who, until his untimely passing, had been Cornelius's right hand man on the farm.

Months before Cousin John's visit, Cornelius, along with two of his elder sons, Evert and Garret, traveled to Albany for a short visit with his mother and family. Leaving Albany along with a small company of ten British soldiers they continued on the coarse, sixteen-mile trek to Schenectady and then along the old Indian trails to William Johnson's impressive, well-fortified three-story stone mansion at Mount Johnson.

The primary purpose of the second portion of the journey, Cornelius had told his wife, was to discuss with Johnson the possibility of using their property near Schaghticoke to build the large flat boats necessary to transport soldiers and supplies on the river. The explanation was true—in part. To be sure there would be much discussion, but the excursion would also allow the Waldron men to take part in the annual sporting games that the hospitable William Johnson so enjoyed hosting.

The magnitude of the event had gone far beyond what Cornelius and his boys had expected. In addition to Johnson's thirty or so

African slaves running to and fro with platters of food, hundreds of European settlers as well as Natives from as far away as the Ohio lands were camped in and around the Johnson house and flanking buildings. For the games Colonel Johnson had painted his body and dressed himself after Mohawk fashion, as did many of the men, all of the guests enjoying the Native dances of celebration well into the night. Rum and beer flowed like water. This meant that most of the attendees did not rise until afternoon each day, awakened by the aroma of freshly roasted meats.

For the boxing spectacle, William Johnson had put his servant, Herman, a muscular German, against his neighbor's powerful African. Johnson had professed loudly that he was confident that his man would be victorious, but shockingly Johnson's servant had taken a terrible pounding from the tall, lean Negro. Those watching the match were astonished that even though the African took many fierce blows to his mid-section, and was repeatedly knocked down, he repeatedly rose up, recovered, encouraged by the deafening cheers of those who'd betted on him.

The fight continued at a ferocious pace, and soon the German was missing a portion of his ear after the African bit off a good chunk. Herman's blood streamed down his neck, yet like a Roman gladiator, the staunch Rhinesman held his ground. Then, after more brutalities inflicted by both fighters, the German's nose was broken. Unable to see out of one swollen, bloodied eye and completely dazed, Johnson's man staggered and fell and did not rise again.

The generally good-natured Johnson had wagered a great amount on this fight, and was so disgusted by his loss that a few days later he offered Herman free to Cornelius if he would only take him out of his sight. Cornelius had sighed and tried to reason with his host. He did not need a house servant as was the position he understood Herman held within Johnson's family, and surely he did not need another mouth to feed if the man could not work in his wheat fields.

'Free' was really not free as Cornelius soon learned after the sporting festivities had concluded. He and his sons took sullen, silent Herman along home. Once back at the farm and installed inside his quarters within the barn where he was shown a clean bed of straw, Herman was no longer mute.

The German, like Johnson's fair-haired German consort, Catherine Weisenburger, spoke little English, but speaking in good Dutch, the man broke his silence first by spitting at the barn's dirt floor. Turning toward the gentle-spoken Evert, Herman angrily proclaimed to be William Johnson's kin by way of Catherine. He insisted he was her cousin. He was insulted that he would be made to sleep in the barn with animals. He stated that these past years he had made his bed in the basement of the Johnson house with other relatives, close to Catherine's mother, near the ever burning kitchen hearth. He would not be made to sleep on the ground like a savage.

Cornelius had started toward the house but turned around when he heard all the commotion behind. He entered the barn hearing the German claim that the woman who lived as Johnson's wife at Fort Johnson had years ago been an indentured girl working in the house of one of the farmers living nearby Johnson's first small farm. Herman said the place is called Warren's Bush.

Frustrated, tears welled up in the servant's eyes. Embarrassed, he turned away.

Cornelius said nothing. Better to let him spit it out. At least a portion of the disheartened man's claim stood on solid ground. He'd heard the tale of William Johnson's desire for, and acquisition of, the lovely servant girl Catherine Weisenburger whilst he was on his way to Johnson Manor. At Schenectady, he and his sons stopped to survey the boatyard there and then spent the night with his Bradt cousins. According to hearsay, Johnson had bought out Catherine's contract and then taken the woman home to his house, and to his bed, and so along came the three youngsters they'd made together.

Cornelius had assumed this was the way of it, but surly no man's business, nor was the servant's other claims such as that after Catherine's first child was born she had begged her beloved Irishman to bring her cousin to their house. Johnson had obliged her by fetching

Herman from the farm where he'd been working and bringing him to Fort Johnson. Thus, according to Herman, he was kin and had been treated poorly by being cast off.

Facing his new master, again Herman resumed complaining about his situation, then and now. His angry words kept coming although Cornelius tried to quiet him.

Herman cried that he had worked as hard as any man to build up Mount Johnson and irately resented that after his many years of good service and being kinsman to not only Catherine but to his Master's own children, Johnson had sent him far away to be used as a common servant to Waldron. Then came what Cornelius thought was Herman's most outrageous complaint. He accused Colonel Johnson of being dishonest! He said that William Johnson had promised to pay him for the fight. With that money the German had thought to pay off what remained on his contract. Both Evert and Garret looked to their father. There could be nothing worse in life than a liar and a cheat. Would this German be so daring as to accuse William Johnson?

Cornelius knew nothing of this agreement, but what did it matter. William Johnson had signed over the indentured paper to him. Herman whined further that he would now be made to work another seven years to gain his freedom, freedom that should be his already. In God's eyes Herman said he knew he had not been treated justly, and if he were a freed man in a better position he would take Johnson to court...kin or not.

Despite his rhetoric, Herman was made to sleep on the straw pallet in the barn, but the following day Cornelius ordered two of his Negroes to cut down trees and then to help his newly arrived servant to build a sturdy, one room log cabin next to the slave cabins behind his house. There, Herman could dwell. Cornelius explained to Herman that on Waldron Farm there were no 'common servants', adding that, by God, he would learn to work in the fields as did everyone else. Cornelius made it plain to all that he did not think William Johnson had acted dishonestly, but had, in angry disgust, turned Herman out. So be it!

Within a short time the new cabin had been built, and the transplanted German appeared to have accepted what had been put upon him.

Months later when Cornelius saw Johnson at Albany, he was able to have a brief conversation with him regarding his former servant. Johnson appeared not to be surprised by Hermans's claim, but insisted that the kinship was long denied by Catherine as well as her mother who lived with them. Although Herman had been born in a town not twenty miles distance from the homeland of Catherine, the German was no relation, and had Herman won the fight, Johnson adamantly declared that he would have been rewarded properly. But Herman did not win (even though he could have, had he put his heart into it, or so Johnson thought). Johnson believed that his servant had deliberately lost, and that was what made him so angry that he could no longer tolerate his presence. Johnson was the one betrayed, not Herman.

Having witnessed the brutal, bloody fight, Cornelius was not so sure that losing was the German's intent, but he gave no further thought to the man's past life. The word of the influential William Johnson was good enough.

Herman proved to be as strong as an ox, and, under Evert's patient supervision, the man became proficient with his new duties around the farm. Cornelius knew that he wished himself free, and who would blame him for wanting it so? Still, Herman ate as they all did which was far better than most in servitude, and his garments bore no more holes than some of his own. However, he continued to complain.

Annoyed with Herman's attitude, Janet spoke her mind. "You would think your man would be grateful."

Cornelius had responded, "One man bound to another by contract and not by friendship is never grateful."

CHAPTER 23

1989

Helen leaned against her kitchen countertop nursing a cup of stale instant decaf. It tasted awful—blah and dead. How she yearned for a cup of fresh brewed java. Ten years ago she'd given up her cigarettes, and now her doctor was on her about the caffeine and her weight. According to the charts in his office, she was twenty pounds overweight and her blood pressure was sky high.

It was foolish not to listen. She knew that. Blah was certainly better than dead, which is what the doc had warned her she'd be if she didn't make some changes, and so decaf it was, and somehow she'd learn to love it. She'd joined Weight Watchers with Chris Mann. Fourteen pounds more to go. What a life.

Pouring the half-cup left into the sink, she rinsed out the blue Hawaiian mug she'd brought back from the Island cruise she and Steve had taken with the Rotary Club a few years ago. Remembering one of their favorite cruise stops, the green slopes of the "Big Island" and all the fun they'd had there, she sighed, almost tasting fresh-grilled Mahi-Mahi. Setting the mug into the dish rack she lingered in front of the window, scanning the backyard, her *Serenity Ville*. A small brown squirrel sat statue-like on the railing of the stained redwood deck. It didn't take her long to spot Rocky, their neighbor's calico cat, waiting patiently under the white cedar Adirondack glider Steve had special ordered for her last spring. Helen held her breath as the squirrel leapt to an outstretched lower branch of a mountain ash, leaving an annoyed Rocky behind.

"You'll never get that one," she whispered, and, as if the big cat heard her, Rocky thumped his bushy, orange and white tail against the deck planks.

As crazy as it sounded, even to herself, she was happy for the distraction. Rocky, the squirrels, and the rare appearance of a migrating flock of endangered rose-breasted grosbeak helped her keep her sanity these days. Although her backyard didn't provide the expansive, glorious view of Hawaiian grassy plains where cattle ranchers took in the blue Pacific Ocean with their morning grog, Upstate New York offered its own untouched majesty. The small space outside her window was a constant stage, and the props and players changed with every season.

As Rocky rambled into the bushes and through the vibrant palette of sun-washed autumn colors, Helen promised herself that she and Steve would get through whatever it was that was going on.

Nervously she glanced at the wall clock, trying to remember what exactly Steve had said to her when he'd called two nights ago. After another late day at work, and then the usual Friday night rush stuff after that—all made worse by a clog in the check-out line at the market—she'd walked into the house after seven, totally beat.

When the phone rang she'd just finished reading the note that Tommy had left on the kitchen table. Now she couldn't get her mind free of what was so important that Steve had to make this latest impromptu trip to Queens. All this weekly running back and forth downstate since his Aunt Clara's death just had to stop. She did understand what the commitment to his family meant to him. Of course she understood. She wanted to help out her mother-in-law, and she'd done as much as she could for Mary Jane, but it was all too much. They just had to move on.

Steve's Aunt Clara had never married, but Helen believed that Clara had loved, and loved deeply, just one person throughout her entire adult life. That person was Laura Ward, her companion, who for many years had been the managing editor of "American Spectrum Magazine".

From the time Tommy could talk he called Laura "Auntie Lar," and over the years the two aunts were *Captain Tommy's Adventure Guides* for one fun week every summer. They introduced him to the Empire State Building, Radio City Music Hall, the Museum of American Folk Art, and Tai food in Manhattan before he was six, and there were multiple excursions to the Bronx Zoo. In October of 1987 Clara and Laura had taken Tommy on the train from New York to Washington to see the "names quilts", the Aids memorial display of quilts that friends and families of the victims of the disease had lovingly spread out all over the National Mall. The following spring Laura had passed away in Clara's arms. It wasn't long thereafter that more crushing news arrived when they learned that Aunt Clara had been diagnosed with terminal cancer.

Mary Jane was by then a retired widow, and although Clara had arranged for in-home nursing care for herself, Helen's mother-in-law wanted nothing more than to help take care of her sister. What was there to think over? After all, as she protested to Steve, Clara was her only sibling. Within days of learning of the seriousness of the progression of the cancer, Mary Jane had packed up one large suitcase and closed up her Saratoga house. Steve had driven her to Queens. After Clara passed, Mary Jane, as Administrator of her sister's will and closest relative, knew that she would have to stay on for a while longer.

Early into the cleanout process Mary Jane had made an amazing discovery. In a brown strongbox tucked far under Clara's bed she'd found a note and the key to a weather controlled storage room located on the other side of the borough near the two aunts' first apartment together. What was discovered at the storage facility made her mother-in-law gasp—thirty-eight taped boxes containing stacks upon stacks of genealogical research files representing several centuries of the Beekman Family as well as others.

Helen's mother-in-law was delighted to learn that her maiden name could be traced all the way back to one Wilhelmus Beekman who had sailed from Holland to New York City, then called New Amsterdam, in the year 1647. As it turned out, Steve's aunt had discovered ancestral links to other Colonial families as well. Clara had left her sister, Steve, and Tommy a fascinating legacy. Mary Jane was completely captivated, and her stay in Queens had stretched from weeks to months.

Helen and Steve had offered their help, but Mary Jane's insistence that they read every single document was a daunting task given the fact that she and Steve both still had demanding jobs. Not that the Beekman family legacy needed further sorting. Clara had expertly cataloged every piece of paper. But Steve's mother was hungry for the duty since genealogy had been a passion that she and Clara had shared since they were girls. As Helen came to understand, so had the two sisters' mother and grandmother as well.

Helen thought that putting together those ancestral trees was mind boggling, but she did admit that when they'd visited Queens throughout the years, they all enjoyed listening to Aunt Clara talk about growing up. Clara, a professional photographer whose expertise was Old Dutch architecture, had past photos of majestic elm trees, horse drawn wagons, and extinct Albany neighborhoods. Steve and Tommy never seemed to tire of looking through her scrap books while Auntie Lar cooked.

Watching the decline of a beautiful extension of their family had been painful beyond words, and after Clara's death, in the beginning, Helen had thought that Mary Jane's journey back through time was facilitating a sense of healing and closure. She felt that for a while it had helped all of them as they tried to fill the hole that had been left in their lives. Now though, Helen was feeling like a third wheel rolling down Carey lane.

What the heck *did* Steve say on the phone? When she had spoken with her mother-in-law last week, it seemed as if Mary Jane was looking forward to returning home. Yet when she discussed things with Steve two nights ago on the phone he gave the impression that closing up Clara's apartment was still weeks off, and he'd gone ahead and paid the rents on Clara's place and the storage unit for another month. He would have to continue to lend his support.

She'd said okay. What else could she say? Steve was his mother's sole administrative as well as emotional support. Helen had gotten that. She'd said as much to him when they had argued about him never being home. No wonder her blood pressure rocketed. Her nerves were shot, and she hated feeling so resentful all the time. She didn't sleep nights, and even the decaf coffee wasn't helping any.

She'd suggested that they move Clara's roomful of boxes into a nearby storage shed complex in Clifton Park just to make life easier on all of them, but it didn't look like her suggestion was going to come to fruition in the near future. When she had asked him if he was worried that they would say something to him at work about all the time he'd been taking off, to her surprise Steve had become very irritated, upset that she would propose such an idea. "End of discussion!" he'd yelled.

For a third time, Helen wiped off the kitchen counter. Although she'd understood, she wished that her mother-in-law had never put them in this position. Earlier that morning, annoyed as she worried whether they would be able to make it in time for Chris Mann's Sunday afternoon birthday party, Helen thought that the sorting and disposal in Queens had gone on long enough.

It was now dark and they'd missed Chris's party. Again Helen pressed her memory. She thought Steve had said when he called Friday night that it was his plan to spend one extra night and be on the road this morning for the three-hour drive back. But if he had gotten going by 5 am, as he had said he would to beat the traffic, he was hours late. Thoughts of a terrible accident stirred in her mind. Nervously she began thumbing through their telephone book looking for the emergency number for the State Police. After writing it down on a pad she picked up the receiver, about to dial when she heard Steve swing onto their gravel driveway. Mentally spent, she replaced the receiver back on the wall and returned to the kitchen to wait for him to come through the door. Obviously, something more had happened in Queens. She hoped it wasn't the discovery of yet another storage bin.

CHAPTER 24

Steve's car keys landed hard on the table. "Sorry I'm so late, Babe."

"Where the hell have you been?!" Helen yelled hysterically. "I've been crazy with worry! Apparently you forgot all about Chris's birthday party this afternoon. You're damn lucky you showed up this second because I was about to call the troopers!"

"Chris's birthday? I'm sorry, but honest, I didn't remember about any birthday party. Listen, something amazing happened to me on the way home."

Taking in a deep breath, Helen lowered her voice while Steve went to the refrigerator. "All this has to stop, Steve. I need you to tell me what's going on."

Steve sipped his beer, observing her pensively. "I actually saw one! After twenty years of reading about them and hardly believing other people telling about sightings, I saw one!"

Helen sank into a chair and held her head in her hands. Talking to him was absolutely useless. Where was Steve? Looking up into his flashing dark eyes her heart ached. Dear God, where was the man she had shared the better part of her life with? She really wasn't interested in whatever his excuse was this time, but words trickled out anyway, "Saw what?"

"A UFO! A real one!!"

"How's your mother?" Helen asked dully.

"She's fine. We made headway together this time around. She'll be wrapping it all up soon. Helen, didn't you hear what I just said? I saw..."

"I heard you Steve, but really...give me a break."

"I'm serious, Helen. It appeared out of the dusk, and it moved straight toward me as if the alien pilot was trying to communicate!"

Helen sighed and readied herself for another of her husband's "visions". He'd had them before but never about a spaceship. For the past year he'd been fixated on the idea of reincarnation, and Helen thought that even his level-headed mother was buying into this latest craziness. That nonsense had begun when he'd found an old rusty bayonet out in their barn. His obsession with the possibility that he was a reborn soldier from the French and Indian War was disturbing enough, but this was something else.

"Okay, tell me about it," she said, watching him posture himself while he obviously tried to figure out what would win her over to this latest delusion.

Finishing the last of his Bud, he reiterated, "I really can't believe it!"

"Just sit down and tell me!"

Steve pulled out the chair across the table. "Well, the Thruway was more crowded than usual, so I got off down near Catskill to take that small road that comes north over the mountain. We've come home that way before. There's never that much traffic there, and besides, I thought it would be a more peaceful ride. I figured that route would help me unwind."

"Yes, I know the one."

"I came over the crest of the hill just before you get to the part of the road that starts up the mountain. You know the spot where the farmer's roadside stand sits. It's where we bought the bushel of apples last month." Steve paused waiting for affirmation that his audience was attentive.

"I know the spot you're talking about, Steve."

Pausing again, "By the way, where's Tommy?"

"Tommy isn't home. As far as I know he's still up at one of his friend's camps at Saratoga Lake helping them get their boat out of the water for the season. He called a couple hours ago".

"I think I'll have a second beer," Steve replied, noticeably disappointed. "That is, if you don't mind?"

"Have at it."

Ignoring his wife's sarcasm, Steve popped the tab. "Well, just off to the right there is a wheat field with a long row of fruit trees on the other side of it. Now, before you think me nuts, hear me out. The thing was just above the top of those trees, just hovering like a wasp around its nest. There it was! Big and silvery and not moving."

"Big and silvery and not moving," Helen chanted hollowly. "Sounds like a scene out of an old Sci-Fi movie."

"Yes, that's right, dear. It was not moving at all, and it had a broad rim around the edge of it with bright colors that kept changing from green to blue and then back again. That's when I saw them, and they were looking at me!"

"Oh God Steve, come on! Now you're really pushing the envelope." Helen rose angrily. "I'm going to dry these few cups, and then I'm going to take a shower."

Steve stood and moved closer, pulling the dishtowel from her hands. "Please believe me. I know what you must think, but I'm telling you I saw it. In fact, I looked at the thing for a long, long time. I don't know how much time went by as I stood there. I didn't move. And it still didn't move either. I looked around to see if there were any other cars or anyone over by the apple stand, but the place was closed up and there wasn't a soul in sight. I figured I'd need a witness because I was sure nobody would believe me, but I'd hoped that you would."

"I'd like to believe you," Helen replied genuinely. "What can I say but that sometimes we think we see something but we don't? Sometimes you might just have an image stuck in your brain. You've had so much pressure on you lately at work and with all this going on down there with your mom. Maybe it's real to you, but it's not real."

Steve was deaf to Helen's explanation. "I figured they were watching me, so I waved. Yeah! I waved. Oh, I can see in your eyes that you think I've lost it, and I suppose if I were you I would think this a silly bunch of malarkey, but it's the truth. Anyway, I waved, and all of a sudden the colors that were spinning around the rim started to change from blue and green to a kind of light pink, and then suddenly it went to red and it started to move toward me very slowly. I couldn't move, Helen..." Steve was breathless.

"That would be understandable," Helen murmured, sighing sadly.

After taking another sip of beer, Steve continued. "No—you didn't hear me. I mean I *really could not* move. I was scared stiff and I wanted to jump back into the car and get the hell out of there, but I just couldn't move. I remember thinking that I had left the engine running in the car, but I didn't hear it anymore. I would have left the car and run down the road, but there I was frozen in place with this silvery space ship over my head and moving toward me. I tell you, I was dying a thousand deaths. Look at my hair. Is there any sudden change to gray?"

"No Steve, I don't see any gray." Helen was wondering who she could call that might be able to help her husband. Chris's cousin worked at the Psychiatric Unit at Saratoga Hospital. Maybe she'd call her.

Steve said, "I'm amazed that you don't. Well, it kept coming very slowly until it was about thirty feet away from me, and then it stopped again. It sure was darn big, and it was almost right over me! Then a shaft of greenish light came out from the bottom of it straight down to the ground, and then it disappeared."

Helen waited in silence for the rest of the story, half of the time daydreaming of a time long ago when they used to picnic by Logan's Pond, lying on their blanket, and taking in the night sky filled with stars. "That's it? It disappeared?"

"That's it." Steve replied.

"Nothing else happened?"

"That's it. The thing, whatever it was, left. It didn't fly away. It just disappeared like someone turned off a light, and then I remember hearing the car engine start running again. I got back into the car and drove here. I will remember that experience as long as I live."

Helen shook her head incredulously. "If that had been me, I would have driven straight to a convenience store or someplace and gotten the number for the State Police barracks; called them about what I'd seen. Why didn't you report this? What I'm saying is that it's hard to believe that you just got into the car and headed home."

Steve was slightly calmer now, but unmistakably drained. "Listen Helen, all a report to the cops would have done is to hold me up to ridicule. I don't want you to repeat this to anyone else; not Chris or any of your friends, Tommy, your mother, or anyone. Understand?"

Helen's eyes narrowed. "Yes, I understand all right, but if you didn't go to the police right after all this, where did you go? Dusk was two hours ago. Where have you been?"

Steve appeared dumbfounded. "What do you mean where have I been? I left my mother's house at about eight this morning, and except for that fifteen or twenty minute stop up there on the mountain side, I came straight home. So what are you talking...?" Steve's eyes drifted up to the clock behind his wife. "Holy shit!"

"That's right. Holy shit. Didn't you notice that it's been dark for hours?"

There was a long hesitation before Steve spoke. He began to pace nervously.

"I know—!"

"Know what?"

"Well, that must be it!"

Helen's lips tightened. "What must be it?"

"If you figure me leaving Queens later than I'd planned, at eight this morning," Steve reflected, "and then, say, three hours travel, even with the heavy traffic, and let's give a half hour watching the UFO, I should have been here before noon! That means there is about six hours missing. Six hours!"

"Seems that way," Helen responded vaguely.

"Don't you see? I don't know where I was for all that time. It's a classic case of alien abduction! I've read about it a hundred times!"

Helen quickly caught a tear. "Please don't say anymore. Don't insult me this way. Let's just get it all out in the open. You're having an affair. Right?"

"No, honey, I'm no cheater." He tried to approach her.

Helen stepped back from him. "Don't!"

"Now look, good grief, it must be that they had me for six hours! What could they have done to me? All the reports I've ever read tell about grotesque physical examinations, and people being marked in different ways. You don't suppose that they—?" Steve turned abruptly and ran from the kitchen toward the stairs.

"Where are you going!?"

Answering on the run, he called back, "I have to get these clothes off and look myself over to see if there are any marks on my body. That would be proof. You would have to believe me then."

Helen let out a long, deep sigh and quickly moved toward the stairs to follow. Despite her disgust with his ridiculous story she was still interested to see how long he would go on with the charade. Reaching the top step, she noticed that Steve had already torn off his shirt and was standing half naked before the full length mirror in their bedroom.

"Oh, they did something terrible to me. God only knows what sort of instruments they used. Look at me! Take a look at these scratches back here! I'm marked! I probably even have radiation poisoning! I read about that, too!"

Helen sat on the bed observing the scratches. The back of his neck was marked up, all right. She made no comment, but she felt nauseous. Either another woman had made those scratches or an alien had truly gotten hold of Steve. Either way, her life was going down the drain.

Moaning painfully, Steve whined, "Look at these bruises on my neck. That must be where they clamped me down. I must have put up a tough fight, but I don't remember any bit of it. My mind is a complete blank. How can they do this kind of thing and the victim doesn't know anything?" Stepping closer to the mirror he tried to see up into his nostrils.

"What are you doing now?"

"Checking to see if anything was inserted into my nose."

"What are you talking about?"

"Implants, Helen. Implants!"

"Through your nose? Be real!" Helen thought that if she was

watching someone else other than Steve in this scenario she would probably not be able to control her laughter, but, this was Steve.

Steve glanced at her over his shoulder. "Look, Helen, I've been abducted and subjected to who knows what humiliation and torture, probably had my body violated six ways from Sunday, and you sit there making stupid comments."

"You are right, Steve, this is no joking matter. If you're telling me you seriously believe that you've been abused by aliens then we need to get you some help. You're sick."

Steve's voice was filled with hostility. "I would hope to get just a little moral support from my own wife!"

Softly, Helen said, "Don't raise your voice to me. From day one I've supported you and you know I have. I've listened when you've told me you feel as if you're living somebody else's life. I've listened when you say that you've seen a man murdered out back in our barn. You scare me, Steve, but I'll hang in with you if you promise that you will talk to someone about all of this, because I just can't handle it all by myself anymore. You need professional help." Helen watched as he sat on the side of their bed and began to weep. She went to him and put her arms around him. Now, she thought. Now it will come out. He'll confess that he's been unfaithful. She didn't know how she'd take it.

Composing himself, Steve said, "I told you, keep all this to yourself. If I want to talk to somebody I'll take care of it. What could the police do about it even if they gave me the benefit of the doubt? The press would pick it up sure as hell, and I'd be a laughing stock in this town." Steve stood up and he removed his slacks and briefs, carefully scanning his lower body. There were no other marks or scratches. Nothing.

Helen looked away as he picked up his clothing and threw them into their hamper. There would be no confession tonight. Of course, there was no flying saucer, but it was apparent that something had happened to him. Maybe he had thought he'd seen something in the sky, pulled the car over, gotten out, fell and hit his head and just didn't remember anything. But then there would be something on his head—a bruise, or blood—not scratches near his neck. This was nuts. What was she thinking? He was seeing someone and that was that. She'd have to accept it or kick him out. She didn't want to kick him out. If only he'd just tell her the goddamn truth.

CHAPTER 25

A Plan for Union, Summer 1754

Governor James De Lancey had accepted the orders of London's Lords of Trade to call together delegates of all British North American colonies who interacted with the Iroquois to meet at Albany for an Indian Conference. The most anticipated meeting of all time in America was scheduled to begin at Albany, the fourteenth day of June.

The very day Cornelius learned of the meeting date, he wrote to his brother, William, at Albany asking him if he would be able to provide accommodations for him and his German manservant during the weeks the conference would be in session. Janet would stay at the farm, preferring not to expose their young children to what she called, "the wicked festive calamity of drunken Indians and British soldiers."

Cornelius did not mind his wife preferring to stay at home with the children, however, before leaving for Albany he must find a woman to stay with her. Janet had been acting strangely for quite some time. Always before she had been an opinionated, talkative woman, but after the loss of their last child the previous summer, his wife had turned inward and hardly spoke to him or anyone else. Many nights he would awaken and find her out of their bed standing by the window staring up at the moon. He was also perplexed by her unexplainable fixation with their servants' cemetery down behind the house. Often she took their young children, Catherine and William, with her to the graves. There spreading her quilt, they would eat fresh wheat bread with her fruit preserves while 'visiting' Dinah and Willie and their Tom who were buried there.

Catherine had told her father that her mama talked to Dinah, and that Mama heard Dinah talk back to her. Mama would ask, did she not hear Dinah? Catherine would reply that she did not hear any other voice. Janet had told the children that they should not be frightened, but they were. After learning of this, Cornelius forbade Janet to take the children to the graves anymore.

Seeing that Janet was not right in her mind, Cornelius asked his sister, Engeltie, to come stay with them. He would be grateful if she would stay at the farm for good. Engeltie said yes and she would come by the end of May. Cornelius remembered that the meaning of the name Engeltie, his mother had once said, was 'angel'. He believed the name fitting. Now he felt comfortable leaving his home and family for the upcoming meeting in Albany.

It pleased him that the place of his birth and where he had grown to manhood would host the auspicious affair. With the King's Colors cornering a field of red, the British Red Ensign had flown dominantly over Albany since 1707. Good Queen Anne had designed the flag, but it would be the implanted Albany Dutch who would host the historically auspicious occasion during the summer! How those now gone—his father, and aye, old Schuyler; the Iroquois' Quidor himself—would have loved to see such a meeting of so many important English subjects converge where the predominant language spoken was still Dutch.

When his brother-in-law, John Yates, a prominent Greenbush smithy with stables in Albany, visited in early May, Cornelius had learned more of the plans for thé conference. Several distinguished representatives from each colony were requested and expected to attend: from Massachusetts, New Jersey, Pennsylvania, Maryland, Virginia, New Hampshire, and, of course, New York. Yet two of the delegates John had mentioned stood out from all the rest. One was the noteworthy Pennsylvania representative, Benjamin Franklin of

Philadelphia, and the other, the thirty-five year old Benjamin Tasker of Maryland.

As a horseman, Tasker especially interested Cornelius since Tasker owned *Selima,* the most celebrated mare in the British colonies. Tasker and his English horse had gained notoriety when a few years ago *Selima* won an astonishing purse of 2,500 gold coins. Edward Collins, Cornelius's longtime friend, had said he might be able to arrange a meeting for him with Tasker, and Cornelius was delighted by the prospect since he and his sons had in mind to begin breeding horses themselves.

This would be the first time Benjamin Franklin would visit Albany, and Cornelius hoped to at least catch a glimpse of him. An introduction and a few words would be unlikely, of course, but he would not rule out the possibility. Albany was not so big as New York, Boston or Philadelphia, and his brother, William, was well connected within the city. So an introduction might be possible. In his nearly fifty years Cornelius had seen many improbable possibilities become reality.

Last year, in addition to a copy of Franklin's *Poor Richard's Almanac,* his Manhattan cousin, John Waldron, had loaned William several other of Franklin's published books on the various Indian treaties that had been made between the Iroquois and Pennsylvania, Maryland and Virginia. These were original eyewitness accounts by an Indian interpreter named Weiser. With William's Albany masonry business booming and his duties as assistant alderman, he had little time for further reading and had passed on Franklin's publications to Cornelius. Throughout winter's lull, in keeping with the custom of his own father, Cornelius had read every word to his wife and elder children. Janet rarely sat for the reading of the Indian accounts, but while Cornelius paid attention to the weather predictions, she particularly enjoyed Franklin's *Almanac* poems and had even managed a smile when Cornelius read the quote 'A house without woman and Fire-light, is like a body without soul or sprite.'

Yet, in his mind's eye, the most interesting of all he had read was the publication describing the events surrounding last summer's

Carlisle Treaty. Franklin had been appointed by his government as a commissioner to sit at the Indian council fire during the Carlisle meeting. According to Franklin's account, it was the first time he had officially participated in a meeting within the Ohio country, and he had listened to the complaints the Indians had made. After reading these passages Cornelius had begun to see Benjamin Franklin much akin to the ambitious William Johnson. The two had keen minds and a talent for negotiating with the Indians. Both men would attend the Albany conference. It would be interesting to hear their ideas.

In addition to listening to the worthy speeches of delegates and, God willing, meeting Franklin and Tasker, Cornelius also hoped to discover what plans were at hand for his country, especially those with respect to the strengthening of the forts near to his farm. After all, the main purpose for the conference, as he understood it, was to satisfy the concerns of the Iroquois, and everyone anticipated that a good plan for building more forts would be forthcoming. From neighboring Schaghticoke Indians he had already learned that the enemy French were building new forts everywhere. His Native friends had made him uncomfortable when they complained to him that the English were weak. No doubt the peaceable Schaghticoke spoke for all the Six Nations when they grumbled that they were losing respect for the English King and his delegations, which had promised them protection but declined to build strong forts.

Cornelius yearned to hear good news while at Albany. It seemed to him his country was falling apart. If provincials like him could not agree amongst themselves and were not united with the Six Nations, surely they were all at risk of domination by the clever French. Enslavement by the French Catholics was a terrible thought, but might not be the worst of their fears, if rumors could be believed. The French and their supporters went about the countryside whispering promises to all held within servitude, be they African slaves or European immigrants bound under contract. All would be freed once the French were victorious, or so they boasted. A good portion of the populace of his country were men, women and children held in servitude. Cornelius wondered how many of them had heard this outrageous French promise. Had his own? He wondered if Herman had taken their lies to heart. He imagined it could be so. Better to keep the servant close where he could keep an eye on him.

During the winter months as Cornelius read Franklin's books, he continued to worry about the legacy he and his countrymen would leave to their children and the children that followed them. What would representatives living beyond New York have to say about the possible new laws for regulating all Indian trade? How would he and neighboring farmers be affected should new restrictions be put into place? And what of this talk of a union of colonies to make a better resistance to the French? Did he want outsiders meddling in his business? As a prosperous farmer and fourth generation American, he wished he could be a part of all this discourse.

Early in June Cornelius pulled out the old Spanish leather trunk. Tradition was that the small trunk had once belonged to Grandfather's father, Resolved Waldron, and had come with him from Holland on the ship *Princess* when Grandfather William was just a boy. Cornelius's elder brother, William, had inherited the Waldron family Bible from father, as was his birth right, but, following their mother's death, to him had come the trunk.

Cornelius instructed Herman to pack it with his good Sabbath clothes—his finely sewn, white linen shirt with leather laces, breeches, and his whale-boned, buttoned, brown waistcoat. To these pieces of proper gentlemanly attire was added a neck cloth that terminated with intricate lace, stockings, and finally the new brown frock coat Janet had made him for the occasion of this special trip. Dressed in his everyday travel clothing, Cornelius, accompanied by Herman, left his wife, children, and his sister, Engeltie, behind at the farm.

They arrived at Albany on June the tenth only to discover that the City was already overflowing with foreigners, many of them delegates invited to participate in the conference. The formal meetings, Cornelius learned, were to be held at Stadt Huys, the Albany Courthouse down by the edge of the river. However, every resident anticipated an overflow of discussions and speeches that undoubtedly would be held within the taverns and openly on the streets. As he had suspected, the talk of a new and improved Indian agreement was on the lips of every man in the City.

That first night he made his way around a dozen pallets strewn throughout his brother's dwelling that were rented to sleeping travelers. Finally he had no option but to share an uncomfortable bed with two of his nephews who snored more loudly than he. As it turned out, everyone's patience within William's household was tried because both Indians and colonial representatives were delayed in their arrival, and the official news was that the conference would not get started now until June the nineteenth.

Cornelius's discomfort was soon offset by the spectacular sights and sounds he took in during the intervening days and nights. Hundreds of campfires could be seen lining both the east and west side of the great North River near Albany. According to William, the fires burned northward along the river all the way to the grand Schuyler house and southward of Albany to their sister Catherine and Henry Van Wie's place. Sloops navigated most carefully as boatmen hired to transport supplies as well as passengers in their smaller, flat-bottomed bateaux boats could barely keep up with the demand.

Since early June, delegates along with their well-dressed servants had been arriving in Albany from as far north as New Hampshire and as far south as Maryland. Benjamin Tasker had arrived safely from Maryland with another delegate, Abraham Barnes. When someone mentioned that one of them made his home at St. Mary's County, Cornelius remembered the stories that his father had told to him about Resolved Waldron, who on orders of Peter Stuyvesant had gone to survey boundaries and dined with the famous Phillip Calvert at St. Mary's City. Recalling his father's tales of old, Cornelius wondered what kind of a man represented Maryland today? Resolved's tale would make a good start for lively discourse with Mr. Tasker.

Most understood that the Lords of Trade greatly desired to make one unified agreement in the King's name with the Iroquois to secure a strong, united front against the French. Such an agreement could come none too soon. War with the French had not been formally declared, yet with every passing day it was more apparent that war was in the wind. This was especially true now that the Virginia militia had engaged in a serious skirmish with the French, killing a French officer.

The fight had occurred within the rich western lands owned by Virginia's Ohio Company where during February a British garrison had built a fort that had been named Fort Prince George. Because France disputed any English rights to the Ohio lands, the British fort did not stand for long. Early in the spring, the French had arrived with a great force of men and forced the small English garrison to leave. They then tore down Fort Prince George and built their Fort Duquesne.

After a week in Albany news came that at the last moment Connecticut had also been invited and their delegates were in the city. New Jersey, most shockingly, had refused to attend. And Virginia had also sent regrets, claiming that they were more interested in meeting with the southern Indians in another month or two. They had little interest in spending money courting the northern Iroquois. This would be an obstacle to the success of the conference. Should the French invade New York who would defend another man's homeland when every colony has their own wants and desires?"

One evening while dining at a local tavern, William and Cornelius shared thoughts about the Virginians. William spouted, "What a foolish, pompous decision Virginia has made in deciding not to attend the Albany meeting. Why, the name Seneca, one of the Iroquois nations, means 'Keepers of the Western Gate', and that gate stands between the French and the northern colonies"

"And, Virginia's borders are...are immediately south," Cornelius added. "The French could...could choose to go south with nothing to hinder them crossing into Virginia."

"They should be here!" William hit the table with his fists. "Just consider the disastrous battle that occurred recently within the Ohio country."

Cornelius agreed. "That skirmish occurred at a place called Jumonville Glen did it not?"

"Yes. The place is near the newly built French Fort Duquesne, I hear. Talk is that the Virginia Governor had sent a young, inexperienced officer, Lieutenant Colonel George Washington by name, out to the wilderness with a small party of Virginia militia. Washington's mission was supposed to be one of diplomacy...to ask the French to leave Fort Duquesne." William grinned, shook his head and then added curtly, "Such a mission was ridiculous. The French had already torn down our British fort and built their own in that place. They consider that land to be French territory. Why would they leave?"

Cornelius sighed disgustedly. "Instead, young Colonel Washington along with some...some Mingo warriors led by a chief called Half King attacked thirty or more Canada French. I think the absence of the Virginians from this conference has more to do with their pro...problem with western Indians allied with the Iroquois than with any future meeting with the Indians in the south."

Leaning closer, William whispered, "After this most recent incident, surely we must strengthen our defenses hereabouts. The Virginians have stripped away the last hope of negotiation."

Cornelius agreed with his brother. *Good leadership is difficult to find these days.*

Delegates continued to arrive, and now Rhode Island men stayed where Virginians were originally anticipated to be quartered. Already many Albany households were hosting one or two representatives, and the barracks capable of quartering two hundred fifty British regulars were overflowing with foreign guests.

William complained that even though he had been contacted about plans to build several new barracks to house over seven hundred, the money was not there. He supposed it would be another year before construction might begin. Should war come, two hundred men would make for feeble protection. In the meanwhile, during the conference, ten more British regulars were being housed in his own cellar kitchen along with his three Negro servants. Most of the soldiers would remain, he suspected, until the new barracks were built.

Later, William grumbled to Cornelius, "My wife and daughters howl for mercy, and I do not blame them. This situation is terrible. I wish to God this conference be over and done with. We await several other Indian tribes to arrive. At least the morning meetings have begun. The delegates filled Mr. Stevenson's home yesterday. He hosts the Massachusetts delegates as you know. Have you heard anything about the discussions?"

"No," Cornelius answered. "I just know what the Al…Albanians are saying."

"Everyone wishes that all the discussions would get on as planned, but our Indian neighbors are the allies we need."

When not seated for daily morning meetings scheduled throughout various houses within the City of Albany, the amicable Benjamin Franklin was often seen out and about the streets. He greeted workmen as he passed by, and later within taverns he held court, often with his arm around the shoulder of one tradesman or another.

William, as well as his son-in-law, Arent Van Deusen, had experienced Mr. Franklin's good humor whilst he jested with them as they lay brick for a new house on Pearl Street. Every laborer liked the Pennsylvania representative because he did not hold himself above them, all high and mighty. The great man always introduced himself humbly and simply as Franklin the Printer, which put both William and Cornelius in mind of another who had once been in the printing trade. Their great-grandfather Resolved Waldron was at one time a printer with his brother in Holland before coming over during the days of New Amsterdam Dutch rule under Stuyvesant.

Still, during the past week the common people of Albany had heard some strange rumors about Mr. Franklin's foolish proposal for a union of colonies and proprietorships. Although there was strength in a unity such as the Iroquois had formed, how could

New York be united with the Catholics of Maryland or the greedy Virginians who claimed unlawful trading rights with the Indians to the west? Meetings to be held in faraway Philadelphia and the appointment of a President General, possibly from another colony, along with a grand council answerable only to the English crown, were not appealing.

New York had problems enough with the French threats of invasion right here in their own countryside. Most thought that visiting representatives should stick to what they had been called to Albany to do, and that was to smoke the pipe with the Iroquois, and, as good English subjects, make the English Lords of Trade in London happy with whatever agreements they came up with.

CHAPTER 26

Albany, July 1754

Two miles south of Albany, at Captain Henry Van Wie's landing, eight jubilant passengers from New York City, bound for the Indian conference at Albany, were obliged to disembark Captain Van Wie's sloop while they waited for full tide. Because of sandbars located in the upper portion of the North River, going on was dubious in the vessel laden with travelers and supplies. They'd have to wait for the river to rise so that the shoals of the 'over-slough' could be cleared. The stopover was expected, and nobody seemed to mind the opportunity to stretch their legs and enjoy a refreshing cool drink.

A cheerful mulatto dressed in brown breeches and pale blue silk shirt greeted them politely at the shoreline. Introducing himself as Andre, he led the visitors up the stone steps to the Captain's tavern where another of Van Wie's servants, a dark young woman no more than fifteen and clad in a starched white apron, stood ready at the door to seat all at a long common table laden with fruits and cheeses.

Later, at high tide, Andre assisted while the passengers re-boarded the sloop. The tall, heavyset and balding Captain Van Wie and his short, portly wife, exuberant in her finest, welcomed all aboard.

Hours later, the happy boisterous group, who by now had enjoyed several glasses of Mrs. Van Wie's tasty secret-recipe— a fruited rum punch—climbed precariously into a dinghy and were rowed to Albany's wharf.

One name was on everyone's lips—King Hendrick, the Mohawk chief. King Hendrick was a longtime friend to both the Dutch and the English, the sole survivor of the four Iroquois who had visited London in 1710 and with whom a captivated Queen Anne had held several audiences. Not long ago, he had again visited London, this time to confer with King George. The great Hendrick's presence would be a sight not to be missed.

Other than the Captain and his wife, none of the passengers who'd sailed up river with them had ever laid eyes on the famous American King. One of the ladies asked if it be true that in olden times before being baptized by a good Dutch minister, the King had scalped many French as well as enemy savages, some being women and children. It was her understanding that the Mohawks were rumored to have gnawed on the bones of their enemies.

Mrs. Van Wie gave no reply but smiled and offered the good woman another glass of punch.

William and Cornelius Waldron, along with their sister, Catherine, and her husband, Captain Henry, all perspired profusely as they stood in front of Lieutenant Governor James De Lancey's prominent two-story home. The four, along with Catherine's servant woman, were part of an enormous crowd that continued to gather and grow around the governor's front stoop. Soon there would not be space enough for another spectator to blend in with British dignitaries, local political notables, their wives and servants, Indians of various tribes, and, of course, the twenty-four Colonial delegates. Catherine Van Wie hated crowds and complained she did not think she could stand in the heat for much longer. Her husband ignored her, consumed with the historic spectacle in front of him. In all his life Henry Van Wie had never seen anything like this.

There were more than two hundred Indians—a colorful assemblage of men, women and children—sitting proudly erect upon ten rows of white pine benches constructed by Albany carpenters for the sole purpose of this day. Not one of them spoke a word as they faced the energized group of colonial delegates seated across from them on chairs that had been hastily drawn out of nearby houses for the purpose of their comfort during these, the final speeches of the conference.

Many important issues, including a plan for unification of all the British colonies, had arisen throughout the beginning weeks. However, for most present, King Hendrick's words today would be the high point of this convention meant to solidify the bond between the Iroquois and the settlers. The staunch old King, the Indian peacemaker who'd long ago given some of his own lands to help settle hundreds of German refugees throughout New York, was expected to implore unification. It was the ninth day of July. Tomorrow the King, along with his people, would return home to their respective villages.

Hendrick had been in Albany for weeks, having arrived in June with his good friend, William Johnson. Thereafter, every morning and every afternoon, delegates and Indians, most days walking to and fro with Johnson, could be seen attending meetings at various places around the city. Many of the gatherings had been held at the State House where Benjamin Franklin had presented his list of points—or 'hints' as he called them—to be considered for the unifi-cation of the British colonies. Several times the distinguished Phila-delphian had met with King Hendrick since the union that he had put forth was clearly modeled after the Iroquois Confederacy.

Today, among the throngs of gawking onlookers were many Ne-groes as well as poorer whites recognizable as those in servitude. Not long after Waldron and Van Wie arrived, Cornelius had noticed that his Herman stood a few hundred feet apart from them under the shade of an elm tree with two of his brother William's servants. Only yesterday, William had been pleased to say that Herman had gotten on quite well with his workers during these past weeks, and Cornelius had been happy to hear so, but watching them now, some-thing made Cornelius uneasy. He thought of Janet and her foreboding dreams and how she'd kissed him goodbye. She had begged him to watch for what he could not see.

It was not unusual to see Albany's people of servitude freely roaming the streets. Cornelius understood this. A servant who was not trustworthy, of course, was not worth his keep. When Herman had been told that he would be working with William's workmen while in Albany, his man was eager to do so, especially when learning he would be paid for his labor and could keep most of his earnings. Thus far, it appeared to be a good arrangement. Now Cornelius began to wonder.

Cornelius tried to shake off his dismal thoughts. He would trust in his brother's judgement. Being allowed to come and go freely did not make a man free, but allowing a restricted amount of independence for one's servant did help keep the servant in a better frame of mind. Oppression breeds revolt. That had been proven multiple times in Manhattan.

Still, Cornelius was surprised and somewhat concerned to see Herman today loitering under the elm, recalling that he had left for work at sunrise with William's overseer just as he had done every morning since they had arrived in Albany. Why was he over there and not at work?

As Cornelius dwelled upon Herman, a young Quaker lawyer who'd accompanied Benjamin Franklin from Pennsylvania, one Mr. Chew, offered Mrs.Van Wie his chair, and a much relieved Catherine sank gratefully into it. However, her servant continued to fan her mistress's face and bosom, at the speed of a hovering humming bird.

Following Cornelius's quizzical gaze, William quickly offered an explanation about Herman. "Rest your mind. I instructed each of my foremen to give leave to all my workers that they would come to this remarkable display. The way I see it, despite a man's position, we are all citizens together here. And surely you recognize my overseer, Jacob, over yonder? He reminds me of Henry when he was that age."

Overhearing, Captain Henry sighted Jacob and grinned. "I do not see the resemblance, but God help Jacob if he fancies a Waldron girl!"

"Amen!" William replied, turning back to Cornelius, "I instructed Jacob that all his men should have beer and roasted meats after the speeches are concluded. I felt such was a just reward. The crew along with your German have done the work of a pair of oxen. The Douw house is ahead of schedule. I am well pleased!"

"Happy to hear it be so," Cornelius replied, surprised by his usually tight-fisted brother's generosity.

William furrowed his brow. "I did not mean to go over your head. Perhaps I should have consulted with you about Herman, but since your man worked so satisfactorily under my overseer, and Jacob, too, praised him, I..."

But Cornelius hardly heard his brother. He was mesmerized watching Herman interact with the men beside him. "He laughs?"

Putting one arm around Cornelius's shoulders, William grinned. "Yes, I see. I, too, have never seen your man laugh. Perhaps he smells the smoking pig. Who is not uplifted by the aroma of a roasting meat? Come now. This is a day to rejoice so let us be light of heart. Stop worrying!"

Cornelius sighed. As eager as he had been to come to Albany for the conference, he was just as ready to return to his homestead, sleep comfortably in his own bed, and enjoy the comfort of his wife's plump, freckled arms wrapped solidly around him. He thought of Janet more than he would have imagined he would have, and this morning he had stopped by Harme Gansevoort's wondrous store on Market Street where he had purchased a piece of fine, light-blue ribbon, fresh in from London. The color would go well in her hair, and he knew that she would be delighted knowing the gift came from Gansevoort's. He could very well expect a loving welcome when he returned home.

"Look there," William said, "King Hendrick has arrived with his followers." Craning his neck to see them better, William added, "And there is William Johnson with his secretary, Wraxall."

Cornelius nodded, "Ah, when the Crown's Secretary of Indian Affairs appears, that must be the signal to everyone that the official time has finally come for final ceremonies to get underway."

Flanked by Johnson and Wraxall, the prestigious King approached with his equally impressive Native assemblage of chiefs following close behind. Cornelius heard the upsweep of combined awe and exaltation gathering momentum from every direction. It was obvious to all that the Native American King had come ready to shore up negotiations.

The Mohawk leader was dressed so magnificently that he outshone everyone present. Nearly hairless, with golden hoops wound tight around one ear, his neck covered with several layers of glistening plated silver, he wore the green satin coat fringed in gold that had been gifted to him by King George. Plainly, Hendrick's opulent, kingly attire was meant to verify his importance. The Mohawk's broad smile demonstrated that he was well pleased with the effect of his grand entrance. Every delegate rose as James De Lancey welcomed Hendrick with a show of genuine respect and friendship.

Much good had already come out of the conferences. Many of the colonies had bettered themselves. Pennsylvania and Connecticut had both purchased additional lands from the Indians in the far west. The Six Nation Confederacy was, for the moment, satisfied that all of the British colonies would work together to strengthen themselves against the enemy French. When Cornelius had shopped for his wife at Harmen Gansevoort's busy store, the buzz had been all about British colonial unification. Many feared that if an Anglo-Iroquois agreement could not be brought to fruition during the conferences, the Natives would continue to court both the British and the French. If the colonies were to withstand an onslaught of French forces they must have the support of the Iroquois.

Benjamin Franklin's points putting forth a union had been debated at great length during the past weeks, but no final draft had been made. With today's closing ceremonies, everyone hoped they would hear of a plan forthcoming. This was the final hour; the summation of all that had transpired was at hand.

The King stood regally silent for several minutes. Turning away from the delegates, he appeared to be studying the irreverent crowd, many of whom were whispering amongst themselves. Several times De Lancey ordered silence. When the audience before them was at last mute, Hendrick began to speak in English. His voice was strong and loud as a man in the prime of his life, but his words reflected the wisdom of his age.

"We wish this tree of friendship may grow up to a great height and then we shall be a powerful people," Hendrick boomed. Turning back to the delegates he added, "We, the United Nations, shall rejoice of our strength as we will have now made so strong a Confederacy."

De Lancey, obviously delighted by the commitment, replied eloquently, "I hope that by this present Union we shall grow up to a great height and be as powerful and famous as you were of old."

A thundering roar went out from the crowd.

Cornelius considered De Lancey's words. Both men saw a new great land with colonies and the Iroquois Nation together under one American sky.

William stood stoically with his arms folded across his chest. "And so it is done... or perhaps not."

"Now, Brother," Cornelius answered contentedly, "let us believe that all the talk amongst delegates, near and afar, will be for the better good of our own country here in New York. For myself, I care not for the haughty aristocratic Virginians who could not be bothered to attend. I only care that New York prospers and that we might all live to cradle grandchildren."

William nodded and sighed. Leaning closer he whispered, "Let us hope that old King George will be of the same mind and heart as those present, but I fear that our English King will not be happy to see his American colonies unified."

"Why would you say such a thing? Unity builds strength."

"Very true."

"And so...?"

Thoughtfully, William replied, "I say what England's German born monarch knows of our distant land is little more than we are one of the lines within the palm of his hand. He has great troubles on his Kingly table. I have heard that France, Russia and Austria have formed a bond against England which now stands with Prussia."

"I cannot believe that our King would not see the benefit of stronger children."

"I hope you are right," William conceded.

All the delegates again stood as King Hendrick took his leave followed by William Johnson and the Governor.

As the crowd dispersed, Cornelius added, "It is time I return to my farm and family, but first, tomorrow I will go by Lansing's and pick up the mare that I purchased from him for Evert. The next day I will take my leave, along with Herman. I thank you and your good wife for all of the hospitality you have shown to me. I feel I have made more than one new friend while here."

CHAPTER 27

Late 1989

Two months to the day after Steve's supposed alien encounter Helen parked her car on Maple Street and walked the two blocks to "Carmella's Roost", Milltown's newest and only café and pastry shop. She was somewhat familiar with the home-style café which specialized in premiering flavored coffees. She had been there once before during the first week that they had opened with Chris Mann who thought the baked-on-premises pastries were out of this world. Helen remembered the deliciously inviting aroma that had filled her nostrils as soon as she had walked in that day.

Coffee and a doctor-forbidden pastry hadn't been a part of Helen's full agenda this Saturday, but an unexpected, off-the-wall call had her quickening her steps toward the shop. Her heart hadn't stopped racing since Darlene Waldron had called saying she had something urgent she had to get off her chest, something about Steve. Helen had tried to press for more details over the phone. She knew Darlene casually, having met her a few times at their Rotary book club meetings. Darlene, a tall, attractive black woman in her late thirties, had moved up from Manhattan about five years ago. She worked as a nurse at the VA hospital, and on occasion had hosted the book club at her Saratoga apartment, but as far as Helen could remember Darlene had never met Steve.

Darlene refused to elaborate on the phone. She insisted that this was something that had to be said face to face.

Approaching the shop she could see Darlene's slim figure through the plate glass frontage. She sat toward the back, a coffee mug already in front of her. Glancing at her watch Helen noted that she was early. She wondered how long she had been sitting there. As she entered Darlene waved. Helen did the same, then went the counter to order a flavored decaf coffee. She paid for it, walked to the table, and sat down.

"I'm sorry if I've gotten you all upset," Darlene began, "but I didn't think what I have to say was something that should be said over the phone. I..."

"Well, I am upset, Darlene, and before I have a heart attack right here and now I think you need to tell me whatever it is that you want me to know about my husband. As a matter of fact, I'd like to know how you know Steve. That would be a good place to begin."

"I don't know your husband...Steve, personally," she stammered.

"You don't know Steve? Then what's this all about?"

Darlene sighed. "I know someone who does know him, and, of course, that Steve is your husband. Something happened that I thought you should know about." Shifting in her seat, she added. "Believe me, I really searched my soul about telling you, but after a bunch of sleepless nights I just have to. That's why I called you this morning."

"Okay, soooooo..."

Darlene waited until Helen's coffee had been delivered to the table and the server had returned to her post behind the counter.

"Well, I have a sweet friend who is sort of a wacky person. Charming and beautiful, but also gullible and flighty. We met in Manhattan years ago and were reacquainted when I moved up here. She knows a lot of influential people and helped me get my job at the VA. My friend is a kind, considerate person who'd never intentionally hurt anyone, but she's got herself involved with something that is just not a good thing."

This is it, Helen thought. *This "considerate" friend is the one Steve is spending his time in the sack with.* "Darlene, let me make this easier for you. You're trying to tell me that my husband is having an affair with your friend?"

Darlene's eyes widened. "Oh, heavens no!"

The attendant behind the pastry counter looked up. "Something wrong?"

"No," Helen snapped back. "Everything is fine, thank you."

"Sorry," Darlene whispered, leaning forward. "No, Helen, your husband isn't having an affair...not that I know about anyway. However, he's got himself in with a bunch of strange, new-age people. My friend doesn't see them that way, of course."

"Steve is involved with the group that she belongs to?"

"Well, yes, it appears so. Let me ask you this question. Has anything strange or unusual been happening lately with your husband?"

Helen did her best to remain calm while she sipped her drink. "What kind of a question is that? What are you getting at?"

Darlene leaned forward. "Did you ever hear of Jane Roberts?"

"I've heard of her. What does she have to do with anything?" Helen thought how only a few days ago she had seen one of Jane Robert's books on Steve's night stand and asked him about it. Since then he'd been coaxing her to read it. Darlene had hit a nerve.

"Well, this group that meets every other Sunday afternoon someplace in Saratoga Springs is studying Jane Roberts."

"So they have a book group. That's what it sounds like, and obviously there's nothing wrong with a book group."

Darlene tucked her dark, straightened hair behind her ears. "It's not exactly a book group, Helen. Nothing like ours. They are into topics like levitation and psychic readings. Jane Roberts is dead; died a few years ago, I guess, but one of these people is trying to channel her the way Jane Roberts said in her book she channeled an entity from another universe that goes by the name of Seth, as I understand it. Of course, you might know that Roberts was a poet long before anything else, and she attended Skidmore College back in the late '40s. One member of the group actually knew her."

Helen sat up straight in her chair. "This is college stuff. I don't know about you, but we were all reaching for something when we were young. It's no secret; Steve and I met in a paranormal class."

"No," Darlene interrupted, "these people meeting in Saratoga Springs are not college kids, Helen. In fact, I know...well, I've been told that one of them is a science professor and another dude is a retired engineer. Then, of course, there's your Steve and my friend who volunteers at the VA, so you'd think whatever they and a few paranormal groupies are talking about on Sunday afternoons must be harmless. Right?"

Helen stared down into her cup. "People have a right to discuss anything that they want, and by the way, how exactly do you know that my husband is truly involved? I'm not clear on that yet. I think I have a right to know who told you," Helen insisted defensively.

Now that she knew where Steve had been the Sunday he'd had his 'encounter' Helen began to wonder about all the Sundays he'd been supposedly in Queens. She was madder than hell, but what business was all of this to this gossipy, in—your-business woman or for that matter anybody else?

"Look, Darlene, I've got a lot of errands to run today. I thank you for letting me know about this crowd, but my husband has far more important matters taking up his time, and I just don't buy into this."

As Helen rose from the table, Darlene asked, "Does the name Van Schaick ring any bells with you?"

Helen paused. "What if it does?"

"My friend is Judy, Michael Van Schaick's wife."

Helen wanted to say *oh come on,* but Darlene's description of Judy was Judy to a T; a beautiful forty-something butterfly who basically adorned Mick's lapel. Occasionally she did volunteer at the VA, and Judy loved everything Manhattan. Helen also knew from Chris Mann that Chris' sister-in-law had some problems. At least one time that she knew of Mick had rushed Judy into the hospital for taking too many pills, although as far as Helen knew she'd gotten some help after that, and that was all in the past. Of course, Mick and Steve knew each other well from being in business, and before things had soured, the four of them had socialized, but Steve always thought Judy was a kook.

Helen sat back down. "What is it that you really want to tell me?"

"What I'm about to tell you I don't want you to share with anyone. Please don't tell your husband."

"I'll try to keep everything you say quiet, but even if you didn't say another word, obviously you know that you've put yourself at risk by initiating this meeting and just by giving up Judy, implying that she is some sort of cult member."

"Okay...here's the whole story as I heard it. Judy believes that she is the reincarnation of a woman who worked as a maid for Queen Victoria in England. Actually, she's obsessed by the idea. She's become very interested in being able to cross over to the other side."

"Oh my God!" Helen gasped.

"Yes, it's frightening, and I've been trying to talk to her because I know how sometimes our minds get flipped around, but it's no use. And, I think she's been taking drugs again. I know the signs, and that stuff can make anybody hug the dead."

"I'm sorry, but I'm missing something. How did you say you met Judy?" Helen was flabbergasted. Last Saturday she'd played tennis with her at the club. Judy seemed fine then.

Darlene took a deep breath. "I met her years ago while I was doing some side modeling in the City. Before I went into nursing I was interested in fashion design. I used to coordinate fashion shows, sometimes model, for a friend of my mother's who owned a glitzy shop on 8th Avenue. Judy was a good customer and a familiar face at after-hours parties. Getting a little high was pretty much the norm, but once I started nursing classes, I never touched it again for fear of losing my nursing license. Judy always seemed to me like two women in one body, and I'll say that my mother never liked her. How the two of us remained friends all these years I'll never know, but that's how it is, and I'd like to help her. I owe her that much. I just don't know how to help her."

"You should tell her husband. Honestly, that would be best for her," Helen said, wondering if Mick had any more idea of whom he had married than she did lately.

Darlene sighed. "Yeah, well now comes 'part two' which might change your mind about either of us going to Judy's husband. Your husband has some of his own issues, too, from what I've heard, but I have a feeling that you are well aware of that. Please don't take me wrong. I'm not judging."

"You sound like you're judging, Darlene."

"No, I just think he needs his wife's help. Judy says that Steve believes that he is the reincarnation of a man who lived in your house back in the middle of the 1700s. So she's convinced that they have a common experience going. They watched the Jane Roberts tapes and are convinced that one person can become another or speak for other people by stepping through a thin barrier. She says that she told Steve years ago about her past life visions. She thinks he's her soulmate brother."

"Wait," Helen held up her hand. "Stop right there. Judy told you that she had told Steve all about this years ago?"

"Yes, those were her exact words. This connecting with the dead stuff must have been going on for a very long time, Helen. Don't you know this?"

Helen shook her head and offered a half lie. "No….no I don't."

Darlene continued, "One Sunday, a couple months ago, they were all gathered together for a scheduled meeting. The house where they often meet, as Judy described it to me, was dark but vibrating with strobe lights, which is supposed to break up the energy."

"They must all have been high or smashed," Helen said disgustedly.

Darlene shook her head. "Judy swears that nobody had anything except your Steve. In his effort to gain access to a heightened altered state he drank some form of drug that someone offered him. He passed out, and, for quite some time, they couldn't get him to come to. Judy was terrified that he was going to die of an overdose. She wanted to call an ambulance, but the others panicked and couldn't decide what to do.

"After a bit, Steve did become more aware of where he was, but he sure wasn't in any shape to drive his car. Apparently, he was scratching at himself viciously, saying that he was being attacked by an army of alien bugs. The engineer in the group decided that they should put Steve into his own car and he'd drive him some-place with Judy following. I guess your husband was with it enough to direct him to a familiar place. After an hour or two, I guess he was doing a lot better so the engineer got into Judy's car and the two of them drove back, leaving Steve to get home in his own car."

Helen said, "You're right. I have to have some time to think about all of this. Time to decide what I should or can do."

Darlene lowered her eyes. "I've never been married, Helen, but if I were, I think I'd like to know if my man was in deep trouble. As for Judy, I just don't know what I can do for her anymore. Her Mick, as Judy always tells it, can be rough. Seems as though every-body down in the Albany area thinks of Michael Van Schaick as a great guy, man of the year and all, but he's hit her a couple times. Did you know that?"

Helen was feeling nauseous. "No, I've never heard anything like that and I've known Mick for many, many years."

"Well, something else to consider—Judy and her husband have a volatile relationship. I'm sure of that. She says they've been to coun-selling. You know, I've been thinking about all of this for over a week. I really didn't want to get in between two marriages, but I couldn't sleep knowing that if something doesn't happen to prevent it, one of these people could end up dead."

Helen dragged herself up from her chair. "I haven't slept much lately either, Darlene. I've thought for weeks that something was wrong. Steve and Judy conspiring though would never have entered my mind. Judy has always been Judy, but she and Steve partnering up... I don't know what to think. So I'll keep silent and I'll ask you if you'll keep all this to yourself. Can you do that for me?"

Darlene nodded and handed Helen a small piece of paper. "I moved last week. I just got nervous about all of this freaky business. I'd rather nobody knows where I put my head down on my pillow. Maybe we all need a fresh start. Here's my new phone number. If you come up with an idea or just want to talk, give me a call. Otherwise, I'll see you again whenever I see you, I suppose."

Helen took the number and without saying another word walked zombie-like out of the café.

Had she ever really known Steve Carey?

CHAPTER 28

1990

Helen slid open the barn door. She took care to avoid tripping over the maze of orange extension wires plugged together connecting the house's electricity to the portable Salamander heater. She looked around at the stacks of lumber piled high, wondering how long the boards needed to warm to be the right temperature. How long would it take to make everything or anything right? Was it possible?

Months had rolled by since she'd met Darlene Waldron at the café. Christmas luncheons with co-workers and friends, and New Year's Eve had howled past. Valentine's Day arrived with a dozen red roses waiting for her on the countertop when she'd come home from work. Through it all she hadn't pushed on Steve...not once. She couldn't justify confrontation because there seemed no reason to rock the boat any further. Steve acted as if his alien encounter never happened, and she'd pretended that she'd never had the tell-all conversation with Darlene who thankfully lived up to her promise and now lived off the radar. It was just as well. Better to accept the lull between storms. Besides, on the recommendation of Father Patrick, who after ten years in LA had been reassigned to western New York, Steve had voluntarily entered a sixteen week program for depression. He referred to his weekly therapy as a mental exercise class. The Jane Roberts book had disappeared, and he seemed happier. Helen thought that a few of her prayers had been answered.

Steve had said that Mary Jane would soon wrap everything up and she had. They'd helped his mother retrieve the last of the boxes from Queens. With their help, Mary Jane had put everything in a rented, climate controlled storage room at an industrial complex a few miles from her house. It was convenient, and her mother-in-law seemed satisfied that she could explore her family's past whenever she felt like it. The grueling trips to Queens were over. Helen was relieved. Should Steve have a relapse there'd be no more excuses for him disappearing on Sunday afternoons.

All and all, things did seem better. Steve reinstated Friday night poker with the boys—three neighborhood men—something he'd not done in almost a year. He left for work at six-thirty and was home by six. He seemed more relaxed, insisting that he and Tommy eat out on Thursday nights down at the Milltown diner. Had it all been just a bad dream? But then, of course, Helen understood she couldn't take comfort in that restful delusion forever. Darlene Waldron had amply provided a good dose of reality. Or had she? Helen had to know. She was through tip toeing around the man she lived with.

Inside the barn, Steve was hard at work sanding boards for a new workstation table. Looking up, he shut off the power tool. "Hey babe, looks good...right? You know, with all that happened to me these past months I never thought I'd get to it. Just didn't think I had it in me anymore. But then something in my head said what the hell, now or never. I thought I'd damn well get to it before more snow flies."

"Where did all this lumber come from? And all these sacks of concrete mix?"

"Oh that; I've decided to build a safe room in here. After all those crazy summer storms last year I thought it might be good for us to have a place where we could hunker down if a tornado hits. Some of the barn wood I'd been hanging on to was just too rotted so I had this delivered from the Goewey lumberyard last Saturday while you were up north shopping."

Helen stood staring at the load in the middle of the barn. "You want to put a safe room in a two hundred year old barn?"

Facing her, he put his hands in his jean pockets, jingling his car keys, a signal that generally meant his wheels were turning. "Why not? It's the safest place on the property because it *has* endured for better than two hundred; maybe closer to three hundred years." He walked toward his workstation.

Helen folded her arms. "Okay. I have something to say to you, and I'm really sorry that I have to say it, but here it is... *I know*, Steve. I know the true story about what happened months ago during those six missing hours... all of it, and it has nothing to do with silvery UFO's."

Steve's happy grin vanished; his mouth opened and then closed. For a brief moment Helen thought she saw a trace of alarm in those intense eyes that at one time could carry her away to another world.

Steve rubbed his hand along a pine board. "Oh?"

Helen continued, her voice steady. "How's Judy?"

"Judy? What are you talking about?"

"Please, Steve. No more pretense. It's better that you just come clean about all of the malarkey that's burying us. Honestly, it's better for me and better for you."

Steve met her intense gaze straight on. "I couldn't tell you the truth, Helen, and that's because you don't believe a word I say about anything. You haven't for a long, long time. I don't know that anything makes any sense to you unless something is right in front of you, like this wood pile."

"Don't lay this on me, Steve. This is about you, and, maybe, just possibly, us. But it sure as hell isn't about you being the poor, misunderstood husband. Understand what I'm saying? I know what happened to you that Sunday, and there was no space ship!"

"You know about the meetings in Saratoga Springs, right?"

"That's right! And, Judy!" Helen shouted.

"I might have done something stupid, Helen, but I don't think of myself as some badass heel. And though you don't want to hear it, I still think that I had an encounter with something not of this world.

I'm not a wacked out idiot, and I'm doing my best to work on it all. And about Judy, well, we just compare notes, that's all. Did George Clark tell you about this?"

"Who's George Clark?"

"Guess it wasn't George. He's an engineer I know who's been doing some experiments." Steve mumbled. "Metaphysical stuff."

Helen was flustered. "Let's just leave it that I have information that you have been meeting with a group that participates in trances or séances, and I know that was where you were the Sunday that you claimed to have been violated by aliens. I know Judy was there and that the meetings in Saratoga Springs have been going on for quite some time."

"It's true that I was invited to sit in," Steve said, "but nobody twisted my arm thereafter. They're amazing people, all of them. But after whatever happened that Sunday afternoon, I thought it best to leave it all alone." Steve folded his arms and leaned back against the half-finished table. "It's funny, you know I've never been one to mix with a group—I've always been a loner—but Jane Roberts fascinates me, and when I heard these people were looking into her life I was drawn in."

"What I don't understand is your secret alliance with Judy. Of all people—Judy."

"Judy's not so bad. She's a lost little girl, swallowed up by an over-bearing bastard. Honest, there is nothing going on now or ever has been with me and Judy."

"Okay. I'll let that go for now. But I have to put this out there, too. I know that Judy likes to shop in New York City, and then I hear how Judy is one of the people who got you involved with this local bunch. So I got to thinking about a lot of your episodes. For example, how about last year when you told me that you were mugged in Manhattan while Christmas shopping? 'Knocked cold' were your words, and left lying in an alley for three hours. You never went to the hospital, though, nor did you want to report that incident to the police, either. You had some scratches that time, too. I believed you then. I thanked God you weren't more hurt.

Ever since meeting Darlene I've been beating myself up, but this morning I stopped. I'm not blind, I just loved you blindly."

"Darlene? Darlene who?"

Helen whispered half to herself, "I shouldn't have mentioned her. That was wrong. You piss me off so much, Steve. It doesn't matter who Darlene is. What matters is that we are not 'we' anymore. I've tried for months. I've waited for you to put your arms around me and tell me what happened that Sunday. Are you having a thing with Judy? For God's sake, tell the truth!"

As Steve stepped back Helen thought he looked honestly shocked. "Judy? You *really* think I'm having sex with Judy? Is that what this is all about? I just told you there's nothing between Judy and me!"

Helen welled up and turned away. She hated it when her emotions trumped. Absolutely hated it.

Steve walked toward her and tried to touch her arm. Helen jerked away, fighting tears. "I kept myself together these past months by remembering the guy I once knew. I kept wishing for that man to return. I prayed things would get better, but now I see there isn't a chance for change unless I have the courage to take a first step. I do love you, Steve. Right now, in this moment, I love you, not some foreigner who might have lived here hundreds of years ago. You...you, damn it! You're the guy I chose. But, I just can't go on like this anymore."

"Helen, you're not going to leave me...are you?"

Helen pulled a wad of Kleenex out of her sweater pocket and blew her nose. "My mother is going down to Florida next week for the end of the winter. I've already talked to her. Of course, I said nothing about any of what is going on with us. She's been wanting her bedroom painted so I told her I'd do it over the time she's gone as a belated extra Christmas gift. I'm going to stay in her apartment in Niskayuna until I can decide whether or not I can come home."

"But what about Tommy," Steve asked anxiously. "What are you going to tell him?"

"Not much, for now. Don't worry, I'd never share any of this with our son, at least for the time being."

Steve turned away. "You never said anything—"

Helen opened the barn door and paused. "Neither did you," she whispered back. "I guess we're both guilty of that much."

CHAPTER 29

December 1755

Despite choosing cautious pathways, the ending date of a man's life is a mystery since the details of his earthly departure are written by the finger of God long before his birth. Such was the flow of Cornelius Waldron's thoughts as he sat at his damask covered table this winter evening with his niece Cornelia's husband, Patrick Clark of Albany, and Israel Putnam, a Connecticut farmer whom Clark had met while marching north from Albany during the summer to join in the British expedition against the French. Putnam, an interesting story-teller, had for the past number of hours taken them away from their troubles, while Patrick, Cornelius suspected, yearned to return to his young family in Albany.

Though late in the hour, the three lingered before the warmth of the hearth, their muskets close at hand, with their discourse turning more toward the sobriety of war.

Much had changed in their country, yet the one constant that remained was the weather. Several inches of fluffy white snow already covered frozen roadways. Within the next few days Waldron anticipated that he and his elder sons, along with neighboring farmers, would pack their wheat onto their horse-drawn sleighs and take it into Albany to be stored in the warehouse. When spring arrived, the grain would be transported to Manhattan where much of it would be shipped to England. Praise be to God; neither the British nor the French had control of the heavens.

As was customary in all Dutch homes during this time of year, wooden shoes would soon be filled with candies for the children, but on this night, as the twelve days of the Dutch holiday approached, little joy was found in any house in the valley. Tonight, despite an apparent win against the French for the British in September, all had much to lament for many good friends and comrades were either dead or wounded as a result of the bloody battles fought around *Lac du Saint Sacrement*. The great King Hendrick had fallen in battle September 8th—William Johnson was wounded.

They had heard news that the triumphant General William Johnson, now the hero of every British subject, had renamed *Lac du Saint Sacrement* to Lake George to honor their English king. Although Johnson's splendid gesture would surly please King George, it did little to uplift folk living north of Manhattan, and especially so for those hunkered down on farmsteads far north of Albany. Hendrick's demise meant a major partnership with the Indians was shaken. Thousands of French troops were quartered for the winter north on Lake Champlain and also in forts to the west. The French enemy was fearfully close.

With deadly battles fought during the fall less than fifty miles away from Waldron's farm, Cornelius well understood that his and scores of other prosperous North Country homesteads along the river were more vulnerable than ever. He was grateful British regulars were garrisoned at both Fort Half Moon and Fort Schaghticoke. Of course, the British understood the importance of defending Albany's outlying farms. Should these farms be burnt and laborers murdered, starvation would follow for thousands. With men not having the strength to draw a sword or fire a shot, New York would be lost to the French.

Troops had been bolstered at outlying fortifications. But would a local force be enough to protect them until help came from Albany? Of course, the English crown, as well as Albany's fine militia, was alert to the protection of these settlers who were courageous enough to stay on their land, and crops had grown in the fields undisturbed. A hefty share of peas, wheat, and corn, along with the pork currently smoking in dozens of smoke houses, was expected to be contributed to help feed thousands of encamped British soldiers.

All the same, Cornelius was giving serious thought to moving his wife and five younger children to Albany. He and his elder sons, along with his Negro field workers and Herman, would stay here on the farm, but he would not risk the safety of the rest of his family. Tomorrow he would tell his wife that she and their children must go to Albany with him when he and Garret took the rest of the wheat to the city.

His brother-in-law, John Yates, had also offered to take in Janet and their young children at Greenbush across the river from Albany. With the onslaught of so many soldiers at Albany, John had said he would welcome the help of two more boys at his Albany stables, and, of course, extra hands at the Greenbush farm would not go idle. Cornelius knew Janet would protest any move, as she always did, but this time he would insist she go stay with their relatives where they could be more easily protected.

Earlier, during the meal, the men had concurred that the greatest loss to their country was that of the great Indian Chief Hendrick Theyonoquin, the most staunch of all their Indian allies. Following the Indian Conferences the previous year, it had been he who at the advanced age of seventy-four had rallied hundreds of his Mohawk braves to follow him into battle and to stand with General Johnson's men against the French and the Abenaki. The three men had talked at length about how the war would fare without Hendrick.

And what would a campaign be without General Johnson? He was seriously wounded during the same battle, but was recovering at his great house where he was tended by his Native American woman, Caroline. Cornelius believed the Indian woman was King Hendrick's niece and that Johnson had lost heart. Rumors were the General had secluded himself in his quarters, but vowed to take care of the deceased Indian statesman's extensive family, many of whom had been encamped upon his grounds for months. In Albany many thought that General Johnson had loved the old Indian as a father and he would never get over Hendrick's death.

Putnam added that he'd also heard that William Johnson had said he was tired of trying to understand the stubborn, foolhardy mind of Massachusetts General Shirley who, in Johnson's opinion, had little experience, yet worse, little respect for the Indians. William Johnson no longer wanted any part of this war. He had resigned in disgust, but first had seen to it that a strong fort at the southern end of Lake George had been built. The walls were an astonishing thirty feet thick. This stronghold was called Fort William Henry after King George's younger son, William, and his grandson, Prince William Henry.

Cornelius shared that Johnson's resignation was the unfortunate news that had changed his course of thinking. He had met the man several times throughout the years. They had done business, and Cornelius thought him intelligent and brave, a man who could move mountains should it please the Almighty.

When Patrick had urged that, considering the terrible circumstances in their country, Cornelius should move his family, he had reluctantly agreed. Without Johnson's leadership he had serious doubts as to the success of the British endeavors.

That the most capable French leader, Commander Dieskau, had also been wounded and was in the hands of the British where he was now a prisoner at Albany had little impact.. Dieskau would be transferred to New York City and then to London when his wounds healed sufficiently. But, it did not matter that Dieskau was gone; the French were a strong enemy, and every man knew this would be a long war. Precautions had to be taken immediately. No person should underestimate the cunning French.

Respectful of Cornelius's wife and young children sleeping soundly in the house, Israel Putnam, or 'Put' as he insisted he be addressed, spoke in hushed tones.

"At thirty-seven, most assuredly, I hope for many years of a good life to come," the soft spoken visitor reflected. "Like you, Cornelius,

I am a farmer and will return as soon as possible to my Connecticut land and my dear wife. But for now we must do whatever we can do."

Cornelius spoke slowly, measuring his words, "And...and will you return to...to your children?"

Hesitating, Put replied. "I have no sons or daughters, but my wife and I still hope for a child. She has conceived twice, but she could not hold the infants long enough that either of them be born into this world."

Cornelius replied sympathetically. "With your permission, I will tell my...my wife of you and your wife's hope. We will keep you both in our prayers."

"I thank you for the prayers, Cornelius, and for the excellent meal your women folk served. I have long thought a man is equally blessed by daughters as well as sons, for what man do you know that can prepare such a feast as we enjoyed tonight? A toast," Putnam suggested, rising to his feet and uplifting his tankard, "to all our wives and daughters. May our women remain safe in the hands of Almighty God!"

Cornelius and Patrick stood, "To the women!"

Patrick Clark drank the remainder of his beer and then sat, thinking of his own young family that he had left behind in Albany. He had not seen his Cornelia, little Nellie, or Will since late summer when he, along with thousands of other provincials, had followed the newly appointed General William Johnson northward toward the *Great Carrying Place* on the east side of the North River. There, he and his kinsmen, had assimilated with three hundred Mohawk braves and thousands more colonials from Massachusetts, Rhode Island, New Hampshire, and Connecticut to fight the French and their allied Indians. They'd hoped to take French-controlled Fort Saint Frederic, the place the English referred to as Crown Point, but instead the wounded General had ordered carpenters to build the new Fort William Henry at the southern end of Lake George.

Cornelius walked to the mantle, and picked up his long-stem, white clay pipe. Reaching for the tobacco box, he smiled. "Yes, my daughter, Geertje, can bake a cake worth the palate of a king," he boasted. "She is...is beautiful, and she is as strong as her elder... b-brothers," Cornelius stammered.

"Indeed she is!" Patrick readily agreed.

"Already my Geertje has suitors, but she is only fourteen, and too...too young to be allowed to place her hand in the hands of any of those who would be happy to have her."

Patrick grinned, quickly adding, "Aye, Uncle, she will make a grand wife for any man when the time be right."

Addressing Israel, Cornelius lowered his voice to nearly a whisper as he packed his pipe. "The older woman who served us in silence is Geertje's aunt, Engeltie, my sister."

Patrick noticed, perhaps for the first time, how haggard his once robust uncle looked. "Uncle, you introduced Aunt to Mr. Putnam when we ate our supper. Do you not remember?"

Lost in thought, Cornelius did not look up. "Our father died when Engeltie was a cheerful maid of seventeen. In those times every man would turn his head when she passed by, but...but after our father's death, which occurred here...at the farm, my...my sister was never the same happy girl. For years we have all sought for her to have a good husband, but...but she rejects every possible suitor we bring to her, and it is not our custom to force a marriage that would make a woman miserable."

"Your sister lives with you and your wife?" Putnam asked.

Reclaiming his chair, Cornelius answered hesitantly, "She... she stays with us much...much of the year since the death of our mother, but...but she still has our mother's house in Albany and a servant who was left to her to see to her needs. Yet, she is most fond of my wife, and prefers to spend her time here, upriver, with my family."

"I see. I watched her earlier with your little Willie. It appears that your boy has a second mother in his aunt."

As these words left Putnam's lips the front door opened and Herman entered carrying a pile of cut wood. Silently, he knelt before the dying fire, refurbishing it with another log. Soon the fire again blazed high in the hearth, and he departed without a word to any of them.

Cornelius sighed and replied as if he had not even seen his servant in the room. "Yes, my...my sister is very attached to...to Willie since she..." Waldron cleared his throat. "Listen to me, I sound like an old midwife."

Patrick turned toward Putnam, anxious to divert the conversation. "Aye, Put, I would advise that you return to your woman soon and forget talk of God's plan for you to fight the enemy again with the Connecticut boys."

Israel Putnam smiled wanly, and Patrick Clark realized that he had drunk far too much and said too much this night.

"I know my duty as I believe in God's miracles," Putnam said, "and so I will go where duty calls, and my wife and I shall continue to pray that this war with the French will soon come to an end."

Grimly, Patrick replied, "I do not see an end in sight."

"We must keep an open heart," Putnam replied. "I have lived long enough to have witnessed miracles. Once, north of here, I was captured by Indians and tied to a tree. The savages stripped me naked and built a fire of brush at my feet, and as the flames leapt about me I thought that I would soon come face to face with Almighty God. I prepared for the end of my earthly life. Strange thoughts come to a man when he knows his life is about to end. As my feet began to burn I remembered the tales my father told of the poor tortured souls of Salem town in Massachusetts where I was born and grew to be a man. The terrible story was of those who, falsely accused of witchery, feared burning as it had been done to others found guilty in Europe." Before again settling his gaze on his two companions, Putnam lifted his eyes in a moment of reverence. "Of course, you know of the history of those dreadful dark days in Massachusetts."

"Yes," Cornelius answered. When Patrick remained mute he added, "I do not think you, Patrick, would know of witch burnings, terrible grievances committed long before your birth."

"I have heard of such in my old country. Ireland is a land that blossoms with superstitions. But I know nothing of Massachusetts witchery, having lived hereabouts in New York less than ten years. There is little time for frightening tales of witches and demons for a hard-working man like me. After carting bricks from dawn till dusk six days a week, I could sleep on a bed of rock."

Putman nodded and continued soberly. "My father and grand-father witnessed the accusations of a crazed mob who, before then, had been the most kindly of neighbors. They observed the subsequent trial of the accused as the workings of the devil within men. Most courageously my father and grandfather spoke against those proceedings, even signing the petition to save old Rebecca, a good Christian woman who had helped birth many of these town's people. It did no good. Rebecca, as well as one of her sisters, was hanged along with many others. There were no Christian burials for them. Fearing demons would rise up out of their corpses, their poor bodies were burnt to ashes and left where they lay. I remember my distraught mother praying for their immortal souls.

"As I faced my death by the hands of savages equal to the cruelty of some Christian men, I wondered if my burnt up, unburied body lying in the wilderness condemned my soul to wander eternally alone, or should I meet others denied Christian burial? I say to you, until that day, fear hath never been my companion. Even as a young man when I faced the she wolf in the cave, I did not fear, yet the loss of my eternal soul was another matter."

Patrick grimaced. Staring into the hearth he mumbled, "I trust the clerics have the answer."

"I am curious," Cornelius interrupted, "how...how is it that you escaped the Indians' fire?"

"I can only say that I am here tonight by the power of the Almighty," Putnam stated flatly. "As I was praying aloud for my life's transgressions, a heavy rain began to fall upon me and soon put out the flames. Seeing this, the savages thought me protected by their Great Spirit and showed themselves so full of fear that they ran away. I, too, believed that God had intervened. Still, being bound and alone, I continued to pray. After several hours tied there and suffering the pain of my burnt feet, a French officer came by with his Abenaki scout, and the Frenchman cut away my bindings, thereafter making the Catholic sign of the cross. Speaking in his own tongue, with which I have little familiarity, I supposed him to instruct me to run for my life, which I did as best as I could do limping through the woods. You can imagine my shock at being delivered by a Frenchman, and more so, a Papist!"

Cornelius winced and rose, fetching the half-filled pitcher of beer from the table. "Catholics are cursed," he declared, "yet it is possible that some still own their hearts."

Putnam stated earnestly, "I do not speak falsely. It is all the truth. I was redeemed, and so now must consider for what purpose I have been saved. Can it be that I remain on this earth solely to kill the French? I would have it not be so."

As Cornelius offered to refresh beers, Patrick waved him away. "My thanks, but I am soon to bed. You say we are to place our mats at the German's cabin out back? Earlier we had thought to ride to Fort Schaghticoke."

Cornelius scowled. "No need to...to wander so far in the dark. My servant understands he is to make you comfortable"

After refilling Putnam's tankard, Cornelius emptied the remaining beer from the pitcher into his own. "I thank you for sharing your story, Israel. With...with war pounding fists at our doors hereabouts we all must consider our future. I...I cannot tolerate that I cannot work my fields whilst we are compelled to house our wives—and our children in Albany for...for the sake of their safety. We must rid ourselves of damn French enemies even if we must go to Montreal and pull them out of their beds to do so!"

Wearily, Patrick leaned back into his chair. "Sixty years ago settlers at Schenectady were massacred by the French, and not so long ago again and not far from here. Aye, we are all sick of the French. All hoped this time with William Johnson and the Indian King at the helm of thousands of brave militia from New York and New England and New Jersey, we would defeat them. We believed we would easily rout these French devils, but, as we have seen, the French and their allied Indians are not so easily put away."

Cornelius responded thoughtfully, "That is because the...the Canada French see no reason to...to be put away. The Canada

French who...who we fight, most assuredly the Canada born French; they see this country as...as much their own, as do we. A Canadian born leader such as Joseph Gaspard de Lery who...who with much cunning led his men to victory at Fort Bull, is like a...a bear with his teeth sunk deep into the flesh of his prey. I know well the heart of this...this kind of a man.

"One hundred years ago here in this country, my...my Holland-born great-grandfather, Resolved Waldron, enjoyed a good partnership with a Frenchman by the name of La Croix. As a boy I...I heard the stories of their adventures just as you, Israel, tell of yours tonight. My forbears, both the...the Waldrons and Stoutenburgs, ate and drank with the French. Although my...my father was never a lover of the French, as a young man I sat at my father's table in Albany with Canada French, friends of olden, people who...who my Manhattan-born father and my mother treated with respect.. This Canadian, De Lery, I suspect, thinks much the same as do I." Cornelius rose and placed another log into the fire.

Glancing toward Putnam, Patrick nodded. "My wife also enjoys telling such tales to our children."

Reclaiming his seat Cornelius began again, "Surely, I am a loyal subject to our King, yet I have never traveled to London town and have no desire to....to go there. This is my country. This was my father's country. His father came over as a boy with his own father and made this land his own, although they never stopped remembering their homeland. I have no fatherland other than New York. England and France have brought their arguments here to...to my country where we Provincials are... are forced to fight and to suffer because of this. We have enough on our plates with the Canada French and their allied Indians and men such as De Lery."

Israel Putnam nodded in agreement. "I believe most of us who have long made our homes here in America would agree."

Cornelius turned toward his kinsman. "Patrick, you...you have told me that soldiers in the taverns at New York speak poorly of this young soldier, the Virginia born George Washington."

"Aye, that was the talk," Patrick responded. "He is either the subject of jest or he is cursed for his foolishness signing the French terms."

Leaning forward, Cornelius continued soberly. "An inexperienced boy was...was sent into the western wilderness to...to face a formidable enemy. This...this, Washington, from what I hear, is not much older than my...my eldest son, and yet Virginia's Lieutenant Governor Dinwiddie expected his newly made officer to...to execute the tasks of a grown man with the skills of a diplomat. I...I hear, too, that he volunteered for the assignment, but courage alone will not stand in for experience."

"That is surely true," Putnam replied.

Cornelius sighed. "General Braddock is...is dead, as is all hope for the Albany Plan of the Union presented last year, a...a good plan which would have brought us strength by unification. Washington is...is no Schuyler or Johnson. As I...I hear it, Washington speaks but one language. Only a fool sends his man to...to negotiate with the enemy when he speaks no French."

"Aye" Patrick returned. "'Tis true that Washington speaks little French, but I do not think the Virginian can be held completely responsible for all errors made with the French. I have heard that when he was at Virginia's Capitol at Williamsburg offering his services to the Governor he came across a Dutchman by the name of Van Braam, a pretender who can only be the worst of liars. It is because of him that Washington finds himself in such a dishonorable position."

"How so?"

"Washington chose poorly in Van Braam. He was over eager to prove himself, I think. And Van Braam...wanting to accompany Washington on the impending expedition west, insisted that he could speak and read the French. He convinced the anxious George that he could act as an interpreter. I suppose the young officer thought the older woodsman a good man to keep at his side as he went out into the wilderness to parley with the French.

"Washington learned too late that this Dutchman, Van Braam, speaks some French, but reads French poorly. Washington thought the terms that Van Braam brought to him from the French were liberal. Of course, Van Braam read them to him. It appears Washington thought he was admitting only to the loss of Jumonville, but, thanks to Van Braam, what Washington signed was an admittance to assassinating a French ambassador on a peace mission."

Cornelius shook his head in disgust. "Yes, I heard this myself. He...he is the cause of a bad situation. Who knows what shall happen now. Washington is fortunate that he has relatives and friends high up in Virginia."

Putnam, too, was obviously tired. Finishing his drink, he rose to his feet. "After my business is complete in Albany, and a short visit home to my wife, I intend to muster in with forces under Colonel John Winslow. A brash Irishman by the name of Robert Rogers is recruiting men as scouts. I talked with him at length a fortnight ago."

Cornelius nodded. "I know of him and his brother, James, who fights alongside him. May God be with you. They...they are both wild men. The soldiers at Ft. Schaghticoke say Rogers can smell the enemy though he be miles away."

Putnam placed his emptied tankard on the table, but did not make his way toward the door as did Patrick. Instead, he walked toward the hearth where he hesitated in front of a fist-sized, crystalized rock sitting on the mantle. Throughout the evening he had noticed that it had often caught the light of the candles, making it appear to sparkle.

Cornelius, seeing his guest's interest, picked it up and handed it to him for closer examination. "It was my mother's and her mother's before. She gave it to me years ago. She...she and my sisters nearly perished that day on a ferry coming across the river," Cornelius said quietly.

"It is very beautiful," Putnam commented.

"It...it came from the Van Rensselaer lands south of here where my grandfather, Cornelius Vandenbergh, settled. I bear his name. According to my mother, her...her father told her that the Natives told him the crystals had rained from the heavens in ancient times.

All her life my mother believed this stone was blessed by God, and she placed it here at Waldron Farm to encourage us all in our faith."

Putnam put the crystal back on the mantle. "It is a priceless heirloom," he whispered, picking up his musket as had Patrick previously.

Cornelius walked him to the door where they joined Patrick. "I bid you both a restful good-night."

"And you, Waldron. Thank you again for your hospitality."

After closing the door behind them, Cornelius glanced over at his mother's legacy and wearily yearned for peace to come to his valley.

As Cornelius had directed, Patrick Clark and Israel Putnam followed the moonlit path behind the house, past the barn and the stable, soon passing a half dozen wooden grave markers rising up out of the snow. Patrick pointed to a small, newly dug grave. Strange for this time of year. They continued on past the cemetery for another two hundred feet or so and in the distance could see Herman's cabin where they were meant to sleep, but they stopped abruptly. A woman clad in a long, fur robe, her head scarfed, stood by the front door with the German. After a short embrace, the woman scurried away through the trees, and Herman went in.

Stunned, the Waldron visitors stared at one another. "By God, I think that was Aunt Engeltie," Patrick whispered.

"I saw no one," Putnam replied in a hushed tone. "I think it best that you did not see either."

Patrick agreed. "'Tis best. My lips will never speak of this to anyone, not even my wife."

CHAPTER 30

May 1756

A s an army of resilient 'peepers' living within the marshlands surrounding Waldron's pond chanted their croaky announcement of spring, war with the dogged French raged on. Hardy farmers tended their fields with muskets close, vigilant of an enemy that might fall upon them at any time. While the Waldron brothers tilled through melted-snow soaked soil, they took turns, along with friendly Schaghticoke Indians, patrolling the farm's perimeters. British regulars patrolled the roads. Living in a state of alert had become the daily constant.

Cornelius Waldron had long enjoyed boasting about the Waldron Farm's reputation for producing the finest wheat in all of British North America. His four eldest boys—Peter, Evert, Garret, and thirteen-year-old Cornelius—had all been behind his team of oxen, plowing by the time they reached their ninth year, and no man could be prouder of the good, God fearing men they had become. His sons knew the land, and Cornelius did not want to imagine his farm without his boys beside him. He was adamantly opposed to any of them leaving for Albany to join General Shirley's campaign against the French. Before anything else, their farm must come first.

But the boys, especially Garret, were all fired up after hearing of the decimation of Fort Bull on the Mohawk River by a group of Canadian militiamen and their allied Indians. Most of the men garrisoned at the palisaded fort had been reported killed and scalped. One of the soldiers, John Vanderheyden, who had been recruited following the Albany Indian conference in 1754, had been a good friend of Garret's.

John Vanderheyden left behind a young widow and infant son at Albany. Garret had angrily sworn to her that he would personally kill a French Canada soldier; an eye for an eye.

Evert, who saw no good in hating any man, tried to talk his younger brother out of joining up, but Garret was passionate about his decision. After weeks of wrestling with his conscience, Evert finally told his father that he would not let his brother go alone, perhaps to face a French hatchet, departing this world with his face buried in a foreign bloodied field.

With tears in his eyes Evert gave over his precious mare and her new foal to his father for care while he would be away during the following months. If he did not return, he instructed him that his horses were to go to his brother Peter, for his intended, Rachael, who loved them as much as he.

The corn and the spring wheat had been planted, and for now, having done their share, Evert and Garret Waldron felt that they had pleaded long enough with their father for his blessing to join the righteous cause. At twenty and eighteen, respectively, right or wrong, they were of an age to make their own decisions.

Peter, the eldest of Cornelius's sons, had also talked to Garret until he was blue in the face. He finally told Garret that whatever his decision, he himself would not leave their land unless absolutely forced to do so. Peter had no desire to take up arms and leave sweet Rachael, to whom he was betrothed. He had no appetite whatsoever for following General Shirley into the wilderness of Pennsylvania or Ohio land, and would gladly stay back on the farm with his father and younger brothers to face their own perils. Rachael was already his life and she would be his wife. They all were his kin and not the unfortunate soldiers slain at Fort Bull. Not even the death of Vanderheyden, God rest his immortal soul, could sway him.

At thirteen, their younger brother, Cornelius, whom they called 'Legs' because he could outrun any white man or Indian in any race, begged to go along with his elder brothers. But he would have to wait his turn to go in another year or so if, as Evert had said, the damn French and the Canadians had not been defeated by then. For now, both Legs and their younger brother, Henry, would have to 'hold their horses' and step up to work all the harder on the farm in the absence of two of their brothers.

Yesterday, with Evert and Garret promising to be back for harvesting, their Negress cook had baked extra loaves of bread which, along with a flask of last year's strong cider, each of them packed inside their cloth travel satchels. They planned to first make their way south to Greenbush and there to lodge with their Aunt Rebecca and Uncle John. While at Greenbush they would enjoy seeing their mother, brothers, and sisters who had not been back to Waldron Farm for many months. Once ensconced at the Yates farm they would ferry across the river to Albany and walk up the hill to Fort Frederick where they would join with the formidable mix of ten thousand other Provincials, British Regulars, and servants who had followed their masters to the encampment.

According to their Uncle William, who had brought the tragic news of Fort Bull while visiting in April, a large number of bateaux stacked high with provisions had arrived safely out west at Fort Oswego. Uncle had heard this from one of the soldiers at Albany belonging to General Shirley's Regiment. They would not be caught with their breeches down this time. Work continued at Schenectady building more boats in order that they be ready for a second trip westward on the Mohawk River.

William Waldron was a loyal British subject, and no man dare say otherwise. However, logically, he could not fathom how the Canadians had managed to sneak up on a British fortification, killing nearly all and destroying forty-five thousand pounds of gunpowder. Nor could he understand why they must wait upon the stuck-in-the-mud, indecisive British commanders, except for the fact that the British had dragged their feet so badly that they were behind in rebuilding their stores of supplies. Fort Bull had been a devastating loss, not only of many good men, but also of supplies meant for use farther west.

Uncle had made his feelings plain roaring, "God save them all! If we lose our country to the French it will be through the stupidity and slothfulness of our British counterparts! How much better all would have been had only the King and his ministers listened in earnest to Benjamin Franklin and agreed to allow the North American colonies to unite!"

Evert had remained quiet, and had been attentive to what his uncle had to say. William Waldron was, after all, one of Albany's most highly regarded masons, and within that position, and others within the city government, he enjoyed the confidence of many prominent Albany folk. Uncle told them that behind closed doors in Albany everyone spoke of the disheartened General Shirley who was rumored to have left his Parisian wife in London, and who mourned the loss of a son killed recently in battle. It was said that their British leader talked gibberish to himself. Evert had no doubt that his uncle had heard many such disturbing confidences. That they must all place their trust in the leadership of such a man was worrisome.

The delay in marching out of Albany made no sense at all. Who, thought Evert, did not know that the French and their Canada Indians had reportedly been seen in places where they should not be trespassing? Why not utilize the information that their own Indian scouts had provided and surprise the intruders who had little knowledge of the land? Indeed, as he understood it, this was what the Canadians had done at Fort Bull.

Evert rationalized that he and Garret knew every back trail and every creek that patterned the woodlands surrounding their farm, just the same as their Albany and Greenbush cousins knew their own territory. Being farmers who lived equally off their cultivated fields and the game that filled the outlying woodlands, most Provincials were excellent shots and knew how to call out the wily, wild turkey.

So, Evert sitting with his father and brothers on the eve before departure for Greenbush, wondered aloud "What does a victory or a defeat matter to an ordinary English soldier, except for preservation of his own life? He has no mother, sister, or sweetheart down the road to defend. If the Englishman survives the battle he will that night dream of England and a glorious return to his homeland where those he loves await his return. The Englishman's sentiments are understandable," Evert supposed. "So why not allow the native born man and not the foreigner to lead the charge?"

Cornelius puffed his pipe a moment, then answered, "Many years ago, during a game of cards, I proposed such a possibility to... to one of the officers with whom I had become friendly at Fort Schaghticoke. As I recall, few words were given in answer. *'Preposterous.'* *The officer said. 'Militiamen are farmers, tradesmen, and such, and surely cannot be compared to the trained British officer. Provincials must be patient and trust that England will see to the good of all.'* After which he laid down his cards—a winning hand— effectively dismissing all my suggestions."

Evert was annoyed. "Father, you are thinking of me as if I were a naive boy and not a man ready to put his life on the line for his country."

Cornelius shook his head. "I meant no injury to your feelings. Most Provincials, of course, are capable of their own defense, but as subjects of the Crown, obedience to English law must be preserved. Of course I understood." He leaned toward his son, trying to make him understand. "Many, especially in New York, have relatives who have been touched in one way or another by the aggressive advancement of the French forces. And those forces are now under the command of a new and capable military leader, Montcalm. 'Twas he who took over the American French command from the defeated Jean-Armand Dieskau , now held in prison in New York City. The rumor is that Dieskau's life was a gift from William Johnson who found him wounded on the battlefield about to be tomahawked. Dieskau would have been killed and his scalp paraded had it not been for William Johnson.

"According to your uncle William, after his capture Dieskau was of little interest to the French. He was swiftly replaced by Montcalm who had recently arrived at Montreal with fresh reinforcements. Your uncle heard that the new commander has three regiments and many companies of Canadian militia. Our Indian friends warn of an imminent attack by French raiders; anyplace, anytime."

"If this be so, Father," Evert asked, "why do you stay here?"

"Come with us to Albany, Father!" Garret extolled. "In Albany there is protection."

Cornelius embraced each of them at length, then vowed "I will never give over my lands into French enemy hands! Do...do not fret over me. I have my strong German servant beside me and am at ease with my situation now that your mother and the children are safe at Greenbush on the Yates farm. I have been assured, should trouble come, that John will take all of them across the river into the fort at Albany."

"But Father—"

"S...Stop, Evert! I have made my decision! I..I..I will stay h....here! Besides, several British soldiers are scheduled to arrive from Albany next week to...to bolster Fort Schaghticoke, and I have arranged that two of the soldiers from the garrison will sleep every night within my own house."

Evert took no solace from his father's optimistic words of assurance, and at every opportunity he pleaded with their father to come away with them. Every other day more bad news trickled into the village. Most recently, American blood had been spilled to the south, west, and north of them, and Evert was beginning to realize that Waldron Farm, a convenient stop along the North River, was a well-positioned and desirable target. He reminded his father that their own cousins on the Vermilye side, the Dolsons, just that past February had been engaged in a fight defending their homestead one hundred miles to the south of Albany. And, of course, in March, John Vanderheyden had been killed. Outlying farms were no longer impregnable for it seemed that many Iroquois who had long been protective friends now preferred to look away from the settlers' troubles. Some preferred to take a stance of wait and see.

Some had joined forces with the French, thinking that the French now held the better cards for a victory over the British.

Even the great William Johnson, who had been at home west of Schenectady at Fort Johnson during the attack of the far Indians and had been warned by his Indian scouts of impending dangers, had been surprised by the quickness of the French attack on Fort Bull. Nobody counted on the Canadians leaving Canada in the depth of the winter. Johnson had gathered together his Mohawk Militia as soon as he heard, but they had arrived days late only to find the fort burnt to the ground. If the valiant and experienced Johnson, with all his Indian allies, could not predict what was to come, then how could anyone else do so?

CHAPTER 31

At six o'clock in the morning, the 18th of May, after a hardy breakfast, Evert and Garret departed the farmhouse, walking across the dew soaked grass leading to the River Road. Some distance out, after passing newly planted fields, the two turned to walk backwards while facing the farm and searched for their father who usually waited ready to wave one final farewell. But instead they saw that Father was already headed toward the barn and the milking. It was obvious that he was still very disappointed.

Odd too, that Herman did not follow behind Cornelius as he usually did after breakfast. Instead, the big muscular man was on his knees and appeared to be digging something out of the dirt. All the more disturbing was the appearance of two Indians who stood off to the side of the barn, talking between themselves.

"Who are those two over there, and what is Herman doing?" Garret asked.

"Something is not as it should be," Evert quickly replied, laying his satchel on the ground. "I am going back!"

Garret, too, threw his provisions down beside his brother's, and without another word, with hearts pounding and muskets cocked, the brothers ran back across the field toward the barn.

As they approached closer the Indians had run into the back woods. Herman, as well, had disappeared, but Evert and Garret could hear scuffling and angry shouting coming from the barn.

"Damn you to hell!" their father yelled. "You...you have ruined her!"

Furiously, Herman shouted back, "I meant only to care for her, but you would not have me as kin any more than your beloved Johnson would have me. I want my money and what you promised to me!"

"You speak foolishness! I...I made no such promises! I would have..." He never finished. Suddenly Cornelius's bloodcurdling scream pierced through the early morning calm.

The brothers came from around the back of the barn and rushed in. What they saw horrified them. The seemingly dazed German was standing over the bloodied body of their father, blood dripping from a bayonet in Herman's hand.

Evert did not hesitate. He grabbed a chair that his brother Peter had just last week finished repairing for their mother and smashed it over Herman's head, causing him to falter, knocking the weapon out of his clutch.

Garret hurried to his father's side, bent down and felt for a pulse. None was to be found.

Herman staggered to his feet. Backing away, with tears in his eyes, he said, "This is not my doing! Your father would have killed me!" As he spoke Garret lunged at him, taking him back down to the dirt floor. Crying out in anguish, Garret held the servant in a choke hold the way Herman had once taught him to do should he be in a fight with the enemy. Evert found rope and soon had Herman secured. The German didn't resist, but tearfully continued to profess his innocence.

"Do not say you are innocent!" Garret shouted. "We saw you from afar digging in the ground. You had something in your hand as you went into the barn. My brother knew something was wrong when we saw the Indians who seem to have gone now, but here you are with the bayonet in your hand, and we both heard our father curse you!"

Glancing over his shoulder to where his father had fallen, Evert tried to come to terms with the fact that, having been stabbed many times over every part of his person, his father was no longer a part of this world.

Garret looked at the bloodied corpse and shook his head in disbelief. "Why would you do this terrible thing, Herman? We have worked together all of these many years. My father trusted you as he would his own brother."

Herman lifted his head and spoke bitterly. "I did not want it to come to this, but I would never be as a brother to your father, though at one time he said that I could be one."

"What are you saying?" Garret asked.

In broken Dutch Herman replied, "I asked for your Aunt Engeltie's hand in marriage long before she was with child, but your hard-hearted father would rather see her shamed than wed. If I had better circumstance and was free, and made enough money for a proper start someplace else, I could have had her as my wife. I wanted her so, and she was agreeable."

"With child! I do not believe you!" Garret shouted back defensively. "My aunt is a Godly woman. She would never have any man. I have heard her say as much many times."

"I speak the truth! My contract for service with your family ended during the harvest last year. Your father asked me to stay here for one year more because of the troubles with the French, and if I stayed on, then he said he would agree to the marriage, but he broke his word to me. When I went to him he lorded over me and said he would have no low Rhinesman marry his sister. After all the years I work for him so hard! And, too, he knowing of your aunt's and my sorrows after our infant child was born dead. The poor babe had not even a Christian burial, but at night was placed into his little grave in the servants' cemetery."

Garret steadied himself against the stall. "So you would murder the brother of the woman you desired for marriage; the mother of your own child?"

Herman turned away and stared at the floor, saying no more.

"What shall we do with him?" Garret asked Evert.

"Find Peter," Evert ordered flatly. "He went quail hunting after breakfast. The three of us will take our father and Herman into Albany and deposit this murderer at the city's goal. We will tell the authorities what we heard and how we came upon him, and then let them do with him as they will. We *will* have justice for our father."

Still obviously stymied by Herman's betrayal, Garret nodded. Though his grief was immeasurable, he could imagine his father saying such a thing to the German if it was true that Herman and his aunt wished to marry. But...how could any of this be true? He never saw any signs that there was anything improper between Aunt Engeltie and Herman. He never saw her so much as cast the smallest smile his way. She never looked large and round as if she was with child.

Of course, now Garret remembered that a few days ago, now that the winter snows had finally melted, he had seen a small mound of dirt in the cemetery grounds near to where Willie was buried. But with his mind on leaving for Albany, he had not given it any thought at all. *Could it be possible that a child was buried next to Willie? And could this be my aunt's baby? This just could not be.*

Their father would never cheat Herman. He was a good, honorable man. But, Garret considered further, it was true that his father preferred their faithful Negroes to Herman as help at the farm, and long ago he had overheard his father speak to his mother of his regrets in having taken him in. He had grumbled that none of their other servants were uppity like Herman and not one of them had ever given him cause for grief, and he had not to worry that their labors would be missed after a few short years like they would be with the 'Palatine Boar', since his Negroes were bound to him for life.

Later, after Peter arrived, he and Evert washed Cornelius's face and then wrapped their father's body within the cherished, colorful Indian blanket that he had inherited from their grandfather, Peter. Carefully they loaded his blood-soaked body into the wagon. With his elder brother seated solemnly beside him, Evert took the reins, while in the back Garret sobbed uncontrollably as he held his father's body close.

* * *

A week later the death of Cornelius Waldron was reported in the New York City newspapers. Copies were distributed throughout a shocked Albany:

Laſt Saturday Week òne Cornelius Waldron of Half Moon, in the County of Albany, was murder'd by a German Servant Man belonging to himſelf, he having ſtab'd him in ſeveral Parts of the Body with an old ruſtey Bayonet, that he had ſharpen'd up ſome Time before, we ſuppoſe for that Purpoſe. The ſame Fellow deſigned to diſpatch Waldron's two Sons, young Men, who accidentally came to their Father's Affiſtance, but one of them knock'd him down with a Chair, ſecured him, and he is now con- fined in Albany Goal.

Surrounded by her eight children, Janet Waldron watched as her beloved husband was interred at the Albany Dutch Reformed Churchyard beside his father and mother and younger brother, Pete.

In June, Herman, starved and beaten, was hanged at Albany on Gallows Hill. Eight strangers convicted of various crimes swung along with him. For days thereafter several were left at the end of their respective ropes, rotting for public viewing. A conspiracy with the two Indians was never proven.

At the insistence of his aunt Engeltie, Evert Waldron claimed Herman's body and buried him between Willie and Herman's infant son, in the same obscure cemetery that provided an eternal home for all the Waldron Farm servants.

Engeltie Waldron never married.

CHAPTER 32

1990

"What the heck are you doing down there on the floor?" Steve asked.

Kneeling in front of the kitchen cabinet's corner crevice, with several small appliances surrounding her, Helen struggled to retrieve a wedged-in Hamilton Beach box tucked into the back corner of a shelf.

"This is the worst wasted space. I want to use my new bread-making machine that you and Tommy gave me for my birthday."

"Need help?"

"No, I've got it, but thanks." Standing, she set down the box on the marbleized, brown Formica countertop. "It's not as heavy as it is clumsy," she added, stooping to put away a blending machine and an old percolator coffee pot that had belonged to Steve's Aunt Clara. "Honestly, I don't know why I have all these things taking up space under here. I haven't perked coffee in years."

Steve laughed. "One day you'll be saying the same thing about that bread machine that you just had to have. By the way, I always liked my coffee perked. It smelled so good in the morning. You know...brings back memories. But I'm sure happy to see you're going to use the bread maker. Wow, fresh bread. How great!"

"Well, let's hope," Helen responded cautiously. "It's a whole lot better than my grandmother's old tin bread pail that she used to hand crank. Her trying to make me into Betty Crocker was a waste."

"Whatever makes you happy, Babe."

Opening the box, Helen glanced over at Steve putting his English muffin into the toaster. "Steve, do you have anything special planned for today, other than working in the barn, that is?"

"As I said last night, this morning I'm pulling down those planks from the loft that I bought at auction. You know, the ones that the salvage company saved from the old Groesbeck place down toward Melrose."

"I don't know, Steve; that's an awful lot of heavy wood to move by yourself."

Steve winked. "No big deal. You're going to have that table I've been promising you for the past three years. I don't know if you know this or not, but that wood wasn't from the barn. The auctioneer told me that it actually came out of the dining room of a house that was built back before the American Revolution. It's walnut. That kind of hardwood is very hard to find anyplace nowadays."

"When you finish with the table, Honey, I know it will be fantastic."

"It will. I can't wait to get those boards down and out into the open in the shop. So, are we having bread with dinner tonight?"

"No, probably not tonight: maybe tomorrow. I was thinking that you and I could go out tonight. How about we celebrate your three months of sobriety?"

Steve seemed surprised. "How did you know?"

"Don't you think I pay attention to milestones? Oh, come on. I know—February 18th, right? I'm so proud of you. I thought that first we'd have a nice early supper at Palma's, and then how about after that we go to see 'Ghost'? I hear Patrick Swayze and Demi Moore are great in it. I know you like Palma's food, and there's no alcohol served there either."

"Perfect. You can moon over Swayze and I'll...."

Helen laughed. "I get the picture."

Opening up the silver Philadelphia Cream Cheese wrapper, he finished with, "Oh crap, this is the last of the cream cheese. Better put it on the grocery list with more bagels."

Helen sighed. "Cream cheese won't help your diet. I also wanted to talk to you about something else."

"The lazy Susan project for that corner down there?"

"No, I've given up on that idea. I'd like to talk about going back to Phoenix to visit my cousin this fall. Her Barbara is getting married, and yesterday I got a letter inviting us to the wedding."

"We'll have to talk it over," Steve answered thoughtfully. "I wouldn't mind seeing Phoenix again, but we'd have to look at the costs with Tommy's graduation party coming up in June and his birthday in July. Yet, on the plus side, all that Native spirituality thing going on out there, big sky and all, sure speaks to me."

"Me too. I loved our trip out west. The purple painted skies were just so beautiful. I can't believe that was eight years ago. Tommy was only ten. Gosh, time sure does fly."

Steve nodded. "Yeah. That was a good trip. Let's see how everything else goes the next couple of months. Maybe we can do it. Now though, I'd better get out to the barn so I'll have time to shower later." Pausing at the back door and slapping the counter for attention, he added, "I'm already tasting Palma's chicken parm, and Babe, thanks for sticking with me through it all. Love you."

Hanging over the bread machine directions, Helen mumbled back, "Love you, too."

In the barn Steve laboriously climbed the ladder to the loft, groaning when rediscovering eight boxes of stored Christmas tree ornaments as well as Helen's mother's old marble-topped end tables and several spindled oak chairs filled the space in front of his prized walnut slabs. Tommy never seemed to be at home these days, and every time he wanted to do something like this he had no help. He stood there looking over the stuff. Like his wife, he wondered why they'd kept any of it. He supposed if Tommy ever did move out they could completely furnish his new digs. Steve began moving the Christmas boxes, listening to bells inside jingling, and right away he knew what the source of the sound was. Helen hung those hand-made, leather backed bells on every doorknob, even the bathrooms, every Christmas. It made him nuts.

One by one he moved the holiday boxes to the side of the loft and then rearranged the end stands and chairs. After maneuvering it all, he was surprised to find something he'd not seen in years. He'd forgotten that he'd stored his great grandmother's wooden trunk up here. Steve sighed. He remembered that the trunk was chuck full of family mementos—things his aunt had saved, and it had taken him and Tommy all they had in them to get it up here after they'd gotten rid of the storage unit. Maybe, he thought, he could get the trunk onto his hand truck and roll it out of the way. If he was going to get at the wood he had to get this out, too. Thinking further, he decided that before he went out to the garage for the hand truck he would take some of the junk inside of the trunk out so it would be lighter. That made a lot more sense. Steve opened the lid. "Oh man," he sighed out loud. "It's loaded."

Searching the cramped loft, Steve found two strong, empty cardboard wine boxes, quickly ripping out the individual protective inserts for the missing twelve bottles. Thank God Helen never found these smoking guns, he thought, putting them down beside the trunk. Anxiously he began scooping out papers that had been stacked on top of multiple stuffed manila folders inside the chest It came back to him how he and his mother had argued over her keeping *everything*. He also remembered her saying, "Even if you decide to throw out most of what I've saved, please keep the trunk and its contents for Tommy."

Exhausted and perspiring, Steve sat on the floor and began shuffling through the loose paperwork, soon discovering that what he had in his hands documented various family lines. Among the papers clipped to a handful of black and white snapshots of antiquated gravestones he found a separate handwritten note about a Garret Waldron born in 1738 who died at Waterford in 1829. Steve smiled, noticing that 'Garret Waldron' had been underlined in red pen. Obviously this guy must have been an ancestor of some special importance.

Skimming through the names of the children born to Garret and his wife, Catherine, he saw a few familiar surnames who'd married into the Waldron family: Clute, Ostrander, Van Der-werken, and that Garret's last child, William, born in 1783 at Schaghticoke, had married Judah Bradt. William's name was as-terisked and suddenly Steve remembered talking with his mother about the Bradt family line and how angry she'd gotten when he'd laughed while she told him that the Bradts descended from the Vikings. He'd apologized, explaining that it was only funny because of his high school basketball teammate, wacko Jimmy Bradt, who fit the bill of the fighting Vikings. Boy, he hadn't thought of Jimmy in years.

A second page explained that William and Judah, both born at Schaghticoke, New York, were buried in the Adirondack Moun-tains at North Creek in the Union Cemetery. *Interesting. Helen might want to take a look at this stuff.* Steve got up and put the handwritten pages and the photos aside on the floor near the loft's ladder where he'd see them later on when he went back to the house. *She'll think this so cool. What a prelude to "Ghost."*

Returning to the trunk and rooting farther down, he found another separate cardboard box that apparently had originally come from an office supplier in Manhattan and probably once contained reams of typing paper. Curious, he opened the lid and reached inside, pulling out balls of crumbled old newspapers from the 1930s, probably packing material meant to protect the precious item nestled below: an odd, irregular-sized quartz rock about the size of a baseball. *What the hell is this?*

Checking his watch, he noted that it was already three o'clock. No time for further exploration. He picked up the rock, walked over to the ladder, and placed it on the floor on top of the few selected pages of Waldron notes. Glancing back at the crumpled newspapers, he figured that later on sometime he and Helen would spread them out on the dining room table. They'd sure be an interesting read. Maybe he could even get Tommy into it. Returning to the trunk, he decided that now he could probably drag it across the floor without the use of the hand truck. Ten minutes later he'd finally cleared the way to some of the walnut planks.

As he stood catching his breath in front of the boards stacked against the back barn wall, he was awestruck by their magnificence even before being cleaned up. The wood was awesome and definitely would come alive again in the table he had planned. Walking one board at a time across the floor of the loft, he pushed the first, second, and third of them off the edge, letting them drop freely to the dirt floor below. As he took hold of the fourth, he noticed that the board seemed far heavier and there was a depression in the flow of the grain. He stepped closer to take a better look. Studying it, he had chills. The board seemed to glow with the aura of another man's face; a man with troubled eyes and a long scar in his cheek below his right eye. Shaken, Steve let the plank go, and it banged hard against the others remaining against the wall.

Remember what the psychiatrist said. "*Don't believe what you see. Fight it. It's not real.*"

Stepping forward, he took a deep breath and looked again. Whatever he thought he saw a few minutes ago wasn't there now. *Forget it. My psychiatrist was probably right.*

He gripped the two sides of the board, his hands shaking. This one was heavier than the others, alright, but he knew he could get it over to the edge where he could drop it down to the lower level. Carefully, as he'd done with the others, he began to walk the fourth board toward the edge. One more step. He backed up and felt something under his heel move, throwing him off balance. Jerking around he saw the obstruction was the rock. *Damn it.* Because of his awkwardness, he'd caused the rock to tear through the genealogy he'd put aside to show Helen. *Double Damn it!* He couldn't let go of the board now. He needed another pair of hands. No good wishing he'd done this differently. Again, stubbornly, he stepped back, feeling for the ladder behind him with his right foot while steadying the board. He found the ladder and then tried to kick the rock out of the way, but lost his balance. He teetered backward. *Oh shit—I'm going to fall!*

Steve hit the pile of boards on the dirt floor below with the fourth crushing down on top of his chest. For a second there was a searing pain...then blackness.

Three hours later, Helen, dressed for their celebratory dinner, realized she hadn't seen any sign of Steve for a long time and it was nearly five. Aggravated that it would be another hour by the time he showered and dressed, she headed out to the barn. They'd miss the early-bird special, and they'd never make it on time for the early movie. He was so annoying. Always it was a fight against time.

With her high heels catching in the gravel pathway, she walked into the barn, surprised by how quiet it was. "Hey Steve, we have to get going! Steve...where are you?"

The pile of boards strewn out all which way were what caught her eye first, and then—Steve on his back sprawled out on them with one single board on top of him.

"Oh my God, Steve—oh God!" Climbing over the lumber she reached out to him and touched his cold, anguished face. Right away she thought he was dead—but maybe just unconscious? She had to get help. Dazed, she managed to make her way back to the house and the phone.

The State Police arrived first. The older of the two officers told her to stay in the house while they investigated. After what seemed like hours, but was only minutes, one returned to her. He said that he was sorry, but it appeared that her husband was dead. He sat with her until Tommy came home.

The coroner arrived almost an hour later and officially pronounced Steve dead. With his hand on her shoulder the kindly older officer told her that the formal ruling was that her husband had broken his neck. She watched from the front window as they put Steve on a stretcher in a black bag and shoved him into the back of the coroner's van.

* * *

At 7:30 p.m. as "Ghost" began at the Country Mall's theater, Helen sat at home beside her son on the sofa. Although Tommy was there, his hand over hers, she was alone. She couldn't cry. She was numb. She wondered where Steve was.

CHAPTER 33

April 2016

Who would have ever thought that he, Tom Carey, would come back to live in Upstate New York? Not Tom Carey, that's for sure. Arizona had been good to him. Even crazier, who would have ever thought that Father Patrick would be the one to help facilitate such a major change in his career, but that was exactly what had occurred. It's the kind of thing that happens when a lawyer and an almost retired priest, who also happens to be a close family friend, play golf together once a week. Helen had called their move the conjuring of miracles.

When the titillating offer for a full partnership with one of the hottest law firms in the country, now branching out into the Albany Capital District area, came in, he and Alison had decided that it was too good to pass up. And so it came to be that early in 2016, Tom, his wife, and son had said good-bye to the west and hello to the east and rural residential Wilton, New York.

After the two service technicians from Hillcrest Home Entertainment finished installing the five flat screens around the house, Tom tipped each of them a twenty. Closing the front door behind them, he did his happy jog to the family room, stepped back, and admired his new sixty-inch installed over the stone fireplace mantle. He wondered what his mother would say when she arrived next month and saw the TV over the fireplace. As he saw it, his newly constructed house had just became the Carey Homestead. He clicked on the TV. Wolf Blitzer's anxious face peered down at him.

Alison walked in carrying another box the movers had delivered two days before. "Some sort of alert?" she asked, glancing up at the screen.

"Yes, afraid so. The Saudi's are pissed off."

"Like your mom would say, all we can do is pray."

Tom put the remote down long enough to take the box from his wife and set it down on the glass coffee table. "Where is our son? Hours ago I told Kyle I wanted him to help you out with these boxes."

"Calm down. He will, don't you worry about that, but I told him that for a few minutes he could do what his father is doing and enjoy playing with his new toy. Just remember, Bucko, you gave the okay for that big one up on the kid's bedroom wall."

While Alison took her scissors to the taped box, Tom returned to the remote and switched to the local news. "Hey, how about this. Hilary Clinton is going to Cohoes High School tonight. Holy Cow! She'll be hitting the 'All American City' and home of the prehistoric mastodon in one swoop!"

Without looking up Alison muttered, "Where's Cohoes?"

"Not too far from here. Maybe a half hour drive. Hey! How about we all take a ride over to the Falls tomorrow. They should be spectacular this time of year."

"Tom?"

"What?"

"How about you take a break from the world on the wall and check out what's in here. I think this is one of the boxes your mom had stored at her house."

Tom clicked off the TV. "Whoever takes on this Presidency next year better be prepared for all out hell on earth."

"I know," Alison sighed. "I just can't listen to it all anymore. Donald, Hillary, Bernie, John and Ted, on, and on, and on. Hey, isn't there a way to make that thing just play music?"

"Yeah, it probably does once I figure out the cable channels. So what do you have there?"

"Don't you remember? Your mom brought a few boxes over to the house the last time she visited us before we left Phoenix. She said it was time you took possession of your things that you left behind at her house, what with our move and her downsizing into her new retirement townhome in Scottsdale. This must be one of those she told me was stored in your bedroom up on a closet shelf. I was surprised that there was anything more she could dump on us."

"Nope. Don't remember a thing about this."

Staring down into the hodgepodge-filled box in front of her, Alison itemized her find. "How cute. Your baseball mitt from when you were a little boy is in here, and it looks like some of your old grammar school report cards from fourth and fifth grades. Hey, look at this drawing of three bull heads and a lion dancing on all this ornate artwork. Nice frame, too. Know anything about this?"

Tom walked over and took the small, framed pen and ink drawing from her. He stared at it for a few seconds. "Oh, now I remember. This used to be on Aunt Clara's dresser in her bedroom along with about a dozen old, family pictures. Every time I'd go down there to visit we'd eventually get to sitting on the bed with a bowl of popcorn, and she'd tell me stories about every one of them. Used to make Auntie Lar so crazy that we were eating on the bed. Anyway, this is a drawing of the Waldron Coat of Arms. I think it belonged to her mother. I'll put it in my dresser drawer where I keep the collection of the wallets your mom gives me every Christmas." He grinned.

"Very funny," Alison said, still fumbling through the box. "Oh, and here are your scout badges, and then there's this thing—no clue," she said, holding out a piece of rough quartz rock in her palm. "Is this something you picked up off the trail during one of your scouting days?" She laughed.

Laying down the frame, Tom took the rock from her. "This was in there, too? My God, I haven't seen that since I was a kid. I think my aunts had it in their curio cabinet." Examining it almost reverently, he added, "I might have seen a box up in my bedroom closet when I was home on leave from the service, but I guess I never cared about it. In those days I had more going on than worrying about junk my mother saved, and believe me, she saved everything: old Christmas cards, buttons; you name it. So I guess I shouldn't be so surprised that she saved this thing."

Alison prompted, "Okay, you have my attention. What's the story on the rock?"

Tom took her by the hand and led her to the sofa. "Sit down."

Alison followed, eager for a break. "I'm all ears."

"You know that my father died when he fell from the loft in our barn, and not long after my mother decided to move us to Phoenix for a new start."

"Yes. You told me how you lived for a year with your cousins and eventually went into the service. I can't even imagine how terrible it must have been for the two of you to lose your father that way and then to start a new life so far away. Are you having second thoughts? We've talked about all this many times, and we agreed to come back to New York. Is the move back what's bothering you all of a sudden?"

Tom tried to control the emotion in his voice. "No, I'm excited about our future here—it's all good. All of that was a lifetime ago, but I never told you the whole story of what happened that day and I'd like to now."

Alison rested her hand on his arm. "You know there isn't anything that you can't tell me. I'm here for you. I hope you know that."

"I do, and I appreciate how good you are with me, and, for that matter, with everyone."

Alison squeezed his hand. "You're easy to love."

"Well, I don't know how easy I am, but here goes. The afternoon of the accident, Dad had wanted to start a project. That's why he was up in the loft. For years he talked about making a new table out of some wood he had stored in the barn. The night before, he'd asked me to help him out the following morning, to move the wood down to his workshop, but I was a selfish little bastard. A couple of my buds and I went out to the stock car races the night before and we all got drunk. I didn't come home in the morning as I'd promised. I called my mother and gave her some halfcocked story about trouble with my car, but in fact, I was hung-over. My dad was trying so hard to keep sober. He had issues going on, drinking was a part of it all, and he'd joined AA. He was really trying so hard. I thought I'd better just stay out of the house until the afternoon, but the hours drifted to near dinner, and then the Police showed up at my buddy's house."

Alison moved closer. "Now you listen to me. If I am sure of nothing else in this life, Tom, it is that you are definitely *not* a selfish bastard. You could never be that kind of person."

Tom smiled at her. "I'm glad you feel that way. Anyway, I guess seeing this rock took me back. I know I was just a kid, but I do have to own up to some responsibility for my dad's death. Nothing can ever change that. It's just that I've learned to live with it."

"Oh God, Tom. I'm so sorry." She put her arms around him, holding him close.

Gently, Tom pulled away. "Now I'm remembering that my mother said that my great aunt, who had the rock to start with, thought that it had some sort of spiritual significance; some kind of family lore was attached to it. Anyway, later I learned that it was next to Dad's body when Mom found him. I remember that she had it on the kitchen table that awful day when I came in. The troopers were with her, trying to console her. My mother believed that it must have been one of the last things that my father had touched, and she always thought that he must have wanted to talk to her about it. That was him. He was a seeker. You know what I mean?"

"I think I do," Alison answered softly.

Tom stood. "Okay, enough is enough."

"Oh, Tom. Don't say that. You listen to my...well, my every 'whatever'. I'm here for you. I'll always be here for you."

Tom stood for a minute admiring the loving California girl he'd found in Arizona. He remembered she'd said something similar to him while he lay in a VA hospital bed deciding whether or not he deserved to recover. Back then he didn't even know her last name.

"I'll tell you what, lady, this is *our* new start. My old baseball mitt, I bequeath to Kyle."

"All right!" Alison bellowed out with two thumbs-up.

"And, when my mom comes to visit, I'll return my grammar school report cards and the badges to her memorabilia pile that I'll bet fills one of her dresser drawers, but what do you say we keep the 'rock' up there on our mantle?"

Alison didn't hesitate. She grabbed the Carey family heirloom and marched toward their fireplace. Placing it next to the decorative, hand painted fish plate her grandmother had once held on her lap all the way from Florida for safe keeping, she turned to Tom, "When my mother and dad visit they will be pleased to see the plate displayed, and we'll tell them we have 'a piece of the rock.'

A sense of relief washed over Tom. "I like it. 'A piece of the rock' sounds very right."

"Alison dug into another box and pulled out several framed family photos. "There," she said, bookending them on each side of the mantle. "Perfect. And, we'll remember your dad and my Grammy every time we watch TV. You know, Tom, my sweetheart grandmother used to say something that I think you should hear about now. I feel her nudging me."

"And what's that?" Tom asked as he headed upstairs to Kyle's room with the baseball mitt.

From the bottom of the stairs she called up after him, "Life is for the living!"

Walking toward another of the village of unopened boxes stacked against the wall of the dining room, to herself she whispered, "Hey up there, thank *You*, and, please bless this house and all the souls within."

THE END

ACKNOWLEDGEMENTS

First, foremost, and always, I thank my husband, Andrew, who patiently read and reread every word of this book and acted as first-wave editor.

And many thanks to editor, Mary Lois Sanders.

Thanks to friend and neighbor, David Fleming, for the use of his photo entitled "Upon This Rock" the image taken on his land in Rensselaer County, New York, which provided my inspiration for this book's cover.

Mega thanks to Donna Lama whose creative vision as cover designer conveys the true 'soul' of my story.

ABOUT THE AUTHOR
AND HER BOOKS

Author Gloria Waldron Hukle resides with her husband in Averill Park, New York. She began her authorship in 2006 with *Manhattan: Seeds of the Big Apple*, the story of the 17th century Waldron family living on Block B in New Amsterdam (which would later be re-named New York City).

A second novel, published in 2007, *The Diary of a Northern Moon*, a mystery generated by family lore, finds a young woman caught in a web of secrets about her deceased father. Set in Albany and the Adirondack Mountains of New York, the reader is challenged to ask "Who was Ben Waldron?"

Two years later, *Threads—An American Tapestry* was published. Hukle's third of her "American Waldron Series Novels" is the poignant early 18ᵗʰ Century tale of the affluent Margaret Vandenberg. Half Dutch, half Native American, Margaret is both loved and hated for reasons that haven't changed among humankind since time began.

Souls of the Soil is the fourth and final of Gloria Waldron Hukle's "American Waldron Series" sometimes referred to as "The Waldron Series Novels". The 'half-seed' for Hukle's wrap-up novel was the actual 1756 murder of Cornelius Waldron, a prosperous farmer living in Upstate New York during the French and Indian War period. The second half of 'the seed' is revealed to the reader through the 1980's character, Steve Carey, a man who *questions everything*.

Hukle, whose inspiration for her book series was rooted in family genealogy and lore, says:

"Genealogy can often be used as a base for the historical fiction writer. Following the lives of our ancestors brings us into a setting such as New Amsterdam or Half Moon so that time and place both encircle and thread the novel. However, in this writer's opinion, the line that is drawn between fact and fiction is one word, and that word is 'possibility'."

I hope *Souls of the Soil* prompts readers to reach out and take hold of their own "possibilities".

All of author Gloria Waldron Hukle's books are available in both printed and e-version. For more information about Author Gloria Waldron Hukle and her work, as well as old maps, lore, reviews, current signings and where to purchase her books, please visit:

www.authorgloriawaldronhukle.com

FLAGS

British Red Ensign Flag

American Flag

In 1707 British Queen Anne adopted a new flag for her country and her colonies.

The old flag of King James I, called "The King's Colors" depicting the Cross of St. George on top of the Scottish flag of St. Andrew, was placed in the upper left hand corner in a field of red. The new Queen Anne flag was called the British Red Ensign or the Cromwell Flag. It would have flown during the time of both Peter and Cornelius Waldron. Queen Anne's flag would fly until the Revolutionary War.

Our present American Flag was established in 1818 when Congress passed legislation establishing the number of stripes at seven red and six white and a star for every new state that made up our union. In 1959 the two final stars were added when Alaska became the United States of America's 49th state (January 3rd) and Hawaii became the 50th state (August 21st).

Made in the USA
Lexington, KY
29 September 2017